"Oh, I beg your pardon, sir!"

Nancy looked up from her position on the floor into the Earl of Selbridge's eyes.

"Quite all right. Please, let me help you up, Miss...Mrs...."

"Browne," offered Nancy, taking his hand and rising gracefully. "I'm afraid that foolish Master Gervaise has let a kitten loose in here somewhere. After all I had to go through to make everything nice again."

"I have noticed such improvements in such a short time. You must be commended on your housekeeping," said the Earl kindly.

The girl's dark eyebrows rose a fraction. Then she burst into laughter.

Her hair! She wore no cap, the Earl suddenly realized, and of course no respectable housekeeper, however young, would go about the house bareheaded.

"Ah, I see you have discovered your mistake," Nancy said gently. "I am Sir Reginald's niece. I assure you, sir, no harm was done. Your response was wholly understandable."

It was amazing, thought Selbridge, that such good humour still sparkled in her eyes and that her smile was undimmed despite his clumsy mistake. What a fool he was, and he was determined to make it up to her in every way possible from this moment on.

Other books by Alberta Sinclair

A HINT OF SCANDAL

Don't miss any of our special offers. Write to us at the
following address for information on our newest releases.

Harlequin Reader Service
901 Fuhrmann Blvd., P.O. Box 1397, Buffalo, NY 14240
Canadian address: P.O. Box 603,
Fort Erie, Ont. L2A 5X3

COUSIN NANCY
ALBERTA SINCLAIR

Harlequin Books

TORONTO • NEW YORK • LONDON
AMSTERDAM • PARIS • SYDNEY • HAMBURG
STOCKHOLM • ATHENS • TOKYO • MILAN

For my brother, Giacomo (Jack) D'Agostaro,
who is the hero of his own story

Published July 1989

ISBN 0-373-31105-2

CHAPTER ONE

"CERTAINLY, SIR...would be very happy to...good day to you," said Jack Daventry, Earl of Selbridge, drawing on his last reserves of patience and hospitality. Finally the library door closed on the backs of his butler and his latest visitor, only one in a long line of callers that day.

It seemed that the earl, unlike ordinary mortals, could not retire quietly to his estate to ruminate and repine over a broken heart. Instead he must continually greet callers like a demmed major-domo.

"What's a fellow got to do to get a little solitude?" he asked the ancient pointer bitch lounging on the carpet, before returning to his comfortable armchair, his volume of poetry and his bottle of madeira.

As Griselda regarded him with her sorrowful eyes, Jack leaned over to give her a pat, then sank with a sigh into his chair. But he turned the leaves of his book almost unseeing. The sentiments contained there were designed to comfort him, to rouse his tenderest recollections, to soothe his wounded heart. Instead, they bored him.

"What a great mooncalf I am," he announced to Griselda. The dog snored gently. Undeterred, Jack continued, "I fall in love with a young lady and I propose. She declines. Then she says she's engaged to another man—but she'd rather marry me. Secret betrothal—and then, demned if I know why, the next day she finds she's mistaken the matter, and it's been the other fellow all along. Females!"

His snort of disgust awoke the sleeping pointer. She stirred uneasily, tottered toward the empty grate, shivered, and then, with an accusing look at the cruel master who denied a fire to a faithful old dog on a breezy June day, settled down again with a whimper.

"Sorry, Grissy old girl. Didn't mean females of *your* species." He sighed again, recalling the myriad charms of his lost love. "But I only wish..." Just as Jack was sinking at last into the dejected mood appropriate to a discarded lover, a discreet knock sounded on the library door.

"Enter," he called out in a tone of resignation.

"I beg your pardon, my Lord," said Jenkins, unemotional and completely unsympathetic, "but Sir Reginald Drakes and Lady Chetwynd are here."

"Oh, very well," said Jack. "Put them in the blue saloon and say I shall be with them in a moment."

"Very good, sir." Jenkins knew the rule. No women permitted in his lordship's library.

Jack plodded to the blue saloon on the floor below. Damn his sociable neighbours! But it would not do to offend Sir Reginald Drakes, Baronet and master of Ellwood Park. Not only was he a crusty old sort, but next to Jack, he was the most influential landowner in the neighbourhood.

Despite his much lower rank, Sir Reginald wielded a good deal more influence, due to his year-round residence there, than did Jack, who spent much of the year in London, Brighton and other people's country houses. Jack scarcely liked to admit it to himself, but he was a little bit afraid of the old man. As for Sir Reginald's daughter, the widowed Lady Chetwynd, though he sometimes derived amusement from her, he was irritated by her airs and stratagems.

"Afternoon, Selbridge." Tall and straight-backed, with curling iron-grey hair, the old man headed straight for a decanter of brandy, waving away Jenkins's offer of assistance.

"No, my good man, I know my way around the bottles in this house. Young Jack's father and I had many a glass in this room, times past."

"My dear Selbridge," cried Lady Chetwynd, extending two plump fingers for Jack to take. She would, Jack knew, be thrown into a paroxysm of delight should he suavely bend and kiss the proferred digits. Though at another time it might have diverted him, right now Jack hardly knew whether he could bear to witness such a performance or whether it was wise to encourage the pretty widow to believe him partial to her.

"Lady Chetwynd, you are looking well. Gervaise and Miss Chetwynd are also well, I trust?" The earl thought it safe to enquire about her children. Thank heaven, thought Jack, she had not yet conceived the scheme of trying to attach him to her daughter, Eleanor. Jack could not think of a pair more likely to drive a man mad between them than these two.

Sir Reginald prevented her from answering. "That devil's cub Gervaise will be the death of me one day," he said from the depths of his glass of brandy. "He's been sent down again. Young scoundrel."

"Papa!" cried Lady Chetwynd. "You always take the university's side of it. They are always worrying my dear boy to death just because he is clever and high-spirited and handsome. They are only jealous—"

"They wouldn't be if they knew what a fool he has for a mother," interrupted Sir Reginald. "And no doubt he thinks his grandfather a fool, too. This time I won't suffer him to play off his tricks again, even if they decide to take him back. He will stay here and obey me, by God, till I de-

cide what to do with him!'' He pounded on the Pembroke
table and rattled the decanter and glasses.

''And Miss Eleanor?'' Jack persevered.

Again Sir Reginald forestalled the proud mama. ''Bread
and butter miss, she seems, but she's always slyly creeping
about. And she watches. Me, the servants, her brother,
everybody. Gives me the horrors, I tell you. Then there are
those insipid airs she learned in London. Faugh!''

He poured some more brandy, apparently overcome by
the thought of them. ''About time we found her a husband.''

''How can you say such things about your own grandchildren, Papa?'' demanded Lady Chetwynd. ''Why,
Eleanor is already an acknowledged Beauty, and she not
even out yet. What you call her creeping about is simply her
ladylike manner. Eleanor,'' she said, turning to Jack, ''has
just returned from the finest academy in London and is
quite accomplished.'' Too late, Jack noticed the specula-
tive gleam in her eye. ''You haven't seen her for a long time,
have you, my Lord?''

''Ah, no... I believe not. And how is Osbert?''

Lady Chetwynd sniffed. ''My brother is still isolating
himself from the rest of us in his study, poring over those
musty old books. I shouldn't wonder if the whole room was
nasty with worms and flies by now....''

''And he refuses to do his duty!'' thundered Sir Reginald's bass. ''Imagine, my son, the heir to Ellwood, refus-
ing to do his duty. Won't go out in company, won't find a
wife and give me a grandson and himself an heir. I don't
count that popinjay Gervaise—fine baronet *he'd* make....''

Jack perceived that it was time to change the subject. ''I
daresay you're all wondering what I'm doing home at this
time of year,'' he remarked.

In truth, he had arrived unannounced and had been hoping for at least a week of blissful solitude to heal his wounded heart before having to exert himself to be sociable. But he'd had the misfortune to be seen passing through the nearby village of Dunscombe the afternoon before, and by now the word was out over the country that Selbridge was in residence at Marbelmeade.

"We wouldn't dream of being so vulgarly curious," said Lady Chetwynd.

"Your own business, my boy," muttered Sir Reginald. "I'm sure a man can settle at his seat once in a while without occasioning the remark of the neighbourhood." He glared at his daughter, who had taken the opportunity to seat herself in the chair next to the one where Jack was standing, so perforce, he had to seat himself next to her.

"And your dear mama left so suddenly for Brighton! I hope she is not unwell?" she continued.

"No, Mama is in prime twig. I just thought it would be best for her to be away from all the dust being kicked up. My architect is arriving soon, and the work will begin in earnest."

In actuality, the countess had steamed off in a huff upon receipt of a letter from her son begging her to leave him alone at Marbelmeade for the summer.

Lady Chetwynd simpered. "I suppose this means that with the new wing, you will be setting up your nursery soon."

Jack felt his face grow warm. Indeed, this had been exactly his intention a year or more ago, when he had decided it was time to marry. And last season he thought he had met the perfect woman. Her perfection was marred only by the small circumstance of her not thinking *him* the perfect man.

Fortunately Sir Reginald saved him the embarrassment of replying. "Time enough for that, time enough! All you females ever think of, marrying and breeding."

"Perhaps," replied Jack, for he was, above all, a very fair young man, "it is because we gentlemen leave them no other outlets for their talents."

At that moment Jenkins and a footman arrived with tea, cake and biscuits, and Lady Chetwynd was distracted. Jack knew very well that even such humble viands as these would be sparse and mean at Ellwood, under Sir Reginald's tight-fisted rule, and he almost chuckled at her ladyship's heart-felt sigh of pleasure at her first bite of a moist slice of plum cake.

Jack prided himself on having a well-run bachelor establishment, both here and at his lodgings in Bond Street. His town house he did not open unless his mother was in London, and it was said that even the countess could not match him in hospitality. But surely he could not owe his run of visitors today to a neighbourhood longing for a taste of his cakes, tea and liquor? No, thought Jack. The sad truth was that he was an awfully popular fellow, and had been a fool to think he could sneak away to Marbelmeade and enjoy his misery in private.

"My dear Lord Selbridge, we shall have to put our heads together and come up with some way to entertain ourselves this summer. You, I am sure, are accustomed to more activity than this dull neighbourhood can provide. And I—" Lady Chetwynd sighed, looking wistfully at the last ratafia biscuit her father had just high-handedly appropriated "—am vexed that not a soul has invited me to visit this summer and that the children and I must pass the months in virtual isolation!"

"Nonsense, my girl, you have callers aplenty and are always plotting to get up some dance or other," said her father. "Enough of that stuff goes on in town; get out and walk in the park, or see if you can wheedle that old dragon of a housekeeper into doing her job for once. Place is going to rack and ruin, and all my daughter and grandchildren can think about is their own amusement," he grumbled to Selbridge.

"Oh!" cried Lady Chetwynd, hand to her mouth. "Papa, I quite forgot. The housekeeper, she has—"

"Finally given notice? She's threatened it often enough lately. This never happened in your mother's day, my girl! Didn't you learn anything about running a household while you were married to Chetwynd?"

"Oh, you know very well that the servants have no respect for me, Papa, no matter how hard I try...." She delved for a handkerchief in her reticule and applied it daintily to the corners of her eyes.

Jack discreetly consulted his watch and slid it back into his waistcoat pocket. Lady Chetwynd's delicate vapors generally lasted ten minutes, more when egged on by Sir Reginald. It was time to intervene.

"There, now, my dear Lady Chetwynd, we all know that you do the best you can. Servants are a terrible problem these days." Her ladyship brightened.

Sir Reginald snorted. "All it means is I have to advertise for another housekeeper!"

Finally, with a last coy invitation from Lady Chetwynd and a brusque comment from Sir Reginald on the plans for the new wing, which he had demanded to be shown, the visitors left Jack to his solitude once more.

For the rest of the afternoon Selbridge tried his best to meditate on his unhappy love, but an important conference with his gamekeeper regarding the pheasants, a call, this time welcome, from his good friend James Phillips, the parish rector, and an interesting event in the stables, the birth of twin foals, kept him from the memory of his faithless beloved.

As he was giving directions for his solitary dinner, there was a racket outside that could only be interpreted as the arrival of a post-chaise full of visitors. Jack cursed under his breath and consigned them to Hades, whoever they might be.

Too late he remembered a casual invitation his mother had issued some months ago. The barking of his dogs, an agitated female voice requesting that the filthy animals be called off at once and a deeper voice greeting Jenkins like an old friend, confirmed the worst of his fears. It was his cousins, Sir Francis and Felicity Garrard.

They were the sort of impecunious and insistent relations that every noble family does its best to either see settled at a comfortable distance or refuse to recognize. Unfortunately, the former solution would no longer serve the earl, as his cousins were now of an age where their quiet country home could no longer contain them.

Eighteen-year-old Felicity had developed a regrettable tendency to hang upon his sleeve, and her elder brother continually importuned him for money and introductions. A more ambitious and less restful pair of houseguests could not possibly be imagined, and Jack had to stifle a groan as he greeted them in the hall.

"By Jupiter, Jack, it's good to see you!" Francis, a slim, handsome, tow-headed figure, bounded into the hall and pumped his cousin's hand.

He reminded Jack of nothing so much as a friendly puppy, but experience had taught him that there was much to be wary of behind that guileless blue gaze.

"Hello, Francis. I'm sorry if you've caught me by surprise. The house isn't fit for guests..."

"Why, Cousin Jack, aren't you going to greet me?"

Selbridge looked down at his petite, pretty Cousin Felicity, her bright green eyes shaded by a bonnet trimmed in ribbon of a shade to match them, her lips tilted at the corners. Had he been a man at all susceptible to the charms of a pert schoolroom miss, Jack might have found himself in difficulty, but fortunately, all Felicity inspired in him was an emotion compounded of equal parts affection and irritation.

He chucked her under the chin. "Why, aren't you rigged up fine, puss! Catch a few mice in that get-up, eh?" He gestured at her fashionable pelisse and bonnet.

Felicity pouted. "How horrid of you, Jack. I'm not a cat, you know." Then her brow cleared. "I'm so glad to be here. Our season was vastly dull—nothing but a few assemblies at Harrogate and a dreary country ball or two. And Aunt Eustacia *would* come down with the gout and insist on Bath. Imagine, when *everyone* will be in Brighton! Then your sweet mama insisted we pay her a visit here...."

By this time the visitors had followed their reluctant host into the much-abused Blue Saloon, while an army of footmen scurried up the stairs with trunks and bandboxes.

"Claret, Francis?" offered Jack, after ordering a more ladylike beverage for Felicity.

Francis gratefully accepted, while his sister continued, "But where is Aunt Margaret? And what are you doing here?"

For perhaps the tenth time that day, Jack explained the circumstances regarding his mother's absence and his own presence at Marbelmeade. His cousins, when informed that they had sentenced themselves to living the summer with plaster and dust, sawing and hammering going on about them, exchanged dismayed glances.

"I was so hoping that you would get up some entertainment for us, Jack. A picnic, or a dinner party or two, or perhaps a ball,'' said Felicity, her eyes shining at the thought. ''You promised me ages ago you'd dance with me, and you never have!''

The pout was coming on again, and Selbridge turned uneasily to her brother, who in his own way was just as disappointed. ''I'm sorry,'' Jack said, ''but you see how it is, don't you, old man? Everything at sixes and sevens... mother not at home...perhaps you'd be more comfortable elsewhere.''

''Nonsense!'' Felicity sprang up and took his arm. ''We are being so selfish, and here poor Cousin Jack will be all alone this summer. We can't simply think of our own amusement when Jack is in need of our company. Besides,'' she added practically, ''we have no where else to go. Birchley has been let till October.''

Selbridge looked at his elder cousin in surprise, and Francis said, somewhat sheepishly for him, ''Had to, Jack, else we'd be in the suds for sure by next winter. Felicity's got some totty-brained scheme of going to London, and we're short of the ready. So when her ladyship invited us to spend the summer here, we accepted an offer to rent the old place out.''

''So next spring we can go to Town. It's a splendid scheme, isn't it, Jack?'' demanded Felicity, quelling her brother with a glance.

Jack agreed, then he poured himself another glass of wine, although he usually did not drink so many as three before dinner.

''Speaking of schemes, cousin,'' Francis continued smoothly, ''I'd like your advice on something—''

But his lordship's forbearance did not extend that far. He pulled out his watch and cried, ''Look at the time! I'd better order two more places set and tell Cook to put dinner back half an hour.''

He busied himself ringing for servants and issuing orders, and soon his competent housekeeper had whisked the visitors away to their rooms.

He dragged himself to his own chamber to change, for now that he had company, he could hardly dine in his buckskins and topboots. There was no help for it; Francis and Felicity fully expected him to entertain them, and he knew from experience that it would be most unwise to leave them to their own devices.

Then the solution came to him. His neighbours would soon be importuning him to join their society. He could easily fob them off with his young lively cousins, while he explained away his absence with the press of business concerning the new wing, the skeleton of which had already begun and was a visible assurance of his being occupied indeed.

Of course, apart from occasional conferences with Mr. Worthington, his architect, there was no need at all for the Earl of Selbridge to concern himself with the thing. He would go fishing.

Jack hummed as he took the crisp white neckcloth from his valet and tied it expertly over his collar. All that was needed was a little ingenuity, and any problem could be solved.

It was with a start of dismay that, some hours later after a lively dinner and a stimulating game of backgammon to the somewhat inexpert accompaniment of Felicity's play on the pianoforte, Jack realized that he had quite forgotten to think about his disappointment in love. He put in a few minutes of recollection and regret while he cleaned his teeth, and fell asleep very shortly after.

CHAPTER TWO

ONE FINE SUMMER MORNING a wagon piled with turnips and onions, its driver a freckled farm boy, trundled over the gravelled sweep up to the front door of Ellwood Park. Perched among the pungent vegetables was a young lady, clinging to a worn trunk that nested among the produce. Her attire, an unadorned but well-cut brown travelling dress perhaps four years out of date, proclaimed her an impoverished gentlewoman, but one with an arresting face.

It was a regular oval set with large, lively eyes the colour of fine sherry, a handsome straight nose and lips the shade of the blush on a ripe peach, all arranged in an expression of singular good humor. Her hair, a rich chestnut brown, glinted in the sun, and while she was not so unfortunately marked by the touch of that heavenly body as was her young coachman, she had freckles enough to give anxiety to a young lady with any pretensions to fashion.

The sight of a farmer's cart bringing an unaccompanied young lady to the door of the country estate of a gentleman like Sir Reginald Drakes may be supposed to cause a great deal of remark. No wonder then, that Miss Nancy Browne, the young lady in question, was surprised to note that her unconventional arrival aroused no curiosity. No one prevented the freckled boy from stopping his sturdy brown horse and wagon before the house, nor from unloading his passenger and her possessions.

Perhaps, Nancy thought, it was because the place seemed to be in turmoil already. The magnificent double doors at the top of a sweeping staircase stood ajar, and shouts and expostulations issued from within. Outside unattended horses wandered and two large pigs happily rooted and rolled in the mud.

At that moment a man in slovenly livery, his hair half powdered, rushed out and down the stairs, and, ignoring Nancy, demanded of a gardener engaged in desultorily trimming a skimpy shrub if he knew that the housekeeper had given notice. The gardener shrugged and continued to wield his shears.

The man in livery bewailed his misfortune. "'Tis a crime! Now I'll have twice as much work as before."

"And what would you be knowin' about work?" enquired his companion, waving his rusting implement, "Had it soft, Bowen, didn't you, all those years when mistress was alive?" He shrugged. "And d'you think it's my natr'l calling to fuss over this lot?" He indicated the sickly shrubs and overgrown lawn. "Lady Chetwynd took me away from the stables since the master fired the gardener."

"Well, you don't expect *me* to do everything, do you?" demanded the younger man, jerking at the tarnished gold-embroidered lapels of his ill-fitting coat. "I'm supposed to be a footman, and since last week, butler as well. Next they'll be wanting me for scullery maid!"

The unofficial gardener snickered and made a rude remark concerning the charms of the current scullery maid, until a gasp from Nancy, who stood nearby, recalled him to the fact that they were not alone.

"Beggin' your pardon, madam. Are you by any chance applyin' for the position of housekeeper?"

She knew she had every right to be offended at this supposition, but only smiled and shook her head. "I'm afraid not. I'm a visitor . . . and I suppose a rather unexpected one at that.''

She could only imagine that her letter to her cousin, Lady Chetwynd, announcing her imminent arrival and her pleasure in accepting her invitation, had been missent or that some emergency had called the family away. They had sent no one to meet her in the village, thus her ingenious method of arrival.

The two men looked with understanding at the trunk by her feet. ''Unexpected it may be, miss,'' the younger man said. ''I beg your pardon, but Sir Reginald hasn't never . . . that is, he doesn't permit any houseguests.''

''Shocking,'' said Nancy calmly, ''but it was Lady Chetwynd who invited me.''

The older one nudged his companion. ''Take the lady's things up, Mister Bowen, and show her inside, being as you're butler and footman both.''

The younger one frowned, but upon Nancy's sweetly apologizing for giving him so much trouble, he hoisted the trunk and she followed him up the stone steps. During this entire conversation, the shouts from the open door had increased, and now it appeared that not only was there an argument raging, but a footrace of some sort was in progress in the high-ceilinged hall bisected by an elegant staircase that swept up to a gallery.

The hall was nearly empty of furniture, and Nancy reflected that this was fortunate under the circumstances. For a young man was pursuing a young woman up and down the length of the room, with not much success, as he did not appear to be too steady on his feet and his prey was considerably quicker.

Simultaneously, a slender, middle-aged female in black was disputing loudly with a heavy, jowled woman wearing a stained apron. The participants of the race were ignored by these two ladies, whose discussion was heated indeed. Still, Nancy found her attention inescapably directed to the runners.

"Aiyee!" screamed the white-capped girl, holding her dirty cambric skirts aloft as she skidded to a stop just short of plunging through to the refuge of the service corridor. The young man, dressed in fashionable, though unkempt, attire grasped her firmly.

"Here now, sweet Bess, give us a squeeze. Don' be so unfriendly. After all, I'll prob'ly be your masser one day. Granfer's old, and Uncle Osbert'll most likely'll have no heir but me. You're a pretty thing, an' I mean you no harm..."

He changed to this coaxing tone after the young maid's expression turned from annoyance to disgust, probably, Nancy thought, at his wine-soaked breath.

"I fancy the girl finds herself unable to place much trust in *that* assertion, my dear sir," said Nancy, smiling kindly at the maid, who took the opportunity of her pursuer's distraction to flee.

"What the devil?" Mr. Gervaise Chetwynd whirled and then reddened as he took in the sight of the destroyer of his amusements. "Beg pardon," he said begrudgingly, as a recollection of the behaviour due a "respectable female" entered his wine-sodden brain.

"I daresay you do," replied Nancy. "Though I am certain you do not remember me, I am your mama's cousin, Nancy Browne. When I wrote to her of my mother's death, Lady Chetwynd was kind enough to invite me to visit."

Gervaise gulped. "Oh, indeed!" A great effort produced the vague memory of some impecunious cousins. He took the hand proffered to him. "Pleasure t'see you again, Cousin...Miss Browne."

"Oh, you may call me Nancy, as you did when we were younger." It had taken but a moment for her to realize that this despoiler of feminine virtue was her Cousin Gervaise, whose mischievous ways did not seem to have changed very much.

The arguing ladies had meanwhile stopped, finally alert to the interesting activity taking place in the rest of the hall. The aproned worthy, known to all merely as Cook, bustled over and shook her finger at the young man. "How many times has I told you, Master Gerry, to leave them gals alone? There'll be no gingerbread for *you* this afternoon!"

Gervaise blushed, casting despairing glances at Nancy, who looked on in undisguised amusement at his predicament. Poor Gervaise! He seemed to want to be taken seriously, but obviously some of the household persisted in regarding him merely as a naughty child.

Cook crossed her arms over her ample chest and turned to Nancy. "You're a mite young, miss, but you don't by any chance 'appen to be wanting the housekeeper's position?" Before Nancy or Gervaise could explain, she went on, "Seeing as this traitor—" she jerked her head at the thin woman in black, who sniffed haughtily "—thinks 'erself so above us that she can't stay another day. You don't see *me* leaving this unfortunate family all but helpless just because her sainted Ladyship is gone and it ain't all cream and roses 'round here no more!" She began to sniff and sob into her apron.

The deserting housekeeper turned to Nancy. "I ask you, miss, what was I to do? Things just aren't the same around here since the mistress has gone, and no one seems to care. I can't get maids to work here any more, and there's no butler, since the old one died, to keep the manservants in line. I'm too old for this job, and I mean to find myself an easier position. I'm sure no right-thinking person would blame me for wanting to leave this godless house!"

She stood firm and cast an unsympathetic eye on the emotional Cook, who merely sobbed harder and cried "Traitor! Turncoat!"

"Oh, dear," said Nancy, "both of you have been through quite a difficult time, haven't you? It is always so, I believe, when a house has the misfortune of losing its beloved mistress. But I'm sure Sir Reginald and Lady Chetwynd would be quite devastated to lose either one of you. After so many years of service you must be quite valuable to them."

To Gervaise's astonishment, at the end of three minutes, Cook was on her way back to her domain promising to produce a small collation, because, "you must be sharp-set after such a journey, Miss!" and the outgoing housekeeper exerted herself for one last duty in commandeering a passing housemaid and ordering her to prepare a room for Miss Browne. But when Nancy cordially shook her by the hand and wished her well in her new position, she appeared to experience a change of heart.

"To be sure, Miss, perhaps it is only temporary, and things will get better. Perhaps I'll wait another week. I haven't got another position yet." Then she asked if the visitor would like anything special for dinner, "seeing as the master eats only roast beef and Lady Chetwynd has no head for menus."

When informed that Miss Browne had a particular craving for some poached fish, baked chicken and fresh peas, she beamed and bustled off to the nether regions to inform Cook.

"And where," Nancy enquired of Gervaise now, "are your mother and grandfather?"

A female voice said, "Oh, Grandfather and Mama heard that the Earl of Selbridge was arrived and are gone to pay a call on him. Gervaise, do comb your hair, you look a positive disgrace. What will Miss Browne think of us?"

They both turned to see that Miss Eleanor Chetwynd had glided silently down the staircase to the hall, wearing a fixed smile and a pretty morning dress of blue sprigged muslin. There was no way of telling how much of the recent drama she had witnessed. "How do you do?" she said to Nancy, offering two fingers. "I expect you don't recognize me."

Nancy smiled and briefly clasped the fingers. "Of course I do, Cousin Eleanor. I should have to have a very sad memory to forget you after only four years. The only difference is that you are even prettier now than you were then. How do you do?"

Eleanor's smile became more genuine at this compliment, for she prided herself on her looks. "Very well, except, I must admit, for being excessively bored in the country."

Though she was all agog to know the reason for her cousin's sudden appearance on the doorstep of Ellwood, Eleanor's rigid idea of manners forbade her to enquire. Fortunately her brother was not averse to explaining.

"It seems, Nell, that Mama had invited cousin Nancy to visit us and, er—"

"You know that you are no longer to address me as Nell, Gervaise," she said automatically. "But Mama said nothing about inviting any—Oh!" Eleanor's glance flew to Nancy's face in apology.

"Well," Nancy said, laughing, "I thought it was only that my letter went astray, but I see that the invitation itself has been forgotten. And Sir Reginald, I understand, forbids visitors. Dear me, what a quandary!"

Eleanor did not know quite what to make of this, and was sure that in Miss Browne's place she would have been most affronted, but hastily bade her guest to step into the sitting-room and take off her bonnet, while her room was being readied. "For in spite of grandfather's nonsense," she said firmly, "of course, you must stay...for the night."

Nancy suppressed a smile, and untied her bonnet strings, looking around the room as she did so. It was a fine, high-ceilinged room at the front of the house, with two tall windows overlooking the lawns. The furniture was beautiful, but in need of polishing. The Axminster carpet could have used a cleaning. The draperies were red damask and coated with dust, the mirrors over the mantel and between the windows were elegant but fly-specked. If the room was representative of the rest of the house, she thought, then the place must have been much neglected of late.

"What a charming room," was all she said to Eleanor, but Gervaise made a wry face. "It was once, when Grandmama was here to look after it, but since then the old servants are inclined to die or desert us. The new ones just aren't up to the old standard." He sighed, as though the entire responsibility was his to shoulder.

"And I shouldn't wonder at it, Gerry," said his sister with some asperity, "if you persist in chasing them about the house like some country lout!"

"And may I remind *you*, my dear sister, that I am no longer to be addressed as 'Gerry'?"

"I suppose Lady Chetwynd finds it difficult to tolerate such a diminished household, when, no doubt, she was accustomed to the best of everything before your papa's demise," Nancy remarked, as though the sibling sparring had never taken place.

Gervaise grunted, but Eleanor looked upon her with new favour. "How aptly you have put it, Cousin Nancy. Nancy, is that your given name? I should have thought...that is..."

"It sounds like a housemaid's name, doesn't it?" said Nancy cheerfully. "That's just what Mama always said, but

Papa would never let her call me Anne. He said it sounded too stiff and formal.''

"Anne is a very elegant name," pronounced Eleanor.

"But she's not an Anne, is she?" said Gervaise, beginning to brighten in his friendly cousin's presence. "She's a Nancy. It suits 'er.''

The effects of his morning intoxication seemed to be wearing off. Nancy thought that some food would take care of the rest, and indeed was eager for some refreshment herself. At that moment a harried Bowen arrived with a tray of tea, cold meat, fruit and biscuits, and Nancy and Gervaise in particular partook heartily of this repast.

The three were actually third cousins, the young Chetwynds being the resident grandchildren of the master of Ellwood, Sir Reginald Drakes. He himself was the uncle of Nancy's late mother, who had married the improvident younger son of a Yorkshire gentleman named Browne. The rather reckless and altogether unfortunate Mr. Browne's search for employment had carried him back and forth across the country for years, and situated his family in a variety of cottages on the estates of more prosperous men, while Mr. Browne worked as estate manager or sometimes secretary, and his wife and daughter inhabited the social limbo of the not-quite-servant.

In consequence Mrs. Browne and her daughter had lived a difficult life for ladies of their station, and had not much contact with their grander relations.

The last occasion of the Brownes meeting the Chetwynds had been four years ago in London, when Lady Chetwynd's husband had been alive and had been prevailed upon to investigate some claim of support for his wife's cousin from her late husband's London relatives.

Having undertaken this duty, to no avail, Lord Chetwynd promptly expired, leaving his widow, who had always thought herself very wealthy, a surprising number of debts and two children who had to make their own way in the world. Lady Chetwynd had retreated to Ellwood Park, the home of her father, and the reunited family had lived more or less contentedly under the joint generalship of Sir Reginald and his wife, the sainted Lady Eleanor, who had died a year ago.

Since then, Gervaise and Eleanor told their cousin, the house was fallen into disarray, Mama was worn to a frazzle, and Grandpapa was simply impossible.

Nancy saw her slim hopes of accomplishing her own dreams falling to dust. Obviously Lady Chetwynd's invitation had been a casual, thoughtless one, and her promise to prepare Nancy to be presented to Society, equally insincere.

Nancy did not wish to be a governess and live in other people's houses or to inhabit any longer the shadowy world in which she had grown up. She lived and breathed the hope of a comfortable home and husband of her own, but had never remained in one place long enough for her to meet any possible suitors. She was determined to find a way to accomplish her goal. Her mama had scraped and saved all these years, unbeknownst to Nancy, to provide her with a dowry, as she discovered at her death. Now she must find a husband or live rootless and alone forever.

Here she was, and here she would stay. This decision was taken in less time than was required for Eleanor to ring for Bowen and have the bellpull break away in her hand.

But Miss Chetwynd only sighed, as if this was not an unusual occurrence, and Gervaise scrambled to his feet. "I'll go," he said, and walking a bit more steadily, he went.

Soon they heard him shout down the hall, "Halloo, Bowen! Come clear this tray, there's a good fellow."

He entered the room again a moment later. Even Nancy looked dismayed at his manner of summoning servants, and Eleanor bridled with disgust.

"You," she informed her brother, "have the manners of...of..." but before she could decide of what ill-mannered creature her brother reminded her, another gentleman entered the sitting-room. Osbert Drakes, heir to Ellwood, was a thin, stooped man of medium height and some thirty-five years. Though he wore no spectacles, Nancy thought he looked as though he ought to be.

Perhaps it was his constant squint or the nervous hand gestures toward his face that made her think so. Though unprepossessing, he was not completely unattractive. He did not have Gervaise's dark good looks nor Eleanor's classic features, but his thick hair was a soft shade of brown, and he had large, vague hazel eyes.

"What's this, children?" he said in a fine tenor voice. "I hear we have a visitor."

"Uncle Osbert," Eleanor began, sighing, "I do wish you wouldn't continually refer to us as children. Why, I am eighteen, and Gervaise is nearly twenty!"

"Stifle it, Nell," said her brother. "Nancy, this is Uncle Osbert. Uncle Oz, Miss Nancy Browne, our cousin from Yorkshire. Mama invited her to stay," he said with emphasis.

"What on earth do you mean, invited to...Oh, how do you do, Miss Browne." His vague glance wandered to her, and as she rose to give him her hand, Mr. Drakes blushed. "I'm sorry for my rudeness. It is just that..."

"We have enlightened Nancy about the situation here, Uncle Osbert," Eleanor informed him crisply. "However, we cannot send her away! She will, of course, spend the night. But if I were Mama, I should certainly speak strongly to Grandpapa."

"If you were Mama, Nell, Grandpapa would've turned us out long ago," said Gervaise. "She's too timid to say boo to a goose, so she always cries, which he detests, but you always manage to irritate him without saying anything at all!"

"That's not so!" Eleanor cried, like the child she was. "I only keep quiet around him because it's much the best way to avoid his temper and stay out of trouble. Not that you'd know anything about that! I heard him say if you went roistering to the village again he would have you locked out for the night!"

"Roistering, you call it? What would you know about it, you milk-and-water-miss! You never look lower than your own nose since you've come back from that fancy academy. I'm surprised you would condescend to discuss it," he mocked in a simpering tone.

"Oh, you two make my head ache," said Osbert, hands to his temples. "I cannot make them stop it. They're always fighting. You can see why I don't come out of my study, most days," he confided to Nancy, blushing as she smiled at him.

"They will outgrow it," she assured him, though personally she doubted it.

"And Uncle Oz, if you *would* come out of that dusty room of yours once in a while, be seen in Society occasionally, you might help matters. Grandfather would be much better-tempered if you went along with his plans," said Gervaise accusingly.

"Grandfather wishes Uncle Osbert to marry," whispered Eleanor, as if she were imparting a scandalous secret.

"And I wish he would leave me alone," mourned Osbert. "I . . . I can't abide females, always wanting to disturb my papers and things and making me eat when I'm not hungry and wanting me to dance attendance on 'em." Then, horrified at what he had said, he gasped. "Oh, I beg your pardon, Miss . . . Cousin Nancy . . . I didn't mean . . ."

"No, of course you didn't," she said soothingly, though privately she thought his lordship's opinions on the weaker sex understandable, considering that he had to live with Eleanor and Lady Chetwynd. "But wouldn't you like to have a wife and a family of your own one day?" she enquired gently.

"No," he said without hesitation. "I only want to be left alone. I am studying the history of the Roman occupation of this area and I do not wish to be disturbed."

Gervaise snorted, Eleanor gave an eloquent shrug, and Nancy nodded.

"Of course, then, you must not be. I shall take care while I am here, Cousin Osbert, never to wander into your study by mistake, even though I should be fascinated to see what you have learned. Why, just to think that the great Roman empire once had an outpost on our insignificant island is dreadfully exciting, and I'm sure your work is most important. I should like to make my small contribution to it by staying out of your way."

Osbert was plainly dumbfounded, and a giggle escaped the otherwise very controlled Miss Chetwynd.

Her uncle did not notice, but stared at Nancy in rapture. "Oh! I say, that is . . . rather kind of you, Miss Browne—I mean Nancy. Do you know . . . I mean I'm sure you're not a bluestocking, but . . . do you know anything about it?" His voice was hopeful.

"Hardly anything," she admitted blithely, "except for the fact that St. Albans, quite near here, was once Verulamium and that Queen Boadicea became very angry with the Romans and gathered a great many tribes and burned it. I suppose there is much more to know?"

Osbert's face bore a look of astonishment and pleasure. "Oh, indeed!" he replied, and launched into his plans for his book on the subject. "And I have a copy of a map... Oh, Bowen!" his fine voice carried out of the doorway to the beleaguered servant who was endeavouring to slip quietly by.

"Will you go to my study and bring the pile of papers in the centre of the desk? Oh, and find someone to help you and bring that stack of books in the corner behind the chair."

Bowen stared as if he thought Osbert had lost all of his faculties. "Y-your study, Mr. Osbert?"

"Yes, you know the place. Bring the things, quickly please!"

Gervaise and Eleanor exchanged glances of amazement, while Osbert continued to expound to Nancy on the importance of his work. Bowen and another servant in livery, who looked like a hastily promoted stableboy, entered with their arms full of books and papers, but after a moment's examination, Osbert claimed they weren't the right ones and sent them after more. Meanwhile he entertained Nancy and bored his niece and nephew rigid by expounding on his pet theories and insisting they read important bits of his correspondence. Nancy smiled at the young people sympathetically, but continued to appear interested and even to ask intelligent questions.

Again, Bowen and his assistant returned, and by now Nancy's questions had made Osbert think of another aspect of his research which might interest his cousin, so he sent the servants back to fetch yet more books and papers.

But while they awaited the arrival of this latest shipment, Mrs. Walker, still at her housekeeper's post, arrived to tell Nancy that her room was ready. Eleanor reminded her uncle that their guest might wish to refresh herself.

Nancy flashed Eleanor a grateful look and sped away in the housekeeper's wake, after assuring Osbert that she was filled with eagerness to see the rest of his discoveries.

Mrs. Walker led the way upstairs. "I must say I'm surprised, Miss, to see Mr. Osbert out of his room. He normally keeps to it all day, except on Sundays, when the master makes him come to church. And, of course, we couldn't clean it on the Sabbath." She shook her head. "I shudder to think what's living behind those bookshelves and under the carpets. That room hasn't been turned out in a year, not since Her Ladyship died. *She* was always able to make Mr. Osbert let us in."

Nancy laughed. "Then I fancy, Mrs. Walker, that if you are quick you might be able to accomplish it. It seems that Mr. Osbert is set on showing me all of his latest discoveries and is having your footman systematically empty his shelves. Soon the study will be all clear for the maids."

"Why, Miss, what a wonder you are!" And she hurried away to drum up a cleaning battalion. On her way back to the sitting-room, Nancy met the housekeeper again in the hall.

"I would never have believed it, Miss, if I hadn't seen it with my own eyes. Bowen's just brought out the last of those papers, and we've got the floor half-done already." She looked at Nancy in admiration. "It's almost like having the mistress back again!"

Thus, a quarter of an hour later, Sir Reginald and Lady Chetwynd returned to find the house apparently turned inside out. The housekeeper, who had given notice only that morning, was going briskly about her duties with a smile on her face, and the sitting-room was the lively setting for a group of young people, including the reclusive Osbert.

Half a dozen volumes on either side of him, Osbert read aloud in Latin, translating into English for the ladies' benefit. On the floor at his feet sat Gervaise, who was buried in an old book and, apparently having resurrected the Latin of his recently interrupted schooldays, was chuckling over what he called, "a *rather* warm passage."

Eleanor had found, underneath a pile of maps, some sketches of ancient costume, and was pointing out to Nancy the similarities to the French mode of several years before, which she had been too young and regrettably too proper to wear, but which she thought would have suited her admirably. Nancy sat amongst them, giving her attention to all three at once.

"Do my eyes deceive me, or is that my son Osbert?" said the gruff voice of Sir Reginald Drakes, standing in the doorway.

From behind him came a squeal. "Eleanor! Don't touch those dirty things or you will stain your gown! Papa, make Osbert take them back to his room."

Sir Reginald entered, and Lady Chetwynd, an older version of her ivory-skinned, pink-lipped daughter, appeared at his elbow. His son and grandchildren stood, looking absurdly guilty, as Nancy strode forward.

"Cousin Verena! I'm so sorry you didn't receive my letter. I'm afraid I have rather surprised all of you. But, of course, if my visit is not convenient, I shall return home," she said, placing a kiss on the cheek of the bewildered Lady Chetwynd.

"Hah! I know you," said Sir Reginald. "My niece Dorothea's girl. You look just like her. What the devil are you doing here? Thought you lived in Yorkshire."

"How do you do, Uncle Reginald," Nancy replied. She felt as though her smile was beginning to wear rather thin, but she persevered. "I'm sorry I descended upon you like this, but cousin Verena was kind enough to invite me to visit back when Mama died, and . . ."

"Hmm. Verena?" He turned to his daughter, who shrank visibly under his gaze.

"Well, I . . . yes, I suppose I did mention it in my letter of condolence . . ."

"And you were *so* generous in offering to take me to London with you next Season, when you present my lovely Cousin Eleanor. I should be delighted to join you," Nancy rushed on, seemingly oblivious to the gasps that filled the air, "and, of course, I shall pay my own way."

"Of course . . . I mean, no certainly, not . . . we shall be happy to have you," blundered Lady Chetwynd.

"The Season, eh? May I ask why I haven't been let into this grand scheme?" Sir Reginald demanded.

"Why, Father, of course you know I must present Eleanor. What other chance does my little girl have to make a respectable match?" she said with a quaver.

Sir Reginald snorted. "With no fortune, it's a waste to take her to London. And what's this nonsense about Mrs. Walker giving notice? She's still here and looks to be hard at work." He considered his daughter with new interest. "Haven't been at my brandy lately, have you, Verena? That would account for some of your recent behaviour—"

"Mrs. Walker has agreed to stay, grandfather," Eleanor interjected.

"Has she? And to what do we owe this miracle?"

"It's Cousin Nancy, sir," blurted Gervaise. "*She* convinced her."

He looked at Nancy with surprise. "I'd like to know how you did that, my girl."

"And I should be happy to tell you, Uncle Reginald," she said, smiling and taking his arm. Before he knew what was happening, Sir Reginald was being led out of the sitting-room.

"I do wish to apologize," Nancy said. "I understand you do not care for houseguests, and I don't blame you a bit. It causes such confusion!" She gestured to the mess in the sitting-room behind them.

"And what exactly is all that about?" he asked, still deciding whether or not to accept her apology. Perhaps his rule about guests was a bit too rigid.

"Oh, it's only Cousin Osbert's Roman things. I'm afraid I revealed an interest, so he became quite enthusiastic and eager to show me what he has found."

"Osbert? Enthusiastic and eager to talk to a female?"

"Oh, he told me how he feels about my sex in general, but I promised I wouldn't disturb his things," she said.

"Wouldn't disturb his—" Sir Reginald burst into hearty laughter, glancing again into the sitting-room where the contents of his son's sacred study were strewn carelessly over the furniture.

"You are an interesting piece of work, Miss. And now I suppose you'll be wanting to stay the night?"

"Oh, it would be so kind of you, sir. Of course, I would leave sooner, but I'm afraid there are no more coaches north till tomorrow morning. And I'm afraid that Mrs. Walker and Cook have gone to the trouble of planning a special dinner . . . they insisted, you see, and I didn't like to—"

Sir Reginald shook his head, laughed again and patted her arm. "I don't know what you did to bewitch them all, Miss Nancy Browne, but I confess this house hasn't seemed so interesting since my dear Eleanor left us." He sobered a minute, then said gruffly, "I suppose next you're going to tell me that Osbert's allowed the maids into his room to clean?"

"Oh, no, Uncle Reginald, I should never tell such a bouncer!" she cried. "He doesn't know a thing about it. They went in just after Bowen took out the last of his papers, and should be almost finished by now. I daresay once all his things are back in place, he'll never know it had been cleaned at all.''

"Baggage!" said Sir Reginald affectionately, completely forgetting that he hated houseguests. But what else could he do, when such a clever young woman was smiling up at him so irresistibly? He thought of Osbert's sudden animation. "You can stay, young lady," he said. At Nancy's profuse thanks, he frowned again. "But only because I am curious as to what you'll do next."

Nancy stared at him, wide-eyed. "Why, nothing that would displease you, sir."

"Hah!" was all Sir Reginald could say.

CHAPTER THREE

FOR THE FIRST DAY of their visit, Francis and Felicity professed themselves content to be entertained at Marbelmeade, and Jack rejoiced that he could postpone his round of social calls. He rode with his cousins in the early afternoon and then retired to his library, leaving them to their own amusements.

But he was not to be left alone long. Soon a knock on the door heralded Francis's entrance. Selbridge sighed, and said, "Yes?"

"I'm sorry to disturb you, Jack, there's something... that is, if you recall I mentioned yesterday..." In spite of the uncertainty of this speech, Francis had by now seated himself in the earl's favourite armchair.

Selbridge reluctantly gave him his attention. "Yes, I know, an important matter. Well, out with it. Worthington arrives today, and I must decide what changes I want made in these." He thumped the plans spread out before him.

"Yes, well, the thing is... I had a mind to marry."

"You, Francis! Aren't you a bit young to—"

"It's no use preaching at me, Jack. I'm old enough to know my own mind," he said quickly.

"Well! Then I wish you happy, and who, if I may ask, is the fortunate young lady?"

"Oh, there isn't one!" At Jack's raised eyebrows Francis laughed. "At least, not yet. I didn't say I'd had anyone particular in mind," he explained gently, as though he suddenly realized that his cousin's advanced age had affected his understanding.

Selbridge clamped his lips together, but Francis did not notice.

"You see, Jack, I've decided it ain't right for me to be a baronet and to be constantly short of the ready. Damme, I want to live like a gentleman, with none of this vulgar worrying over bills."

"If I can be of help..." Jack began, facing up to the inevitable and reaching for the keys of his strongbox.

"No!" Francis stood and began to pace the room. "I mean, thank you, Jack, you've always been generous, but I'm not talking about you tiding me over. I'm talking about the rest of my life, and Felicity's too. If I married well, I could introduce her to all the right people."

"I apprehend that by marrying well, you refer to a young lady of large fortune," said Jack.

Francis sat down again and leaned forward. "Exactly! Now I'm not usually in the way of meeting any heiresses. But you, Jack! You spend every Season in London, you attend Almack's and all that, surely you must know a host of 'em!"

"And you wondered if I would be kind enough to invite them all here so they could parade before you," Jack queried, smiling.

"Well, no, but I say, that would be famous of you, coz!"

Jack sighed. "I'm sorry, my boy, but you see, my acquaintance is rather deficient in heiresses right now. The last one I knew—" here at last, his lordship experienced a pang of disappointed love "—was a beauty I was after for myself, only she married another. After that I swore I'd have no truck with them!"

"Oh...I see," said Francis in some awe. "But don't you...that is, I know there is a great house or two hereabouts. Haven't they any...?"

"To my knowledge, there are no heiresses secreted in the neighborhood, my dear fellow." Francis's face fell. "But there is a monstrously pretty girl at Ellwood Park. She's Sir Reginald's granddaughter."

Francis brightened for a moment. "But has she any fortune?"

"As her father left the family in debt, she has only a very small one, I suppose," said Jack, thoroughly tired of the subject.

"Oh." Francis's face fell. "Well, I mean to go after the largest I can find. I have Great Ideas, Cousin, and if this heiress scheme falls through, I—I'm going to try one of them."

"Indeed?" Jack yawned.

Francis correctly interpreted this as a signal that he had tried his cousin's patience long enough. He rose. "Yes, I shall. It's a bit drastic, but...if I must, I shall." His smooth young jaw was determined.

"Very well, then. Just don't do anything dangerous, noisy or dirty," Jack called to him as he made his way to the door.

Francis turned to him and grinned. "Cut line, Jack. You sound just like my old Nanny on a rainy day in the nursery!" and left.

The earl tried to return to the contemplation of the projected facade for the new wing, but he could not completely suppress his curiosity where Francis's "Great Ideas" were concerned. When the boy spoke that way, he knew he ought to be worried, but there was precious little he could do about it, except to find his cousin an heiress, and this he was not foolish enough to attempt.

Soon, a gentle tap again summoned his attention to the door. This time it was Felicity. Jack suppressed his annoyance. Felicity was well aware of his rule regarding the library, but obviously thought herself above the general ban on females. It was tiresome, but last night at dinner he had noted that the girl seemed to have developed a real tendre for him. He stood at her entrance.

"Cousin Jack, I don't mean to disturb you, but—"

"But you do, nonetheless," Selbridge said with a smile. "I'm sure it is something important. Sit down, my dear." He indicated the chair he had just vacated and when she took it, quickly reclaimed his armchair. He hated to have anyone else sit in it.

"It is only that...you see, Cousin Jack, I'm worried about Francis. He seems to have gotten some strange ideas lately..."

"Not strange ideas, my girl," he corrected her wryly. "According to your brother, great ideas."

"Oh, he's been here first!" She looked put out. "Well, I must say that his main idea, to hang out for a rich wife, seems perfectly sensible," she said. "But he's...he's been messing about with some very odd things lately, and—" her fair forehead wrinkled in concern "—Cousin Jack, I'm frightened!"

Jack was alerted. "Frightened, my dear?"

"Oh, Jack," she said, drawing closer and putting her hands in his. "He has bought all these strange, thick books with odd symbols in them. And he has taken over the old still room and put them all there, along with foul-smelling bottles and stalks of dried herbs and—" she shuddered "—a lot of awful-looking shriveled things. And there's a spirit lamp and some glass jars and a big kettle and—"

"And a batch of eye of newt and toe of frog on the boil, no doubt," said Jack, unable to repress his amusement at this picture of Francis as an alchemist.

"It's not at all funny, Jack!" cried Felicity.

"I'm sure," he said soothingly, as soon as he had regained his composure, "that there is a reasonable explanation for this. If you simply ask him—"

"Oh, but I daren't!" she exclaimed. "I tried to once, and he . . . he threatened me!"

"Threatened you!" Jack's expression grew serious.

"Yes, he threatened to tell my governess—that was when she was still with us—that I was painting my face in secret."

Jack was smiling, but she was not looking at him. She examined her small white hands now back in her lap.

"And when he found me in the still room one day, looking at a page of a book that was open on a table, he flew into a rage! He said if I didn't mind my own business I would be sorry, because then he wouldn't take me to London. But I told him you and your mama would, and that he could take his smelly herbs and his old books and lock himself up with them forever if he liked."

Jack fervently hoped that neither he nor Francis would be reduced to such an extremity. The prospect of having his cousin Felicity at his heels in London was not to be borne. He would warn his mother in his next letter not to encourage the girl to think of it.

"Shall I speak to him about it?" he said, realizing this was the only way to end the matter.

"Oh, if you would! I know you can make him see sense, Jack. He always respects your opinion." She fluttered her thick lashes at him. "As I do, of course." She contrived to blush prettily.

Jack gently extricated his hands. "Then I shall give you my opinion on another matter, child. I advise you not to paint. It ain't becoming to a young girl, and—" he pinched her cheek avuncularly "—it's plain you don't need it."

Felicity looked as though she did not know whether to be pleased at the compliment or annoyed at his supposition that she was still a little girl, but correctly took this as her dismissal and left him alone.

But Selbridge had neither the leisure nor the inclination to approach Francis on the subject. His architect, Mr. Worthington, arrived, and the earl spent the latter part of the day in a much more productive manner than he had the morning. Although young, Worthington had been a pupil of Soane and had worked under Nash as well. Selbridge had at once agreed with his plans, and now he enjoyed their conference in which they worked on further details of the new construction.

The earl had high hopes of unifying the somewhat jumbled appearance of Marbelmeade by this new wing. The seat of the Selbridges had originally been an Elizabethan manor, shaped in a traditional "E," but the bottom and middle of the "E" had long since burned in a fire, leaving an inverted "L," which had been unsuitably renovated over successive generations. Jack had taken a liking to Mr. Worthington and had decided to treat him as a guest, hoping that his cousins would restrain themselves in the presence of a stranger.

But to his dismay, at dinner that night the architect's presence did not repress the spirits of either of the earl's cousins. Felicity hung on his lordship all evening, flattering, flirting and inquiring about all the scandals of the ton, while Francis beat him soundly at backgammon, and went so far as to ask Mr. Worthington if he knew any heiresses.

"Any Cit's daughter will do, you know, so long as she is pretty."

Fortunately the architect was a good-humored young man. His eyes twinkled as he assured Francis very solemnly that he would, upon returning to town, canvass all the heiresses of his acquaintance.

By the next day then, Selbridge was eager to begin calling on his neighbours and to introduce his cousins to them. He felt that the charm of the two was best appreciated when spread over a varied society, and he began enlarging their acquaintance by a visit to Ellwood Park.

When their carriage drew up to the entrance, Jack wondered if they had arrived at the right place, so orderly was it. Outside there was a servant he did not recognize expertly rolling the already neat lawn. The scraggly shrubs had been trimmed to a pleasing symmetry, the gravel sweep was neatly raked and the steps swept clean. All of the livestock seemed to be in its correct abode, for today he saw no horses, chickens, pigs or ducks wandering at their leisure over the formal grounds, as he had so often before.

"Sir Reginald must have had the latches on his pens repaired, at least," he murmured to himself. The door was opened, though, by a familiar servant, attired in clean and well-fitting livery.

"Good day, my Lord," said an unusually cheerful Bowen, ushering the visitors in with some ceremony.

"Ah, Bowen, take our cards up to Sir Reginald and her ladyship, will you? I must say, the place is looking splendid. Amazing when you consider you've been left without a housekeeper."

Bowen looked perplexed. "We have got a housekeeper, my Lord," he said.

"Well, that was quick work!" Never before had Sir Reginald replaced a servant so easily.

Bowen put them in the sitting-room and left.

Just as Selbridge began to notice that here, too, things seemed to be more orderly, the door flew open and a young woman in a plain blue cambric gown, a white apron round her waist, burst into the room and began to crawl about the floor.

"Here, kitty...here, puss...that naughty boy...he shouldn't have taken you away from your mama just for his own amusement and then left you—Oh!" The girl, who had directed her attention only to the area beneath the furniture since entering the room, looked up to see a pair of tasseled Hessians before her. Her surprised face was reflected in their mirror finish.

She looked up further and met Selbridge's eyes while Felicity and Francis nudged each other and exchanged amused glances. "Oh, I beg your pardon, sir! I didn't know anyone was in the room."

"Quite all right. Please, let me help you up, Miss... Mrs...."

"Browne," offered Nancy, taking his hand and rising gracefully. "I'm afraid that foolish Master Gervaise has let a kitten loose in here somewhere. After all I had to go through to make everything nice again..."

Selbridge was enlightened. "It is to you, then, that the family owes the improvements I've noticed at Ellwood. Quick work, Mrs. Browne."

Nancy smiled. "Well, I can hardly take the credit for all of it, but when I arrived and it seemed so obvious that help was needed, I could hardly ignore it."

Selbridge was amused. "Indeed, how could you? I must felicitate Lady Chetwynd on having found a jewel of a housekeeper on such short notice."

The girl's dark, delicate eyebrows rose a fraction. Then she burst into laughter. Her face was, Jack found himself

thinking, extremely pretty. He recalled a particularly fine
sherry in his cellars that was exactly the colour of her eyes,
and while he wondered at her sudden laughter, he thought
it quite delightful the way the morning sun from the window picked out the red in her hair.

Her hair! She wore no cap, and of course no respectable
housekeeper, however young, would go about the house
bareheaded. He perceived his error. The girl stopped
laughing, seeing the expression of chagrin on his face.

"Ah, I see you have discovered your mistake. No, I am
not the housekeeper. I am Sir Reginald's niece. Though I
suppose I may take credit for inducing Mrs. Walker not to
desert the family, I fear I am no closer to her position than
that." In spite of his embarrassment, he still had wit enough
to notice that her smile was extraordinarily lovely.

"Please, I hope you will forgive me, Miss Browne! It was
a shocking mistake." He bowed for good measure, while his
cousins looked on, astonished.

"Oh, it was really rather amusing, sir. I assure you, I am
not at all offended," Nancy replied. It was amazing,
thought Selbridge, that such good humour still sparkled in
her eyes and that her smile was undimmed despite his clumsy
mistake. What a fool he was! Surely no matronly housekeeper was ever this graceful or lively.

Felicity, perceiving her cousin's apparent fascination with
the shabbily dressed young lady, spoke up.

"It is very kind of you, Miss Browne, to forgive Jack so
quickly. You ought to be quite vexed with him. I know I
would be if he mistook *me* for a servant!"

Francis frowned at his fashionably attired sister and
apologized for her to the pretty Miss Browne. He had dis-
cerned at once that she was obviously no heiress, but she
certainly deserved better treatment than either of his relations had offered. "You must forgive my sister, Miss

Browne,'' he said, bowing over her hand. ''I fear she is young and has not yet developed manners.''

Nancy looked kindly at Felicity. ''Oh, but she is charming, and I doubt very much that Miss...?'' she looked a question at Francis.

''Garrard is our name, Miss Browne, and this is my cousin, Lord Selbridge,'' said Francis, indicating the bemused Jack.

Nancy smiled and said, ''How do you do?'' to both gentlemen, and then, ''I doubt Miss Garrard would ever show herself downstairs in such a manner that there could be the slightest danger of her being taken for a housekeeper.''

Felicity's hackles were smoothed at these generous compliments, and she decided at once that it was only the oddness of the lady's appearance that had caught Cousin Jack's interest.

''While I am, I fear,'' Nancy went on, ''a sad hoyden, and always will be. Now if you will excuse me, I shall let Cousin Verena know you are here and go and mend my appearance a bit.''

''But Miss Browne, will you so quickly abandon your design in coming to this room?'' enquired Selbridge. ''I would not like to think I have turned you from your errand.''

''Oh!'' Nancy felt herself blushing, for meeting these elegant people and being mistaken for a housekeeper had been so distracting that she had quite forgotten the poor kitten, and now it seemed the earl was laughing at her. ''Well, I suppose while I am here, I ought to—''

''Splendid! And we will help you,'' said Jack.

''That is not at all necessary, I assure you,'' she said, dropping to the floor once more and resuming her search.

"But I insist," said Jack, and soon he and Francis were down among the furniture legs peering about and calling, "Here, kitty!" while Felicity snickered at the sight. But as she hated to be left out of anything, she soon added her own mewing cries to attract the fugitive feline.

"I think I see something!" cried Francis. "Is it very little, Miss Browne, and a fluffy pale gray?"

Before Nancy could reply, Selbridge called out, "I think I have him! Here, little fellow," and he extended his hand under a heavy armchair, wiggling his fingertips in a manner curious cats cannot resist.

Felicity crowed with laughter as her brother, the knees of his pantaloons smudged, his hair in disorder and his neck-cloth crooked, cried triumphantly, "You're out there, Jack. I've got him!" He made a grab under the sofa and emerged with a large gray dust ball in his fist.

"Oh, my!" said Nancy, eyeing the ball with chagrin. "I'll have to tell Mrs. Walker to speak to the downstairs maid again."

Just then a shrill, protesting, "Meeeuw!" sounded from Selbridge's corner, along with a muffled curse from the earl himself, and from the door, Sir Reginald's deep voice.

"Why is it, Nancy my girl, that every time I enter this room I find everyone in confusion on the floor?"

The occupants of the room all stared guiltily up at him, as he was joined by Lady Chetwynd, who, with handkerchief to her mouth, gave a little cry of surprise.

Felicity had joined Selbridge in the corner and was kneeling beside him, dabbing at his scratched hand with her handkerchief, Francis was still crouched before the sofa clutching his dust ball, and Nancy was peering out from under the draperies. "Oh, Uncle Reginald, how odd this must seem to you," she cried, extricating herself from the embrace of many yards of damask.

"Odd, indeed," he said gruffly, though Selbridge knew he was repressing a chuckle. "What's this, my Lord? I suppose crawling about sitting-rooms is going to be this year's fashionable activity, eh?"

Selbridge leaped up and helped his cousin to her feet. "Good day, Sir Reginald. I would like to make known to you my cousins, Miss Felicity Garrard and her brother, Sir Francis," he said, as if nothing out of the ordinary had occurred.

Nancy stared at him with frank admiration.

"Pleasure," grunted the old man, and introduced his daughter, who stared suspiciously at the young people while attempting to fawn over Selbridge at the same time. At that moment a white blur raced across the blue carpet and snarled itself in her skirts.

"Oh, help!" Verena did a sideways dance and twitched her ruffled skirts back and forth while a tiny white kitten clung gamely to them. Finally Nancy, repressing a gale of giggles, ran forward and detached the truant.

"Now I've got you, you little bundle of trouble," she said triumphantly. "I'm so sorry, Cousin Verena. I should have warned you there was a cat loose in here, I know how you dislike animals. You see, I came in to search for him, and—"

"And made our acquaintance instead," Selbridge continued. "Then, I'm afraid, we all volunteered to help search for er...trouble, yes, I should recommend you to name him that, Miss Browne," he said, glancing at the kitten, unconcernedly washing one paw while clutched against Nancy's bosom. "That is, if you haven't named him already."

"Trouble," Nancy repeated. "An excellent notion. Thank you, my Lord," and with a last smile, discreetly removed herself and Trouble from the sitting-room.

After depositing the kitten back beside his mother in a basket in the kitchen, Nancy hurried upstairs to change. Though she had tried not to show it, her embarrassment at being taken for a housekeeper by her uncle's distinguished visitor had more than equalled her amusement, and she blamed her careless appearance and casual manners for the mistake.

These ragged ways of hers just wouldn't do, she told herself, if she wanted to be presented to Society.

Emerging from her room, she met her cousin Eleanor. Though she had changed her old blue cambric for a demure white muslin dress, she felt hopelessly dated beside Eleanor's fashionable figure.

"There are visitors downstairs," she told Eleanor, trying to suppress a note of excitement that unaccountably crept into her voice.

"Oh?" Eleanor enquired, brushing an infinitesimal speck of lint from her sleeve. Nancy sighed. How she wished she could summon up that look of sophisticated unconcern Eleanor managed so well!

"Yes, the Earl of Selbridge and a Sir Francis and Miss Felicity Garrard, his cousins."

Eleanor betrayed some interest at this. "I know Selbridge, of course, but with the cousins I don't believe I am acquainted. Shall we go down?"

"Yes, but . . ." Nancy hesitated. "Something rather distressing occurred just now." Hastily she explained about her search for the cat and Lord Selbridge's mistake. "I'm afraid he was a little shocked that I did not appear more affronted. It is simply that . . . well, I thought it amusing at the time and I really could not blame him for his mistake. And now he probably thinks I am terribly ignorant and unladylike and ought to be a housekeeper after all!"

Eleanor unbent enough to give her a sympathetic smile. "Dear Nancy, though you've only been with us two days, I begin to wonder how we got along without you before, and I would like to help. I know you wish to come to London with us next spring, do you not?"

"Oh, yes, I was hoping your mama would be kind enough to teach me how to go along..."

"Nonsense," said Eleanor. "Mama hasn't any more notion of how to get along in Society than has a baby. *I* shall teach you what you need to know. Of course, I have not yet been presented myself," she offered as a disclaimer, "but I read all of the fashionable journals and have been to an exclusive academy in London and correspond with many friends there in the ton. You really cannot do better than to let yourself be guided by me, Nan," she said, gracefully leading the way down to the sitting-room.

Nancy tried to imitate her stiff-backed posture, and tilted her chin up a little. *There,* she thought, catching sight of herself in the hall mirror, I look much more the thing now. So she re-entered the sitting-room in Eleanor's wake, prepared to imitate her manner to perfection.

Selbridge looked up eagerly at the entrance of the two young ladies. The conversation had grown dull, Sir Reginald, it seemed, not approving of Francis, and Lady Chetwynd equally unenthusiastic about Felicity, whether on her own or her daughter's account one could not say. Felicity clung close to Selbridge and tried in every way to stamp him with her ownership, while Lady Chetwynd rambled on about dear Eleanor and the brilliant Season she was sure to have.

"Dear Eleanor" was introduced to the Garrards, and though Felicity's expression was sour, Francis's was admiring, and he immediately engaged her in conversation. Selbridge wondered if Miss Chetwynd's lack of fortune would prevent him from amusing himself with her, decided that his cousin's scruples were not that strong and glanced quickly past Eleanor at Miss Browne.

Gone was her friendly smile, and in its place was a rather haughty expression. She was much more conventionally dressed than before, and instead of answering his frivolous question about "Trouble" as he expected her to, she merely thanked him rather stiffly for his assistance.

He stared at her in surprise and then nodded and turned away to speak to Eleanor. Nancy felt chilled for a moment, as if the sun had gone behind a cloud, but briskly told herself not to be nonsensical. Of course, he was surprised to find that she was a proper young lady after all. Likely he was deciding how he ought to change his manner toward her.

"I daresay you've noted the improvements, Selbridge," said Sir Reginald abruptly.

Selbridge replied, with a glance at Nancy, that he had.

"We owe it all to this girl, too." The baronet indicated his niece, but her wish that he would not mention it was as in vain as it was fervent.

"The day before yesterday, everything was on the point of collapse. Mrs. Walker had given notice, the whole estate was at sixes and sevens, my daughter with no more idea of how to go about fixing it than a monkey." Lady Chetwynd frowned at her father's bald description.

"An angel sent from heaven, that's what Nancy is," said Sir Reginald, uncharacteristically effusive.

Nancy laughed. "But Uncle, I sprang upon you all unawares. It was the least I could do."

"Nonsense, child." The baronet turned to Selbridge. "This girl will prove to be the gem of the family, mark my words. Knows how to make herself useful. As far as I'm concerned, she can stay as long as she likes."

Selbridge said, "Indeed, I am sure we all hope that Miss Browne will be making a long visit," and favoured her with a smile, which she returned much more quickly than she had meant to.

Felicity frowned, and Eleanor looked peevish, and first one, then the other quickly claimed Selbridge's attention. Francis's handsome face took on a sulky look at the lovely Miss Chetwynd's desertion, and he was left to Lady Chetwynd. Jack nodded at him, attempting to convey the reminder that if he wished to progress with the daughter he ought to try to charm the mother, but Francis did not get the hint and listened to her ladyship's chatter without interest.

Though refreshments were brought in and the conversation became general, Nancy did not feel comfortable. She found it difficult to keep her glance away from the Earl of Selbridge. He was a handsome, somewhat stocky man, energetic, rather than fashionably languid.

His brown hair was thick and curly, his eyes bright and merry, and his complexion that of a healthy outdoorsman. In short, she could not help but admire him and wish to engage his interest. Of course, being of so elevated a rank, he could never have an equal interest in her, but it would certainly be excellent practice for her forthcoming Season.

But how was she to conduct herself in an earl's company? She watched and listened to Eleanor carefully. Eleanor spoke of London. Nancy had only been there once and had little to say about it. Eleanor talked of the theatre. Nancy had never seen a play, though she had read all of Shakespeare. But how would one bring the subject around to a play one had read but not seen? Just as she was about to attempt it, the talk turned to music.

"Oh, you must hear my dear Eleanor play the harp—she is grown quite improved this past year," Lady Chetwynd was saying with a smile for her daughter and a significant nod to the earl.

Felicity Garrard was impressed in spite of herself. It was quite clear to her that this odiously beautiful Miss Chetwynd was trying to attract Jack's attention, and it irked her, but some native cunning made her realize that her advantage lay in emphasizing her family relationship with the earl and thus allaying suspicions that she might be trying to attract him for herself. A girl like Eleanor Chetwynd, she thought, could be an unwitting ally in this situation.

So she graciously expressed a wish to hear Miss Chetwynd play and timidly offered to return the favour by entertaining her with some selections on the pianoforte. "For Cousin Jack has been so kind as to offer to have his mama's instrument tuned for me, and with a few days practice I shall be a tolerable again." She favored her cousin with a sweet smile.

Miss Chetwynd, not at all fooled, for as she came into the room Miss Garrard had been flirting with her Cousin Selbridge in a very obvious way, gave a chilly smile and said she looked forward to it. Finally Nancy, who, though she had no truly fashionable accomplishments, had at least had some knowledge of music, sighed, in a fair imitation of Eleanor.

"I miss my own music most severely, Miss Garrard. I used to pass many hours of enjoyment on my harpsichord."

She was thoroughly unprepared for the quickly suppressed smirk on Felicity's face and for Eleanor's lifted eyebrows.

"Why," said Felicity, "how endearingly quaint of you, Miss Browne. I declare I have never even seen one. I believe my grandmother used to keep one in her rooms at Bath."

And thus Nancy's one poor accomplishment was reduced to a completely old-fashioned and uninteresting pastime more suitable for invalid old ladies than to marriageable young ones. She lapsed into silence, but not before she caught the ghost of a smile on the earl's lips. It heartened her somehow, though she realized that he, too, must be laughing at her lack of sophistication.

When the talk turned to next year's Season, she watched her cousin carefully and managed to look creditably bored with the whole process Lady Chetwynd excitedly described.

"I shall take a house I have been promised in Mayfair," she said to the earl, "and vouchers to Almack's are assured me, as at least two of the patronesses are my very dear, er, acquaintances." Nancy tried not to smile, but just then Selbridge glanced at her. Their eyes met for a moment, but Nancy quickly looked away, aware that it was most unsuitable for a young lady to stare so boldly at a gentleman.

There. Now he would know that she knew how to conduct herself properly. Somehow this did not make Nancy as happy as she thought it ought.

"And you, Miss Browne," Selbridge said, "shall you make your come-out this year as well?"

"I expect so, my Lord," she sounded as bored as she could. "Lady Chetwynd has kindly offered to sponsor me along with my Cousin Eleanor."

Eleanor gave her a sideways glance of approval, but Sir Reginald looked at her oddly. "What's the matter with you, niece? Have you got the headache? You're looking peaky."

Nancy was abruptly thrown into confusion by this enquiry, and she felt Selbridge's gaze on her, watching, measuring, perhaps, whether he was not correct the first time in believing her no more than a servant. Her company manners certainly needed polishing if she could not even cope with such a question from her own uncle!

"I am very well, Uncle Reginald," she said with as much composure as she could muster.

"Perhaps," said Felicity with elaborate kindness, "Miss Browne has knocked herself up with all her exertions here. What with cozening your housekeeper to stay and running after stray kittens..." She gave a silvery peal of a laugh. "I confess it would be enough to make me take to my room with the headache. To be sure, how busy you are, Miss Browne, is she not, Jack?" She leaned confidentially toward the earl.

Nancy was hurt, but her understanding was excellent. Miss Garrard was making it as plain as possible that she did not appreciate any other females making themselves interesting to Lord Selbridge, and Lady Chetwynd made it equally obvious that she considered him her exclusive property, or Eleanor's. Even now she was securing his acceptance for a dance she planned to give her daughter quite six months away.

Eleanor, too, though she had kindly offered Nancy her assistance, had now cast her adrift and set about to charm the earl herself. Nancy, her heart sinking, immediately withdrew from the fray. How could she possibly compete? As the guests finally took their leave, the earl bestowing only a casual goodbye on her, she promised herself she would work to acquire all the requisite graces and accomplishments, and by the time the Season began, she vowed, would learn to put them to good use.

CHAPTER FOUR

LORD SELBRIDGE AROSE EARLY the next morning and crept out of the house, hoping the hour was sufficiently uncivilized for his guests not to be abroad yet.

He entered his stableyard and soon had one of his favourite horses made ready for him. So far he had not resorted to this kind of early exercise while at Marbelmeade, but as he rode away, blessedly alone, and observed how the sun shone gently on the old stone buildings and peace lay upon the estate, Jack wished he had not wasted these precious early hours in past days.

When he had first arrived at Marbelmeade he had expected to retire to a sleepless couch late every night and lie abed every morning thinking of Her, whom he had lost, but although he had certainly lain abed till almost nine, he had found himself thinking mostly of his breakfast or if he ought to have stucco or brick for the first storey of the new wing and if he ought to overhaul the old kitchens as well.

Now Jack laughed for having deluded himself that the morning must be devoted to languishing in bed, and decided that he would have an early ride every morning as long as the weather remained fine. He almost changed his mind, however, when, having ridden along a path through park and fields and along the side of the lake that lay between Selbridge lands and Drakes lands, he saw an unmistakably female figure, well-mounted and habited, riding toward him.

For a moment he was horrorstruck, thinking it might be Lady Verena or the slyly insipid Eleanor, but then he realized that the one did not ride and the other would never allow herself to be seen on a horse alone and at such an unfashionable hour. The female rider slowed her horse, seemed to hesitate, and at that moment Jack realized that it was Miss Browne. Without thinking, he urged his mount forward and went to greet her.

"Good morning!"

"Oh, yes, it is a glorious morning!" Miss Browne replied, looking about her with appreciation. "You are very fortunate to live here, Lord Selbridge." Then she turned pink, as if afraid she had overstepped the bounds of propriety.

Selbridge found this fascinating. "I have never thought of it that way," he said, as side by side they began to walk their animals around the lakeside path. "Although I have always loved Marbelmeade and used to know every wood and field intimately, I really haven't spent enough time here of late." He looked around, seeing here a tree he had once climbed, and there the spot where he had always dropped his clothes before bathing in the lake. "But you are right, I am fortunate."

Nancy was silent. Only last night she'd vowed to learn her Cousin Eleanor's rules of behaviour, and here she'd blurted out the first thing that had come to mind. But she'd not been able to help herself. The spell of the place's beauty had been upon her.

When she had arisen not long after dawn, as was her habit, Nancy had permitted herself a walk in the garden before beginning the household duties, which should have been Lady Verena's but had become, by unspoken agreement, hers. There to her surprise she had met Sir Reginald, who had already ridden and was returning to the house for his own breakfast. Finding that his niece could ride and possessed the necessary attire—thanks to a kindly governess at her father's last place of employment who'd given her the mistress's castoffs—the baronet had sent her up to her room to change and had given orders to the stables to prepare Lady, a well-behaved chestnut mare, nominally Eleanor's, for Miss Browne's ride.

Dressed in what she considered her one becoming suit of clothes, Nancy had all but forgotten the duties awaiting her and had been enjoying the dainty-stepping Lady and the lake shimmering in the morning sun, and had been taken by surprise when she met the earl. Now he was looking at her strangely, and she suddenly realized that she had not replied to his last remark. Her cheeks felt hot, and she wondered how long she had been staring at him in stupid silence.

But Selbridge saw her distress and though he was puzzled at her sudden shyness, he spoke kindly to her, attempting to draw her out, though with little success at first, for he questioned her about her former life, and naturally enough, Nancy did not want him to know how sad and humble an existence it had been.

"My mother was Sir Reginald's niece, and my father's people were small landowners in the north. Other than that, my Lord, it is a dull story, one I am certain would bore you."

She did not smile, and Selbridge thought he might have offended her, so he gradually drew the conversation away to his plans for Marbelmeade.

In this Nancy could not help but take an interest, and as the earl described his plans to her she had to stop herself several times from interjecting a comment. She loved big, old stately houses, and at one of her father's places of employment she had been privileged to witness just such a building project as Selbridge's, but quickly realized how unsuitable it would be for a fashionable young lady to have any opinions on the subject, and confined herself to saying she thought his plans sounded charming.

Selbridge started and looked keenly at her, wondering if she was bored or making fun of him. But Miss Browne's mobile, expressive face was pursed in a prim expression more suited, he thought, to her cousin Miss Chetwynd. What has gotten into the girl, he wondered, and began to regret his impulse of joining his ride to hers.

"I hope you don't mind," he said, as they came to a turning where the path roamed away from the lakeside and traversed the edge of his own lands. "I usually have a good gallop here." He saw at once the disappointment in her eyes.

"Will you join me?" he continued, surprised at his invitation. To his astonishment, she did not decline nor show offence at his questionable manners, and her eyes glowed softly and becomingly.

"Oh, may I? This mare has such a sweet pace, and I have been longing to let her have her head."

Cheered at this sign of animation, Selbridge smiled and said, "Why not make it a race? To that hedge, where your Uncle's property begins."

"Agreed!" Nancy quite forgot all else in the excitement, and in a moment they were off. It was glorious to feel the wind in one's face and the warm sun on one's back, thought Nancy. She had no hope of winning, for she saw that his lordship's horse was far superior, and, of course, she was hampered by not being able to ride astride, but it was a joy just the same. It was only when she reached the hedge almost on Selbridge's heels that she realized she had once again proved herself a hoyden. But strangely, the smiling Selbridge did not seem to care. He even congratulated her on running a good race.

Of course, Nancy told herself, it was only his good manners. He no doubt thought her ill-bred. She was about to withdraw into her imitation of Cousin Eleanor when Selbridge, who saw the dawning of severity in her eyes, swiftly engaged her attention by commenting on the cows grazing nearby.

To his amusement, for he expected her to say that they were very pretty cows, or something equally inane, Miss Browne delivered firm, intelligent opinions of her uncle's livestock, and before he knew it they had progressed from Sir Reginald's cows to his pigs to his poultry to his stables, on all of which Miss Browne appeared singularly well-informed.

Selbridge was generous with his approbation. "How delightful that you know all about these things! I've never spoken to a young lady with such a good head for estate matters, Miss Browne."

Nancy, disarmed by this praise, said simply, "Father helped manage some of the finest estates in the north, and as a child I followed upon his heels and learned a lot." She stopped, remembering that this was hardly the kind of background she ought to admit to, but the earl did not seem at all disgusted. He began to talk about his own estate and interests, and before Nancy knew they had embarked on a lively discussion of dogs, both of them deprecating the fact that Sir Reginald did not keep any and imagining which breeds would best suit the household at Ellwood.

"For Sir Reginald, a spaniel," said the earl.

"A pug for Cousin Verena," Nancy decided. "A little fat yapping one with bad breath."

Selbridge agreed. "Lady Verena is not fit to own a *real* dog."

Nancy suppressed a giggle. "For Gervaise, a pointer," she suggested.

"For hunting housemaids," said the earl. This time Nancy laughed aloud, and the earl joined her.

"No dog for my Cousin Eleanor," she said when they had recovered.

"Is she frightened of them?" enquired the earl.

"Oh, no!" replied Nancy, shocked. She could not imagine the self-possessed Eleanor afraid of anything. "A dog would not frighten her, but she does like to keep herself neat, and one cannot have even a lapdog without getting untidy sometimes."

"True," agreed Selbridge. "You know, you must come to Marbelmeade soon and let me introduce you to my dogs. My mother won't have them in the house, except for Griselda, who is so old and lazy that she does nothing but sleep, but I think you will like my kennels."

Suddenly mindful of her untidy appearance and the sinking feeling she had proven herself worthy only of his lordship's kennels, Nancy murmured that she would be delighted, then said, "I must go now, my Lord. The housekeeper—I mean Lady Chetwynd—will be expecting me. We are embroidering a pelisse with worsted—all in satin-stitch," she announced, for she did not wish the earl to think she was totally devoid of feminine accomplishments, though in fact her aunt and Eleanor were teaching her the art of the needle. "And then there will be an appliqué..."

But his lordship did not seem appreciative. "Very well," he said, and bade her good day.

Nancy was disappointed, but, of course, Lord Selbridge did not wish to hear her run on about her embroidery. How silly of her to think that she could impress him that way!

Jack, in fact, did not know exactly why his immense enjoyment with Miss Browne had ceased. It was as if suddenly she had turned into a different young lady altogether. But he put it out of his mind and went off to his breakfast.

When he approached the breakfast parlor after changing his attire, he heard the voices of Francis and Felicity raised in a quarrel.

"It's none of your affair, Felicity, and I won't have you interfering with my plans."

"Oh, piffle to your plans, Francis! It certainly is my affair if you are going to continue doing those same strange things here as you were doing at home. Jack will be annoyed and send us away, and then what shall I do all summer? I will not go to Bath, and I am determined to spend the Season with Jack and Aunt Margaret next year, so you had better stop whatever nonsense you are planning or else Jack will be angry with both of us!"

"Sisters!" said Francis in disgust.

"How can you be so unkind?" Felicity was saying, and hearing the tears in her voice, Selbridge expected a storm and decided, albeit reluctantly, that he ought to make an entrance.

The two looked up guiltily as the earl entered. They turned their attention to their breakfasts, but as Jack sipped his coffee he noticed that they both continually glanced up at him, Felicity's face pleading, Francis's wary.

Selbridge sighed, put down his cup and looked at them enquiringly.

Sister and brother both began to speak at once, glared at each other and stopped.

"Well, what is it?" said Selbridge, his patience suddenly grown short.

"Francis is being horrid to me, Jack," said Felicity piteously. "He is trying to disgrace me."

"That's nonsense, Felicity, and you know it. I'm only trying to do something with my life, and yours too, for how do you expect to be comfortably settled without my help?"

"If you are so determined to help me, Francis, then why won't you tell me what was in that trunk they delivered this morning from Birchley?"

Francis grew red. "I cannot. Not yet, at any rate. You will just have to be satisfied, Felicity, that I have your best interests at heart."

"Oh!" Felicity cried, flinging down her fork and pushing herself away from the table. "Not that speech again! Can't you do something, Jack?" she demanded.

Selbridge said coolly, "Not until you learn to behave better, my dear. That is no way to speak to your brother."

"It isn't fair. You are all against me," she cried, and fled from the room in tears.

Selbridge sighed, for he knew he would have to confront Felicity later. He turned to Francis. "Would you mind telling me what that was all about, sir?"

Francis's handsome face took on an expression of sullenness tinged with slyness. "It is only... You recall I told you that I had plans, Jack."

Jack said he recalled the occasion perfectly, and waited.

"Well, I have decided that it is unlikely that I will meet any heiresses and that I ought to waste no time in carrying out my plans. And today I will begin."

"How very interesting," his cousin commented. "I wish you good fortune. However, this does not explain your sister's outburst."

"Oh, Felicity doesn't understand. A man must do what he must do," he said stoutly.

Jack yawned. " Doubtless, but must he be a bore?"

Francis looked pained, but remained adamant.

"Well, I beg of you do not upset her. I shall not ask you to explain your plans to me unless you wish it, and I will do my best to calm your sister, but you must tell me one thing," he said, remembering the promise Felicity had extracted

from him the day of her arrival. "It is not anything dangerous or foolish, is it? Your sister seemed to have some idea of
your dabbling in alchemy or something of that sort."

The young baronet's brow cleared. "Oh, no, sir, certainly not! Just the sort of rubbish she *would* think! In fact,
it is about as harmless, and if it succeeds, it will make me a
rich man."

"Ah," said Jack, as if he completely understood, which
he by no means did. "Well, then, I can tell your sister with
a clear conscience that I have spoken to you and that your
plans will have no detrimental effect upon her situation."

With that he went on with his breakfast. Francis slipped
away to examine and arrange the contents of the trunk that
had arrived from the coaching inn in the village, having already wheedled the housekeeper into letting him have an
unused room in one of the old towers.

When Francis appeared for luncheon, he seemed ab-
sorbed in his own thoughts and was no trouble to his cousin.
Felicity, however, had sent word that she had the headache, and after the mercifully quiet meal, Jack knocked at
the door of his mother's sitting-room, which Felicity had
taken for her own, to find her sitting red-eyed near a window, torturing a piece of silk with a needle and thread.

She rose, obviously about to fling herself on him, but
Jack held up his hands and said, "I have spoken to Francis, and he assures me that what he is doing is completely
harmless and will bring no trouble to you in any way."

"Oh, Cousin Jack!" exclaimed Felicity.

Fortunately, Selbridge had managed to barricade himself behind a large table, so all Felicity could do was stare at
him with worshipful eyes.

"And from now on I do wish you would remember your
manners, my dear. I do not wish to enter my breakfast parlour and hear my houseguests engaged in a loud argument.

If you do not promise to behave, I will leave you home tonight. Sir Reginald, I know, will not tolerate that sort of thing at his table."

Miss Garrard's dramatics dissolved instantly, and she put on a pout. "I know very well how to behave, Jack, but Francis put me all out of temper. I was so certain that he was up to something dreadful. But now I promise I will be good," she said, and sidled up to him kittenishly.

Selbridge retreated farther around the table, but smiled. "I hope so. And now why don't you take some air? It is too beautiful a day for you to sit in this stuffy house. You can have my carriage and a maid and drive into the village if you like."

"Oh, thank you, dear Jack!" Away went Felicity to change, while Lord Selbridge made a quick escape to the estate office, where he conferred with various employees and tenants, until it was time to change for dinner at Ellwood Park.

He had been looking forward to seeing his cousins more securely introduced into the society of the family at Ellwood. Although their first visit had not been promising, he had not entirely lost hope of the young people all becoming friends. He had also, since that surprising meeting and ride that morning, been looking forward to seeing the unpredictable Miss Browne again. Although she seemed to waver between her charming self and being someone else entirely, the earl could not but admit to himself that he found her intriguing.

To his severe disappointment, when they were shown into the drawing-room, Miss Browne appeared insipid once more, and although Selbridge talked to her for some five minutes, he could not disengage her from her Cousin Eleanor, and, to Lady Chetwynd's apparent delight, had perforce to talk to her as well.

Felicity frowned, but Gervaise was looking at her admiringly, and she was soon lapping up his compliments. Sir Francis enjoyed himself much less, as he was undergoing examination by Sir Reginald on the subject of his meager patrimony, his education and his politics. From Sir Reginald's occasional snorts Selbridge apprehended that his cousin was failing miserably, thus pleasing his host, who loved nothing better than to disapprove of something or someone.

Finally Jack tired of trying to elicit a spontaneous word or smile from the very proper Miss Browne. Francis was shooting him looks of despair when he was not casting longing gazes at Miss Eleanor Chetwynd, so, dexterously leaving the two young ladies, Selbridge went to rescue his cousin from Sir Reginald's inquisition.

Unfortunately Lady Verena intercepted him, and, shrugging helplessly at Francis, he was made to sit down with her ladyship and listen to a discourse on Miss Chetwynd's beauty and talents.

Dinner was no better. Jack was placed between Miss Chetwynd and Miss Browne, and while he now felt ready to continue his attempt to talk to the latter, the former occupied his attention for a good part of the meal. Felicity, placed across from him with Gervaise on one side and the silent and gloomy Osbert on the other, laughed shrilly at all that was said to her and flashed looks like daggers at Miss Chetwynd.

Miss Browne, meanwhile, appeared to be watching Eleanor carefully, and Jack could not help but wonder if she was confused about which fork to use. When he escaped Miss Chetwynd's insipid chatter and managed to address a remark to her, Miss Browne was tongue-tied, until he recalled his promise to show her his kennels and attempted to fix a day for her to visit.

"Oh, that is so kind of you, my Lord," Nancy replied, "but I am afraid I will be much engaged for the next few days."

This was what Eleanor, for whose advice she had applied after the morning's ride, had told her to say. She had been correct in thinking that she had made the wrong impression on the earl, for her cousin had said, "How shocking, dear Nan, to invite a young lady to see a lot of noisy, dirty animals. He should have invited you for a drive or to see his gardens or hothouses, but a kennel! Most unsuitable."

Nancy had been disappointed, for she was truly interested in seeing his lordship's dogs, but she had bowed to her cousin's superior knowledge of the proper thing.

Selbridge was taken aback and then disgusted at her politely worded refusal. He said, "I am so sorry. I beg you will let me know when you are at leisure," and then Eleanor captured him again.

It was a relief to Nancy when Lady Chetwynd led the ladies from the room, but her relief was short-lived, for Eleanor and Felicity began a conversation in which she could take no part, as she had little knowledge of current fashions, knew little popular poetry or music and could not boast of any conquests at local dances and assemblies.

Felicity, despite her lack of fortune, had been accustomed to being made much of in her little circle, and, of course, Eleanor fully intended to be a great success next Season in London. Felicity was full of "Cousin Jack," while Eleanor smiled patronizingly and said how much she was looking forward to having him at her coming-out ball.

Nancy sat dumbly, wondering what she could say to impress Lord Selbridge and thought for a moment that, when he returned, Eleanor and Miss Garrard would very likely tear him apart between them. She found herself smiling at the thought.

The door to the drawing-room opened, and the men appeared. Nancy saw her cousin and Miss Garrard sit up straighter and sweeten their expressions, saw Eleanor put a hand surreptitiously to her hair, saw her bite her lips to redden them, and her heart sank. But to her amazement, Lord Selbridge ignored these signs of readiness to be flirted with and came straight to where Nancy sat with Lady Verena.

Quite without thinking she replied naturally to his first remark about the progress of Sir Reginald's crops, and it was at least two minutes before lady Verena could spoil their enjoyment by entangling Lord Selbridge in a discussion of his mother's health and from there to searching out a nonexistent connection between the earls of Selbridge and the Drakes family, who, although they had been neighbours for a century or two, curiously had never intermarried.

"Not yet, my Lord," said her ladyship, glancing at her daughter. "But time will tell."

His lordship squirmed, but Nancy hardly noticed it, so deep was her sense of disappointment. It was not because her aunt had interrupted her conversation with the earl. No, that was obviously only because she'd been talking to Lord Selbridge about inappropriate subjects. But she knew nothing of his family, nor indeed much of the Drakes, her mother's family. She was, in fact, an outsider, in more ways than one.

However, she soon noticed that her Cousin Osbert was sitting alone, looking eager to slip away, which would only earn him a scold from Sir Reginald, so she went to him and let him talk to her for a while about the Romans, till she heard Sir Reginald bark at his granddaughter, "There's that harp of yours collecting dust in a corner, Miss Eleanor. Let's hear some music, or were all those expensive lessons for nothing, eh?"

Although obviously disgusted with his manner of requesting music, Eleanor could not quarrel with her grandfather, and indeed was eager to perform before Lord Selbridge. So she disposed herself gracefully at the instrument, casting a quick glance in his direction, to be certain that the earl was watching, as indeed he was, but only out of politeness, and began to play. She seemed scarcely to notice Sir Francis Garrard's more eager attention, and the fact that he moved his seat so as to be able to observe the fair performer more closely. Nancy noticed it, and felt sorry for the young man, who so far had not had much luck in attracting Eleanor's attention.

As for the performance itself, Nancy had heard her cousin practising a few times and found that she generally had one of two reactions to harp music. The first, when she was tired enough, was to fall asleep; the other was to become irritable, and right now it was a struggle as to which reaction would claim her. Fortunately she was far too anxious to sleep, so it was the latter, which she controlled with difficulty while the maddening string-plucking tinkle went on and on.

Apparently Sir Reginald was easily convinced that his money had not been wasted, for to his own disgust it was he who had paid to send his granddaughter to her high-flown London academy, and he soon called for someone to play on the pianoforte.

Felicity, who had been gnawing her lips in frustration, for she assumed that the expression on her Cousin Jack's face at hearing the heavenly music was rapture, and not boredom, was quick to oblige, and soon had gathered all the young people about her at the instrument. She and Francis sang a duet very prettily, and Lady Verena, not to be outdone, clapped and said, "How delightful. Eleanor and

Gervaise always used to sing charmingly together. Why don't you sing something now, my dears?''

But as the duets referred to had taken place some years ago in the nursery, and the songs would have been unfit for adult company in any case, her request could not be obeyed. In any case, as Nancy swiftly observed, wondering how she had missed it before, Gervaise was not with them.

''Why, where is your brother, Eleanor?'' Lady Chetwynd asked, as though she were surprised, but Nancy knew that it was not at all unusual for her cousin to absent himself in the evening. Even she, however, had not expected him to leave while there were guests, and she was ashamed for him.

''How should I know, mama?'' Eleanor retorted.

Nancy saw trouble brewing and stepped in boldly. ''Oh, I am so sorry, Cousin Verena. I'm afraid it is all my fault. You see, Gervaise took me aside earlier and said he wished me to make his excuses and apologies to everyone. He was not feeling well, and I know I ought to have told you, but somehow it slipped my mind.''

Selbridge stared at her in admiration and delight, for he had never heard such a barefaced lie more gracefully told. He realized, if no one else did, that Gervaise and Nancy would not have had a moment to confer that evening, as they had been seated well away from one another at dinner, and Gervaise had partaken deeply of the port afterward and had last been seen following the gentlemen back to the drawing-room. It was then, Jack mused, that the young devil must have slipped away.

Fortunately Lady Verena was too embarrassed to do more than grab gladly at this straw, and said, ''Oh, the poor boy. One of his headaches, I suppose.''

Sir Reginald's lined face grew mottled with anger, and Nancy was afraid of what he might say, so she hurriedly begged Felicity to play again, and made Osbert sing a duet with her, which startled Osbert's father so much that he forgot about Gervaise and listened. Nancy had discovered that Osbert was fond of music as well as ancient history, and had made a point of asking his opinion on a song she was trying to learn, for Eleanor had graciously allowed her the occasional use of the pianoforte, so that she might wipe away the disgrace of the harpsichord.

Gratified at her great-uncle's approval of the duet with Osbert, Nancy was too relieved at having averted a scene to notice the look of speculation that crossed Sir Reginald's face or the admiration on Selbridge's.

Meanwhile, the absent Gervaise was already feeling the effects of a prolonged drinking bout with a motley collection of male companions in the village tavern. That most of them were not of his own class did not trouble him, or at least it did not after he had disposed of several glasses of spirits. He was already quite boisterous, and boasted of having escaped a dinner party at which the earl of Selbridge had been a guest, after which he made several drunken wagers, which he lost, and finally, quite late, he and the others were ejected from the tavern.

He was going to make his way home alone, but was not loath to stop and take one final challenge.

"I'll wager," cried Tom, the well-known ne'er-do-well son of a yeoman farmer, "that the young genlem'n couldn't lead my father's prize bull through his lordship's garden without rousing the house."

"Oh, you do, eh?" Gervaise was eager to defend his honor. "Well, lead me to that bull!"

At his drunken bravado, Gervaise's companions jeered, but the bet was accepted and much furious wagering took place.

Then the party of eight men straggled along a lane to the farm, where the farmer's son deftly brought out the bull, who allowed himself to be led along the empty moonlit road to Marbelmeade.

By this time Gervaise began to have second thoughts about his wager, but when Marbelmeade was in sight, he was still flushed with liquor and boldly took hold of the bull's rope, urging him through a small gate that led into Selbridge's park, along a path and so to the gardens, which some Italophile ancestor of the earl's had adorned with marble figures of every size and form.

Now statuary in the moonlight may be romantic to some, but to a bull that has been awakened from sleep, dragged hither and thither on the end of a rope by a band of rowdies and now put into the care of a very drunk young man totally unaccustomed to large farm animals, it was maddening.

No sooner had Gervaise given an unwise tug on the rope and an even more foolhardy slap on the animal's side, than its eyes rolled around, it began to snort alarmingly, and a horrified Gervaise let go of the rope, some remaining sense telling him that if he did not he would be dragged through the garden and end up flung into a marble urn.

The angered animal picked up speed, his hooves scattering gravel and thundering on brick, his sides brushing the hedges, and as he turned, offended at the sight of a figure in marble draperies glowing eerily in the moonlight above his head, his mighty rump crashed against a narrow pedestal opposite the statue, and a smaller statue fell with a crash. Pillars toppled, and the more delicate of the urns and benches were doomed.

Now the bull was not the only one to be shocked at these occurrences, and the brave men of the tavern set, after shouting loudly enough to wake the house, were disappear-

ing into the night, except the yeoman farmer's son, for fear
of his father's wrath should he lose the bull.

The unfortunate animal became trapped in a maze of little paths, where at every turning, there was a bench or pedestal, rosebush or flowerbed to be upset or trampled. Finally
the bull could stand no more, and working his way to the
edge of the garden, headed for the open ground, gored his
way through a gap in the hedge and left, his owner's son on
his heels.

Thus, by the time the earl of Selbridge, his gardener, who
slept in a cottage not far away, and several of his servants
appeared in the garden, Gervaise was alone with the wreck-
age.

"Who's there? Come forward where I can see you," ordered Selbridge, angry first at being awakened, and now
that the damage in his mama's precious garden was revealed to him, furious.

"I...it is I, Chetwynd, my Lord," said Gervaise in a
strangled voice. Many had been the pranks he had faced up
to and paid for at Oxford and before that at Eton, but this,
he thought, facing the fury of Lord Selbridge, was worse
than any of them.

"Chetwynd! I thought there was something havey-cavey
going on tonight. You owe it to Miss Browne, sir, that your
grandfather did not rouse the entire house to go out and
search for you after dinner. Now I believe you owe me an
explanation, young man."

As mild and easygoing as Jack usually was, when he was
roused to anger he could chill a man to the bone with a look.
As this frost swept over Gervaise, he endeavoured to explain what had happened.

"You see, some of the fellows—not gentlemen, you
know, but good fellows—at the tavern were making wagers, and before I knew it they had wagered that I couldn't

lead a bull through your garden without waking the house,"
he said miserably. There appeared no spark of understanding or humour on the earl's face. "I think it was the statues
that startled him, my Lord. I couldn't hold him any more,
and he trampled everything to pieces trying to get out. I am
so dreadfully sorry, my Lord. It was all my fault for being
such a fool—and drunk besides." Which last to Gervaise
was a brave admission, for he had often boasted to his ig-
noble companions how hard was his head.

By this time there were unmanly tears in his eyes, and he
was cowardly enough to half hope Selbridge would see them
and pity him, but he received a rude shock.

"I see. I will send a message to your grandfather tomorrow—no it's already today—this morning, sir. And if some
mutually suitable scheme of reparation can be worked out,
I suppose I shall not find it necessary to bring you before the
magistrate."

This last, Gervaise thought, was said with regret, and he
decided that he would pray that the mutually suitable reparation would be acceptable, for, naughty as he had been
all his life, he had never once been threatened with arrest.

"Thank you, my Lord. That is, please accept my most
sincere apologies, and I will do everything in my power to
see that reparation is made." These last words came to him
out of desperation, and Gervaise hoped they would save him
now.

"You will, young man, you will," was all the earl said,
and without another word, turned and left the chilled and
sickened Gervaise to find his weary way home alone.

CHAPTER FIVE

IT WAS NOT ONE OF THE housemaids of Ellwood Park who banged perfunctorily upon the door of Mr. Gervaise Chetwynd's chamber before entering that morning or who, after resting on the bedside table a tray laden with strong tea and toast and fresh butter, flung the curtains aside and cheerfully proclaimed that it was a wet miserable day.

"You had better get up, Gervaise, because Lord Selbridge is already here and your grandpapa is in a towering rage," said Nancy Browne.

The mound of misery on the bed unwound itself from the sheets and poked out a bleary face.

"Go away! That is," he amended, seeing his cousin's hurt expression, "it ain't the thing for you to be up here—not proper. But thank you for the tea."

While he sat up and occupied himself with his beverage, Nancy considered his remarks. "I daresay you are right, you know, and, of course, I have come to your mama to learn what is proper, but in this case I think I could be forgiven. If I waited for the maid to come up you would still be asleep and Uncle Reginald would be even angrier with you for making him wait than he is about what you did last night. And Cousin Verena is downstairs as well, half-asleep and crying into her chocolate, poor thing, so you had best get dressed. I'll leave you now."

"No, wait! Please, Nancy..." Gervaise, almost forgetting his state of deshabille, leaped out of bed, clutching the covers with one hand and reaching out for Nancy's arm with the other. "How do you know about last night? Good Lord, I had no idea the news would be over the whole house so soon." He slumped down again and hid his face in the blankets.

Miss Browne ignored these histrionics. "Oh, the whole house doesn't know—only your mama and myself. I was in the breakfast parlour when Lord Selbridge came to see your grandfather, and Uncle Reginald did not wish me to leave. Although I think it was horrid of you to frighten that poor bull and wreck his lordship's garden, I won't scold you, because Uncle Reginald will take care of that. I am sure you are already very sorry."

Gervaise made a wild, mournful sound. "Of course, I am! What a fool I was, first of all to drink that much, and secondly to take that ridiculous wager. It's just that I'm so damned bored all the time—I beg your pardon, Nancy—but you know how dull it is here."

"I suppose it is dull for you," she conceded, though she herself had not been at all bored since arriving at Ellwood, "and I am sorry for it, but you know it is your own fault for not applying yourself to anything and allowing yourself to do these silly things. I haven't asked what it was that got you sent down from Oxford, but I am sure it was something just as nonsensical as what you did last night."

"Quite," replied Gervaise, reddening, for that particular escapade had involved females of a sort a young man ought not to be discovered harboring in his rooms.

"And, of course, you were found out, and you will be lucky if they ever take you back." Nancy sighed and gathered up the tray, for though Gervaise had rejected the toast, he had now finished the tea and his eyes looked a little clearer. "Before I leave you, I just want to know why you have never told anyone about your drawings."

At this swift change of subject and, indeed, at the subject itself, Gervaise was so startled that he jumped and almost lost the sheet that was protecting his decency. "Drawings? But how did you—"

"Oh, I saw you one day when you were sitting in the orchard with your drawing things, doing a view of the house. It looked very good from where I stood, but I didn't want to disturb you. Eleanor said you had always drawn since you were a child, particularly houses. She showed me some of your work," she added, to the accompaniment of an angry outburst from Gervaise, of which she took no notice, "and I thought it was excellent, but Eleanor said no one had ever made any fuss over it."

"And I don't want them to do so now," said Gervaise firmly. "It's just a childish thing I do sometimes when I feel low. Papa used to dabble in architecture, and he used to let me copy out of his books when I was a child. But what has this to do with the punishment that is awaiting me downstairs?"

Nancy sighed and looked at him in despair. "Never mind now. It was just a thought. Now you had better get dressed, quickly." She left him.

Downstairs, a tense little group had removed itself from the breakfast parlour to the morning-room. Lady Chetwynd, who had been ordered out of her chamber long before her accustomed time by Sir Reginald, had watered her chocolate with her tears until her father irritably told the footman to take it away from her.

Sir Reginald, though calmer now than when the earl had first informed him of his grandson's misdemeanor, was ready to burst into rage again at any moment, and Selbridge, having had his say, was quietly awaiting his chance to interview the culprit. It had not surprised him, when he arrived earlier, to find Miss Browne already up and eating breakfast with her great-uncle, but it had made him a bit uncomfortable when Sir Reginald insisted she stay and hear what he had to say.

It had had the effect, however, of reminding Jack to remain composed, however outraged he felt, for the sight of his mother's trampled garden in the grey wet morning had aroused all his anger again. But when he was shown into the breakfast parlour at Ellwood and saw Miss Browne, looking fresher than the day in a plain but becoming, straw-coloured morning dress, smiling sweetly up at her great-uncle over her coffee, he had stated his business firmly but without heat.

To his dismay, Sir Reginald had begun to curse his grandson's existence. "I'll tan his young hide for this! Deliberate, wanton destruction of property!" he shouted, his face dangerously purple. "Get that idiot of a grandson of mine down here at once!" he ordered a footman who had come in to clear away the breakfast dishes.

Nancy had slipped away to warn her cousin herself, and now she came down again, hoping that her plan would work. Gervaise, she reflected, was so foolish and childish that he didn't deserve to have so much trouble taken over his future, and she very well ought to let Lord Selbridge order him to spend the rest of the summer mucking out his lordship's stables or doing some other disagreeable work to make up for what he had destroyed. But out of gratitude to Lady Chetwynd and Eleanor, she could not let Gervaise suffer such a fate.

Thus Nancy waited until Gervaise received the tongue-lashing he deserved from his grandfather, had formally but sincerely apologized to Lord Selbridge and had been alternately abused and comforted by his weeping mother. When the subject of the reparation was entered, Nancy said softly to Selbridge, "It occurs to me, my Lord, that my cousin might be of some use to you in your project at Marbel-meade. You might make him assist Mr. Worthington.''

"That's right, make the lazy young slug dig some ditches or carry bricks. That'll teach him to destroy other people's hard work,'' interjected Sir Reginald. "He'll have plenty of blisters and aches to remind him of it when the day is done,'' he added with obvious relish.

Gervaise looked frightened, and even Jack had to laugh silently at the thought of this slightly built, languid young fashionable handling a pick and shovel.

"I am sure that would be a salutary lesson, Uncle Reginald,'' said Nancy, "but that is not precisely what I had in mind. You see, Gervaise has a talent for drawing and design that no one seems to have taken any account of, and I think he should be put under Mr. Worthington for the summer and see what could be made of it. Of course, he should make himself available to Lord Selbridge for whatever else his lordship might want, but by helping Mr. Worthington, he would learn to apply himself to something useful.''

"Could be the making of him,'' mused Sir Reginald.

"My boy articled to a common architect? Is he not a gentleman's son? He must not actually take employment!'' cried Lady Chetwynd, fresh tears springing from her eyes. She looked pathetic and charming, and she obviously knew it, but Jack, to whom these looks were directed, was not impressed. He happened to catch a glimpse of Miss Browne's face at that moment, and she was so obviously thinking the same thing of Lady Chetwynd that he had to stifle a laugh. Miss Browne's delightful sherry-coloured eyes were full of warmth and humour, and again he wondered at the changes in her behaviour. He liked her much better now than when she cloaked herself in chilly reserve.

Meanwhile, Sir Reginald gave his daughter a scathing glance. "Nonsense, Verena. I'll admit I would rather none of my family be connected with a trade, but Worthington is a gentlemanly fellow, and I'm sure Gervaise couldn't possibly learn any worse habits under him than he already has acquired at Oxford. Would you rather see him up before the magistrate for his crimes?"

"If I may be permitted," Gervaise said loudly, and when every one was silenced he looked startled at his own audacity. Nancy gave him an encouraging smile, and he was emboldened to continue. "If that is agreeable to your Lordship—" he bowed a little to Jack "—I should do my best to give satisfaction and would do anything required of me by you and Mr. Worthington."

This time Nancy's smile held approval, Sir Reginald muttered that he hadn't thought that the boy had it in him, and even Lady Chetwynd was moved to tears of pride by the change in her boy. Everyone looked at Jack, awaiting his decision.

He looked at Miss Browne, who was obviously somewhat of a master architect herself to have drawn up such an excellent plan, but she was suddenly shy and averted her eyes. Young Chetwynd was obviously repentant, though Jack was not sure if this was due to his most certainly having woken with an abominable head or to fear of his grandfather and the magistrate or, perhaps, to a genuine willingness to give up his idleness and put his talents to work.

"The plan seems satisfactory to me," he told Sir Reginald at last. The whole room seemed to sigh in relief. "But mind you, sir," he addressed the sagging Gervaise, "I shall expect you promptly at eight every morning, and you must stay at your work as long as I or Mr. Worthington need you."

"Yes, sir, of course," said Gervaise eagerly.

"I wouldn't want to put you to the trouble of giving bed and board to this young scapegrace," said Sir Reginald, "or I'd tell him to pack his traps and stay at Marbelmeade for the duration. But I shall see to it that he gets there every day, and leave the rest to you and Worthington."

Even Lady Chetwynd was silenced by the swiftness of this judgement, and it was arranged that Gervaise would begin his new life on the following day. Lord Selbridge took his leave, but not before drawing Miss Browne aside and complimenting her on her idea.

"Oh, it was nothing at all," she said, pleased but embarrassed and wondering how Eleanor would have reacted to such flattering attention. The earl, though not very much taller than she, was smiling down at her, and his merry brown eyes stared straight into hers for a moment. A sudden shortness of breath came upon her, and she had to look away.

"But it was very clever of you," the earl continued, apparently unaware of her distress. "You saw immediately that young Gervaise's ills stemmed from not having enough to do. If he really does draw well, works hard and learns from Worthington, he may end by finding a career."

Nancy could no longer hide her pleasure in his approval, and she allowed herself a wide smile. But in a moment she stopped, worry creasing her brow.

"What is it, Miss Browne?"

"Oh, my Lord, I have just thought of something dreadful! There is someone whose wishes I did not at all take into account."

Selbridge was momentarily puzzled, but she was quick to enlighten him. "Mr. Worthington! Suppose he does not want an assistant?"

Jack was so delighted by her expression of dismay that he burst into laughter, at which Miss Browne looked shocked, until she started to giggle herself.

"I suppose," said Jack, "that he will have to tolerate having one thrust upon him for a little while. He can always let young Chetwynd sit down and copy plans and drawings, I suppose."

"Or dig ditches or carry bricks," suggested Nancy sweetly, eliciting another laugh from Selbridge. Then a swish of skirts alerted them they were not alone.

Eleanor Chetwynd stood at the foot of the stairs, looking with disfavour upon the tête-à-tête, and Nancy's lips closed upon a stillborn laugh. Before the earl's very eyes, she changed from a warm and delightful girl to a fashionably indifferent young lady, who began to bid him good day very properly. Miss Chetwynd's eyes invited him to stay and chat with her, but he left hurriedly.

"It is a pity, Nancy, that you let yourself become so carried away when Lord Selbridge is here. His opinion of you is not likely to improve if you cannot show him that you can behave with dignity," said Miss Chetwynd.

"I know, Eleanor, but I am afraid that I am just not in the habit of being so reserved, and I cannot grow to like it," Nancy replied. "But I will try harder next time."

Eleanor softened at Nancy's look of distress, for she had really become quite fond of her gauche cousin. "Do not worry, I am sure you will learn." And the two girls went for their daily stroll in the garden, during which Eleanor drilled her cousin on the proper way to behave to an earl.

The next morning, a pale but determined Gervaise appeared at Marbelmeade. Jenkins showed him in with silent disapproval, knowing full well, as did most of the earl's servants, who had been responsible for the destruction wrought in the countess's garden. Gervaise bore it bravely and was rewarded by the arrival of Miss Garrard. Felicity had risen unusually early and had decided that since the garden was in a dreadful state anyway she might as well brave the sour looks of the gardeners and cut some flowers for the house. With her bright curls swept up behind and sheltering under a chip straw bonnet, a basket over her gloved arm and a pair of scissors in the opposite hand, she looked, Gervaise thought, like the picture of summer. He hurriedly got to his feet and bowed.

"Oh! I thought you were Jack," she said unpromisingly. She did manage to blush a little at her rudeness, and then reflected that Mr. Chetwynd was a most handsome young man, even if he had been horridly drunk and ruined Aunt Margaret's garden.

"I daresay you've come to begin your work with Mr. Worthington. Is it true that you draw?"

Gervaise admitted he did. "But I really cannot tell you if I do it well. I shall have to let Mr. Worthington see my work and decide." He nervously fingered a thick, leather-covered book on the table at his side.

He was so obviously dreading this moment of judgement that Felicity felt sorry for him and decided at once that if Cousin Jack was not kind to him, he would hear from her on the subject.

Miss Garrard and Mr. Chetwynd entered into a mutually agreeable conversation, and so pleased was Mr. Chetwynd by the young lady's beauty and her interest in his affairs, that he became quite courtly. Felicity basked in the refreshment of for once being taken seriously.

This did not prevent her, however, from sidling up to Jack when he came in and inquiring with a bewitching smile if he had slept well.

The earl appeared unmoved. "As usual, Felicity. The child is looking particularly charming today, is she not, Mr.

Chetwynd?'' Jack let his glance rest fondly upon her, because when she was not being irritating Felicity was very charming indeed.

Felicity had dimpled at this casual compliment and was now firmly planted at her cousin's side, but Gervaise said, "Indeed, my Lord, I certainly agree, but I fear I must take exception to one thing. Miss Garrard is no longer a child, but a young lady."

Jack hid his amusement at this piece of chivalry.

"Well," was all he could say, "I suppose we had best begin. Worthington is waiting for us in the estate office. Ah, you have brought your book of drawings. Very good. Now, Felicity, don't get into any mischief in the garden."

Gervaise thought the earl was going to pat his cousin on the head, and told himself he would not stand for it, but fortunately his lordship did nothing of the kind, and Gervaise had to follow him, bidding a respectful goodbye to Felicity, who was saying, "I can hardly get into more mischief there than Mr. Chetwynd did, can I, Cousin Jack?"

Gervaise was shocked by this betrayal, but her parting smile was so sweet that he forgave her instantly.

As for Selbridge, all he desired was to introduce this young nuisance to Mr. Worthington, then escape to his library for an hour or so, where he thought to sit in blessed solitude and look over the bit of poetry he'd penned to Her, and sigh for a little while over his lost happiness. Unfortunately, Mr. Worthington, though prepared to receive Mr. Chetwynd as his assistant on trial, had need of his employer's opinions and orders on certain matters, and Jack found the morning flew by. The verses languished unread in a compartment in his lordship's desk.

Nancy, after sending Gervaise off with bracing encouragement, had gone about her usual household duties, so that by the time Lady Chetwynd descended, all at Ellwood had been smoothly set on the daily routine, and Nancy was free to do as she pleased.

The day before, after judgement had been passed on Mr. Chetwynd, the ladies of Ellwood had received a neighbourly call from Mrs. Phillips, the wife of the local rector. She and Nancy had instantly taken to one another, each recognizing in the other, perhaps, that managing but kind disposition so necessary to the successful running of any enterprise, be it a household or a parish. The visitor had brought with her a new arrival to the neighbourhood, Miss Caroline Phillips, her husband's younger sister, and though this young lady seemed shy and Nancy had some difficulty in drawing her out, she had liked her very much. More to the point, some intuition told her that Miss Phillips could be very useful in a plan she had just begun to make, and she was determined to visit the rectory and increase her acquaintance with its ladies.

Lady Chetwynd and Eleanor declined to accompany Nancy on her visit to the rectory, the one pleading lassitude and headache, the other avowing that she had many letters to write to other perfected young ladies who had been released from their fashionable academy and were now set loose upon town and country, so Nancy expressed her regrets politely and thought that it could not be more perfect for what she had in mind.

She marched purposefully up to Osbert's den, which, newly cleaned and kept very neat since her arrival, was still a chamber of solitude from which the scholar scarcely emerged.

"Damme, you've made me lose my place—Oh, it's you, Nancy. Please do come in. I thought it was that pestilent niece of mine. She often comes in to annoy me when she is bored, you know."

Nancy, though objecting to his description of the elegant Miss Chetwynd as pestilent, wisely held her tongue. She wanted Osbert to accompany her to the rectory and felt it would not assist her cause to correct him now.

"How are the Romans today, Osbert? Have you found anything new?"

Osbert's face grew animated, and once again Nancy thought that he should be wearing spectacles because he looked as though he ought to be pushing them up on his nose. As it was, all he could do was rub the top of his head to indicate his excitement.

"Indeed, I have. I have just received a letter from a noted antiquary correspondent of mine..." He rummaged through a pile of letters, but was unsuccessful, to Nancy's relief, for she knew that if he had found the letter he would have read it to her in its dull entirety.

"It doesn't matter, I suppose," Osbert said. "The important thing is that he tells me there may be some important Roman remains right here, or practically here. Somewhere along the western border of Selbridge's lands, to be precise."

"Wonderful! I should love to see them, and Lord Selbridge is so kind, I don't suppose he would mind at all letting us look for the site."

Osbert frowned. "I fear that even his permission would avail us nothing, Nancy. You see, I shouldn't begin to know where to look. The source that my antiquarian friend quotes is an old diary of a local farmer who had the land before it came into the Selbridge family by marriage two hundred years ago. It seems the original owners, while digging a well, found some tiles and shards and brickwork that sound suspiciously Roman."

"Would it not be a simple matter to find the well and dig again?"

Osbert sighed and closed a ponderous tome that lay open in front of him. Dust flew up in his face and clung to his eyebrows, and that he did not immediately sneeze was a matter of wonder to Nancy.

"I am afraid not. You see, the well died down to a mere trickle, so it was filled in again a few years later. After two hundred years, it would be impossible to locate its site, at least not without a map of the land at the time. And Selbridge would not have such a map, because the land did not belong to the earl of that day."

Nancy thought swiftly. "I think I know who might have such a map, Osbert," she said, and was rewarded by a look of hope. "Mrs. Phillips was telling me about how she and the rector had found some ancient parish records in an old box in the church crypt not long ago, and she did say some of them were legible. There could very well be maps or some other clue. I was planning to pay a call on Mrs. Phillips and Miss Phillips. Why not come with me? Perhaps the rector will let you look over the contents of the box."

Osbert pondered this, torn between the excitement of a possible discovery and the reluctance to leave his comfortable den and have to associate with females. The former emotion triumphed to Nancy's delight, and he made himself ready to accompany her.

As it was a fine-enough day for an open carriage, Nancy had already ordered her great-uncle's gig prepared, and had had every intention of driving it herself, but to her surprise Osbert took the reins himself and acquitted himself creditably during the short ride to the rectory.

Osbert was not such a dull fellow after all. In fact, Nancy and her cousin found much to talk about, and over the past few days he had proved himself quite willing to except her from the general mass of despised females, even going so far as to stay in the drawing-room with the family after dinner, instead of retiring to his study, in order to continue a conversation or sing a duet with her. Nancy saw her great-uncle's pleasure in this and was happy that she had been able to have an influence on Osbert.

They drove up to the neat little rectory, which, like the church, was built of stone, mellowed by the years and set in a lovely garden. Mrs. Phillips received them warmly and led them to her drawing-room, which ran the length of the first floor and overlooked the gardens. Nancy, from her seat on a sofa by the window, could see a bonnetted female figure walking about slowly below, and Mrs. Phillips said, "I have asked the maid to tell Caroline we have visitors. She will be delighted to see you again. And I don't believe you have met my husband's sister, have you, Mr. Drakes?"

Osbert gulped, and Nancy saw his eagerness for the contents of the old box dissolve in his fear of yet another female entering his life. But Miss Caroline Phillips, when she entered somewhat breathlessly a few moments later, was so very unthreatening that, after the introduction, Osbert visibly relaxed and was able, when Nancy brought up the subject of the discovery in the crypt, to contribute to the conversation and even to beg permission of his hostess to view the rector's discovery.

"You see, ma'am, I hope to find an old map which will help me locate some possible Roman remains."

"Maps..." Mrs. Phillips crinkled her lively brown eyes. "I have not seen all the documents, but James tells me there are a great many, some legible, some not. I do not know if there are maps."

Miss Phillips, who was a tall, slender girl with dark blond hair and soft grey eyes, said in a small voice, "There are maps, Jane. I have seen them."

Her sister-in-law made encouraging sounds, and Miss Phillips went on timidly, "I am sure Mr. Drakes would be able to read them."

Nancy was delighted to see Osbert's eyes light up. "Do you think so, Miss Phillips? But that is wonderful!" and he beamed at her in a way that would have quite startled Sir Reginald and Lady Chetwynd.

Miss Phillips was silenced by embarrassment again, and beneath her almost translucent skin, one could see an entrancing tide of rosiness ebbing and flowing. Osbert observed this phenomenon with a curiosity that was by no means detached and scientific.

Mrs. Phillips met Nancy's eyes, and in an instant all that was necessary flashed between them. The rector's wife came to her sister-in-law's aid.

"How clever of you to have taken note of the maps, my love. And I am sure, Mr. Drakes, that the rector would be happy to have you look at them. He would be glad, I am sure, of your learned opinion."

Now it was Osbert's turn to colour, and Nancy swiftly engaged his attention to distract him from his embarrassment, while Mrs. Phillips gently put questions to Caroline as to what she had seen in the box, and before very long the two shy people were actually talking almost comfortably with one another. Nancy, having managed to discover that Caroline Phillips had often assisted her late father, a noted scholar whom Osbert had revered, saw the two of them safely embarked on this line of conversation and slowly eased herself away, to turn with satisfaction to her co-conspirator.

"How charming Caroline is," she ventured, a knowing smile on her face.

"Indeed," replied Mrs. Phillips, "and how good it is for a shy girl like her to meet a quiet gentleman like Mr. Drakes."

This established, they exchanged self-congratulatory looks, and their conversation turned to Ellwood Park.

"I do so admire what you have done there, Miss Browne. Why, after her ladyship died, the place became sadly run down. You have put new life into it, my dear."

Nancy took the compliment calmly. "I have done very little. Ellwood simply needed someone a bit more forceful than Cousin Verena, and now it runs itself, as it ought to do. Besides, I am so grateful to Sir Reginald and my cousins. It is my pleasure to do anything I can for them."

Encouraged by Mrs. Phillips's obvious sympathy, she talked about her former life and described her plans to the rector's wife. "I do so wish to have a Season and meet some eligible gentlemen. All my life I have lived in other people's houses, you know, and I long for one of my own. Without a husband and home," she said without a trace of self-consciousness, "I shall always be just Cousin Nancy. It is unjust and hateful, but there it is."

Mrs. Phillips looked on her with compassion. "I hope you get your wish, my dear, because obviously you would be the perfect mistress for any home. As to eligible gentlemen..."

The rector's wife stopped and looked meaningfully out of the window, where, in the distance, the towers of Marbelmeade could be seen. It took Nancy a moment or two to discover what her hostess meant by this gesture, and when she did, she was distressed.

"Oh, no, Mrs. Phillips, it could not be! Why, Lord Selbridge is..." To her irritation, she felt her face grow warm. "He would never...it would never occur to me...it would not do, you must see that," she finished lamely.

"If you mean because he is an earl and you are only the daughter of a gentleman's younger son, then perhaps you have a point, but I do not think it would weigh very much with Selbridge if he found his affections engaged."

"He would never think of me, I am sure, Mrs. Phillips," Nancy insisted, knowing she was right but, remembering his lordship's delightful smile, wishing she was not. "Why I haven't the air, the manners, the appearance. Compared to my Cousin Eleanor and his cousin Miss Garrard, I am a bumpkin!"

This discussion was interrupted by the arrival of the rector himself. James Phillips had known Lord Selbridge since their student days. He had prematurely grey hair, wise, steady blue eyes and a whimsical expression, which endeared him to Nancy immediately. He and his red-haired, pert wife made a pleasing contrast, as they exchanged looks of affection.

"What do you think, my dear? Mr. Drakes thinks there may be some Roman remains about, and he would like to look at those old maps you found in the crypt."

"Roman, eh? Papa would have liked that, wouldn't he, Caro?" The rector smiled at his sister, who began to describe to him just what Mr. Drakes had discovered and why he wished to see the maps.

Mr. Phillips agreed to show Osbert the contents of the box, infected by his sister's and his visitor's enthusiasm, for Osbert readily joined his voice to Miss Phillips's.

Nancy declined to accompany them to Mr. Phillips's study, where the old trunk was ensconced, preferring to talk to her new friend, from whom she received much in the way of helpful household advice and quick sketches of the inhabitants of Ellwood Park, which quite agreed with her own summations of those individuals.

"Above all, you must never let Sir Reginald think he has frightened you or has you cowed. He can be a dear, as he has a soft heart beneath all that growling, but just look at Lady Chetwynd and you will see what happens when one does not stand up to him."

"Oh, Uncle Reginald and I understand one another," Nancy confided. "In fact, I have become very fond of all of them, even Lady Chetwynd, though she can be most trying at times," she admitted.

"As you seem to have them well in hand," Mrs. Phillips said with a smile, "let me tell you about the rest of the neighbourhood." She offered her opinions of the inhabitants of the area, then said, "As for Lord Selbridge himself, he is kind and charming and a very good friend to us. I hope I did not alarm you earlier with my little teasing, but we think it would be so good for him to become interested in another young lady, after what happened to him in London last Season."

Nancy's curiosity was aroused, and Mrs. Phillips was most willing to satisfy it. Thus she heard the entire story of Lord Selbridge's engagement gone wrong, which the rector's wife knew she could entrust to Miss Browne, perhaps, as that lady possessed the true matchmaker's heart, with the hidden motive of awakening Miss Browne's compassion for the lonely, rejected bachelor.

But Nancy, hearing that Lord Selbridge was suffering from unrequited love for a beautiful, rich lady, felt her heart sinking to her feet and immediately scolded herself for being so foolish. How silly she was to entertain even the most tiny and secret hope that she had impressed him. She forced herself to sound sympathetic, which, indeed, she was, although she was also disappointed.

"And so his lordship has retired here to try to forget the lady? How brave he is! Why, one would hardly know that he was suffering from such a heartbreak!" In fact, Nancy thought, if Mrs. Phillips was not obviously such a reliable source, she might have thought the story untrue. Lord Selbridge seemed, except for his anger over Gervaise's destruction of his garden, entirely free from care and in excellent humour.

The others returned, triumphant and dust-streaked, Osbert proudly bearing a crumbling piece of thick paper marked with almost indecipherable lines and scrawls, which, nevertheless, he assured them, was a map of the lands that were now Lord Selbridge's and on which some former owner had once attempted to dig a well and found Roman remains.

Nancy was pleased to see Caroline Phillips flushed with excitement instead of shyness, and even the rector himself appeared infected with antiquarian lust. But Nancy considered that she and Osbert had by now long overstayed their welcome and concluded the visit by arranging that they would all, along with whoever else was interested, make an outing to the spot, which Osbert undertook to pinpoint on a preliminary expedition of his own, first, of course, obtaining permission from Lord Selbridge. Mr. Phillips assured them this would present no problem.

"If I know Jack, he will be as enthusiastic as you are, Mr. Drakes, and will want to make a picnic excursion out of it. I'll speak to him about it tomorrow."

Osbert and Nancy agreed that Mr. Phillips, as the earl's closest friend in the neighbourhood, would be the proper person to obtain his permission and departed, after bidding goodbye to their host, hostess and Miss Phillips.

Nancy was glad to see that his enthusiasm carried Osbert through the awkward farewells, and he took the hand that Caroline tentatively offered him without a hint of discomfort, his mind plainly on the quest for Roman remains and not on Miss Caroline Phillips's pretty face and soft manners. But that, Nancy thought, could no doubt be changed.

CHAPTER SIX

EVERY MORNING FOR the next few days, Mr. Francis Garrard climbed to a musty but brightly lit room in one of Marbelmeade's two towers. These structures were a folly of the fourth earl, the present earl's grandfather, and in the last century one of these romantic rooms had been improved by the addition of a glass-paned window and a coal brazier to be used as a sewing-room, but it had again lapsed into disuse, until this visit of the Garrards.

Francis, who had refused the assistance of the footman who had carried his boxes and parcels up for him and had unpacked them all himself, now presided over an old trestle table and a few rickety chairs. In his second day of tenancy, clad in shirtsleeves protected by a broad apron, he looked upon his handiwork with satisfaction. It had taken one entire morning to unpack, but today he had his books, retorts, bottles and pots, his crocks, mortar and pestle and his spirit lamp, all laid out and ready. He had already gone so far as to begin distilling some essences and crushing some herbs.

Still, fear and uncertainty clutched him. Suppose his previous experiments, undertaken at home in a dark, dank stillroom with his sister pounding on the door, proved false? Suppose his recent lucky find, the receipt sold to him by an old Gypsy, was fraudulent? Common sense at once came to his rescue. Whether or not the formula worked, he might induce people to believe it did. As the concoction on which he had laboured would, in his opinion, do no one any harm, he felt perfectly justified in trying to sell it.

Now he put in a good morning's work until summoned to a midday meal. To Francis's relief, his sister and Jack seemed quite uninterested in his activities. The former was busy flirting with Gervaise Chetwynd, who, Francis saw to his disgust, was already in a fair way to becoming her slave. He had at first looked upon this young man with contempt for his foolish stunt with the bull, but the day before he had observed, while taking a brief respite from his labours, that Mr. Chetwynd was not as foolish as he had at first seemed. Francis had seen him work willingly and hard under Mr. Worthington, and had noticed how respectfully he attended the earl.

As for Jack, today Francis sensed impatience under his calm affability, and though he had been tempted to invite his cousin up to view the tower and discuss his work, he now vowed he would not trouble him about his undertaking until he had ceased his labours and found success.

He was pleased when his cousin said, "I'm riding to Ellwood this afternoon. Would you care to join me?"

Francis accepted with pleasure and went up to his room to change into riding clothes, but when he came down he found that their departure had to be put off temporarily, for the rector, Mr. Phillips, had arrived.

"Roman remains?" Selbridge was saying incredulously, as he handed his friend a glass of wine. "Is this some new fit of Osbert Drakes's? I only hope he does not mention it to his father. Sir Reginald is unlikely to prove sympathetic to such nonsense."

James Phillips smiled. "I think, my friend, that he is too happy to have his son out of the house to quibble about reason."

Selbridge then introduced his cousin to the rector and explained that Mr. Phillips had come to ask permission for Osbert Drakes to search Selbridge lands for some Roman ruins.

"Of course, James, I have no objection, as from this map," the earl was now squinting at the map that had so excited Osbert, "it appears that the spot he wishes to search is in some waste land beyond the northwest meadow. A pretty spot, actually, but too much clay for any crop."

The rector smiled at this agricultural digression. "My word, Jack, you have become quite the gentleman farmer. The country breezes have blown those London cobwebs right out of your brain."

Selbridge grinned. "Gentleman farmer indeed! How dare you diminish my consequence? I own that since my first Season in Town I haven't paid much attention to matters here, James, but I am not entirely ignorant of country matters."

"I beg your pardon, my Lord." Mr. Phillips bowed sardonically, and Francis marveled at the casualness with which his noble cousin accepted this teasing.

The rector continued, "I appreciate your giving permission about the ruins, Jack. Mrs. Phillips and my sister are charmed with the idea and hope you will join us. We might have all the young people from Ellwood, and your cousins as well," he said, with a friendly nod to Francis.

Jack, always eager to shift the responsibility of entertaining his cousins onto someone else, agreed readily. His expeditions with Francis and Felicity had left him most undesirous of their exclusive company. Now he offered to host a picnic excursion to the spot, exactly as his friend had predicted the day before.

"Excellent!" said Mr. Phillips. "Caroline will be pleased, and so will Miss Browne. You know it was she who brought

Drakes with her to ask about the map. Her presence seems to have done a world of good at Ellwood, has it not?''

The earl agreed thoughtfully that it had indeed.

The rector made ready to depart. ''I shall send word to Ellwood that permission has been granted, and let young Drakes search out the spot. Then the ladies can set a day for our picnic.''

''You need not trouble, James. Francis and I were planning to call there, and I shall have the pleasure of informing them myself,'' said Selbridge, wondering if Miss Browne would be pleased.

When they did call, to his disappointment, Miss Browne, though thanking him very prettily for giving his permission, was firmly in control of herself that day, and her smile appeared patterned strictly after Miss Chetwynd's—chilly with a hint of a simper. Lady Chetwynd, however, was delighted at the prospect of a party, though she considered the search for Roman ruins a very odd reason for having one.

''I daresay, my dears, that Osbert and the other gentlemen will completely ignore us, once some mouldy old piece of brick captures their attention,'' she said with an arch smile.

Jack felt like writhing but could do nothing except protest that, of course, no gentleman would find a bit of mouldy Roman brick at all interesting when there were such charming ladies present.

''Except Uncle Osbert,'' said Eleanor, for once quite forgetting decorum in her sense of injury. Osbert could have made himself quite useful to his niece, since he was a relatively young man, by bringing eligible young friends into the house. He had never troubled to oblige her in this way, and it rankled. ''He is very likely to be so busy with his ruins that he will forget about us altogether.''

Nancy quietly promised that she would see to it that Osbert did not forget his social obligations.

Lady Chetwynd smiled. "Of course. My brother has become quite devoted to our Nancy, my Lord, and she can do with him as she pleases."

Jack's curiosity was piqued, as this was the second instance he had heard of Miss Browne's influence on the reclusive Mr. Drakes. But before he could remark on it, the man himself was in the room, uncharacteristically talkative and full of gratitude to the earl for his permission.

Osbert then proceeded to engage Lord Selbridge in a lengthy discussion of the site of the potential ruin, going on about how many labourers he might bring and how large a hole might be dug.

But Francis, who until now had sat quietly between Nancy and Eleanor, was never one to ignore the ladies, and soon he was engaged in a flattering but wholly confabulated report of how clever Gervaise Chetwynd was, which much pleased Lady Chetwynd, though Miss Chetwynd rolled her eyes expressively at Nancy when she knew no one was watching, having no faith in her brother. "Imagine," she whispered to Nancy, "Gervaise actually working!"

The earl heard her, and to her distress, looked up and said, "But I assure you, Miss Chetwynd, your brother is proving himself very useful and is already far along the way to repaying his debt. The garden, except for the broken statues, of course, is almost back to normal, and Mr. Worthington assures me that his sketches are excellent. He is already working on some elevations for the new wing, and I like some of his ideas better than Worthington's!"

"Oh, I am so glad," said Nancy sincerely, unaware of her cousin's disapproving looks. "I did so want Gervaise to stop being bored and make use of his quite considerable talent."

Selbridge turned to Nancy. "Yes, I am very happy, too, Miss Browne, and once again I congratulate you on your idea. But tell me, do you still ride in the morning? I confess I have not been able to manage it for a few days, but I fully intend to do so again. Perhaps we will meet by the lake again. Will you ride tomorrow?"

Nancy, who had, on her brief rides, been disappointed not to have seen him, was surprised and delighted. "Why, yes, my Lord, if the fine weather holds."

Lady Chetwynd, still jealous of her own and Eleanor's chances, forestalled any more intimate conversation between the earl and Nancy by saying, "Yes, the weather *is* lovely, is it not? You young people should be outdoors. Eleanor, do show his lordship the garden. It is looking uncommonly fine today."

Nancy subsided, reddening, suddenly aware of the impropriety of making what almost amounted to an assignation with the earl, and allowed her cousin to guide Lord Selbridge out into the garden. Lady Chetwynd and her brother remained behind to quarrel comfortably, so Nancy had perforce to stroll out into the garden with Francis. She did not altogether mind, although Francis looked longingly at Eleanor, but as the party arranged itself, she could have sworn that Lord Selbridge turned to her with a rueful smile before Eleanor drew his attention away.

When Francis managed to divert his attention from the lovely Miss Chetwynd to the companion circumstances had forced upon him, Nancy found that she enjoyed talking to him. He spoke divertingly of Marbelmeade and of his pretty sister, who, he assured her, was a troublesome minx. "The sooner I have her married off, the better," he said.

Nancy enquired if there were any prospects, and then wondered if she had been too forward, but Francis, perhaps tired of the lonely hours in his tower, seemed disposed for a friendly gossip.

"None," he admitted. "In fact, I had hoped that if I could find a wife, she could introduce her to Society, but I have given up the idea. I shall have to make my fortune another way. You see, I have a *plan*."

He was so obviously waiting to be questioned further that Nancy could do nothing but oblige. "How interesting. Perhaps you would like to tell me about it."

But Francis had suddenly stopped walking and was gazing at her face with new interest. If Nancy had been paying proper attention to her lessons she would have blushed and looked away, but as it was she just gazed steadily and questioningly back at him.

Francis seemed struck by something. "Yes! Perhaps...forgive me, Miss Browne, but I notice that you have freckles."

To any other female this would have been among the highest of insults a gentleman could bestow, but Nancy once again proved false to her cousin's training and simply said, "Yes, unfortunately. They are a nuisance, but if I stay out of the sun they are not so noticeable."

"Well, you and I may be able to assist one another a great deal, Miss Browne. This is quite confidential, you know, so I beg you won't say anything about it to anyone just yet..." He began to look uneasy, for it had occurred to him more than once that what he was doing was not, strictly speaking, any occupation for a baronet.

Nancy vowed secrecy. They were now out of sight of the others, Eleanor having skilfully steered the earl into the more intimate confines of the walled garden, more in obedience to her mother's instructions than because she sought to fascinate him.

Selbridge endured her company, wondering what his cousin and Miss Browne were finding to talk about all this while and praying that Francis would have the sense and Miss Browne the compassion to rescue him. He had heard their voices, Francis's eager, Miss Browne's interested, but now the sound had died away and he was left to Miss Chetwynd, who endeavoured to extract from him some London gossip. Sighing, he obliged, wishing that Miss Browne were with him instead.

But Miss Browne was otherwise engaged. Francis, glad of their seclusion from the others, had proceeded to regale her with an account of his search for a way to make his fortune, his fortuitous discovery of several old books containing formulas of cosmetic preparations, his meeting with the Gypsy and the miraculous receipt, and his present effort, the search for the perfect freckle eradicator.

Nancy was every bit as fascinated by this as Francis could have wished. Had not freckles plagued her throughout her life? Had not Eleanor and Lady Chetwynd ordered her to apply, all to no avail, various lotions and creams to her face? Removing those horrid brown dots would, she was certain, bring her a step closer to being the perfect young lady.

They entered eagerly into conversation about Francis's undertaking, and by the time the other strollers approached again, Nancy had agreed that when Francis had completed the formula, she would be the first person to try its efficacy.

Selbridge did not, owing to Eleanor's and Lady Chetwynd's vigilance, manage to have another word with Miss Browne that afternoon except for goodbye, but he did ride out the mornings in the next week and, to his delight, she was always there.

On these occasions he admired her riding, but took care not to compliment her, for he soon discovered that this only threw her into that stiff reserve. After the second meeting he learned that if he wanted to elicit the warm, sweet and natural Miss Browne he had first admired, he must immediately plunge into conversation about the things that interested her most.

These subjects were not hard to discover, for when he hit upon them her eyes glowed and her words came forth with energy. Whenever the weather was good enough, they rode side by side talking of local matters, of the family at Ellwood and their affairs and of Selbridge's new wing, which was slowly taking form. The earl wanted badly to bring Miss Browne back with him and walk with her over the place, but so far she had politely resisted any invitations that did not include Lady Chetwynd or Miss Chetwynd. Jack was disappointed because Miss Browne had seemed such a sensible, knowledgeable girl and not at all prudish.

One morning Jack had looked doubtfully at the clouds and wondered whether he ought to venture out, but as a thin ray of sunlight won its way through, he scolded himself for being faint-hearted and took his usual ride. To his disappointment, Miss Browne did not appear. It was growing cloudier, the false promise of that little sunbeam luring him out for nothing. He was about to turn back, when he heard hoofbeats.

Nancy in her elegant habit, her seat graceful and her hands impeccably correct, rode down to the lake. Jack smiled at the sight of her—a little voice reminding him that he was being untrue to the memory of Her. The little voice, however, was easily silenced, as these days his lordship could only spare the time to pray at the shrine of his goddess on the rare occasions when his presence was not wanted elsewhere. At these times he would elude his guests and go fishing, and just when he had pondered himself into a soulful mood, he usually fell asleep and had to jerk himself awake lest he lose his line or his seat in the boat or on the bank. Today he brushed his memories of the lost love aside impatiently. Miss Browne looked worried.

Jack found himself riding up to her and extending his hand impulsively. "What is it, my dear? Is something wrong?"

Nancy looked a little startled and quickly withdrew her hand, seeming unaware that she had put it in his. "It . . . it looks as though it is going to rain, and Uncle Reginald is feeling his rheumatics, Lady Chetwynd is angry with me because I did not behave properly when some young ladies came to call, and Eleanor has insulted Cook and I had a dreadful time smoothing her down and, oh, I do wish I hadn't come here at all!"

"I am wishing nothing of the kind, Miss Browne. I am, in fact, excessively glad that you came to Ellwood and that today you braved the weather and your relatives and rode to the lake. But you are certainly right about the rain," he said as the clouds began to drop their burden of moisture.

"Come, we'll go to the old gatehouse—it's not far."

He led the way past the lake and up a steep, narrow path Nancy had never explored, until they came to a small house of stone and brick, obviously untenanted, secluded in the trees. There was a shed of sorts attached to the rear, and there his lordship dismounted and helped Miss Browne from her horse.

Nancy was chilled, for the air felt more like November than July, and it might have been for this reason that she was shaking a bit as Selbridge helped her down from her horse. But she herself had a suspicion that it was because he was very handsome and because she admired him more than any man she had ever met. She knew that it was highly improper that she had come out at all, but she so enjoyed their rides. Now it seemed that they would be secluded here till the rain stopped. Nancy hushed her thoughts before they could go further.

"Come inside," said Jack. Nancy hesitated, wondering if they could just shelter in the shed until the rain stopped, but a return of her shivering decided her. Besides, Lady Chetwynd and Eleanor did not have to know a thing about it.

Selbridge opened the rear door, which led down a few steps into a small stone kitchen. To Nancy's surprise, it looked used, and Selbridge informed her, while he swept out the grate and found some wood, that his gamekeeper sometimes took shelter there.

"Have you had breakfast?" asked Selbridge, rummaging about in the little kitchen.

Nancy shook her head. "I didn't have time today. I woke much later than usual, and I didn't want to—" She stopped, horrified. She had been about to admit that she had forgone breakfast simply so she would not be late in meeting Lord Selbridge.

His lordship, however, only smiled briefly and continued to search for something. "I am sure, then, that you would like a cup of tea as much as I would. It is a little primitive here, but my gamekeeper manages to make himself comfortable, and I know he keeps some tea... Ah, here it is." He unearthed a small package of tea from a cupboard, and, to Nancy's surprise, competently set about brewing it.

Jack laughed at her amazed expression. "I am not entirely helpless, Miss Browne. I can make tea, and even grill a chop if I must."

While Nancy digested these wonders, the earl went outside to draw some water. By the time he came back she had found kindling and flints. They made a fire, set a little copper kettle over it, and it was not long before the tea was ready. The rain continued, and they sat cosily on a small bench at a little table shoved against the wall, drinking out of thick cups.

Sensing his companion's discomfort, Jack began to talk about innocuous subjects, but Nancy lacked her usual attention. The tea was finished and still they sat, listening to the rain, watching the flames die down. Nancy absently traced a design with her fingers on the wall beside her. She turned to say something, but saw that Lord Selbridge's eyes were on her and removed her hand from the wall, clinging instead to the lingering warmth of her cup.

"Don't be frightened, Miss Browne."

His voice was low and pitched deeper than normally. She could not meet his gaze and was annoyed with herself for losing the coolness Eleanor had tried to instill in her. His presence seemed very large and near, though in a drawing-room they might have shared a sofa and been no farther apart. But this, she reminded herself sternly, was no drawing-room.

"I . . . I'm not afraid, my Lord." Nancy tried to laugh a little, but succeeded only in producing a little gasp, because he was now leaning over her, his hand on the wall next to her. He smiled. "I'm not a very alarming person, really, and I thought . . . that is, we have spent some very pleasant mornings together. I had hoped you would consider me a friend."

Though the room was chill and damp beside the fire, it had a comforting smell, the scent of loaves baked and joints roasted and soups simmered. Nancy took a deep breath.

"How kind of you, my Lord," she said softly. The breath she had taken had proved inadequate. Another was necessary, but did not help. The earl had moved along the bench until their knees were almost touching and had dropped his hand down along the wall until it rested on the bench on the other side of Nancy. She had only to lean slightly to be in his arms. Her heart hammering at this discovery, she kept herself upright with a great effort.

"I don't wish to alarm you, Miss Browne. I only want you to know how much I admire what you have done at Ellwood. That family was in a sad state before you came. But you..." His smile grew warmer, and Nancy, who had gathered the courage to look up at him, cast her eyes down again, for his eyes suddenly seemed as bright as the sun, and one could certainly be hurt staring into the sun. She knew she must speak to break this spell, or she would do something foolish, like fall back against his arm or perhaps stroke his cheek.

Then she recalled what Mrs. Phillips had told her. Lord Selbridge was suffering from a broken heart. Nancy was the more distressed to realize that these apparent advances of his were therefore nothing of the kind. The thought acted as a jolt to her common sense, and she straightened up. The poor man was seeking comfort; perhaps he wanted to foster an illusion of intimacy in order that he might confide in her about the loss of his love. She tried to cheer herself by thinking that it was an honour to be sought after as a friend and confidante by a man like the Earl of Selbridge, but it did little to ease her sudden sharp pain.

"I want only to help, my Lord, in return for what the family is doing for me. You know that I wish to go to London next Season. I have a small dowry, and I must establish myself. I was going to ask you about London, my Lord, but perhaps you don't wish to talk about it, so soon after..."

She saw that he did not lean so close now, and was looking at her, puzzled. "I hope you do not mind," she continued, "but I have heard of your broken engagement. It must have been very painful." There, thought Nancy. She had done her duty, and now he would talk about what troubled him and feel better.

To her surprise, he abruptly pushed the bench back and stood up, holding out his hand to her. "Yes," he said. "It was painful, but I do not think of it. The rain seems to have stopped. I should let you go back. No doubt you have many things to attend to, as do I."

Nancy felt tears spring to her eyes. What had she done wrong? But his lordship gave no clue. He was polite but reserved, behaviour she had ceased to expect from him.

The rain had ended, the sun was struggling again through the clouds, and though he rode with her a little way along the path to Ellwood, Nancy said that she could manage to return home by herself. "The paths are muddy, but I am sure I will have no difficulty."

He nodded and took her hand for an instant before he began to turn his horse. What could she do to bring back the smiling, jovial Lord Selbridge she had so unwittingly chased away?

"Lord Selbridge," she called after him. To her relief, he looked back at her, and his face held no annoyance.

"May I come and see your kennels soon?" In a moment she told herself it was the most foolish thing she could have said. He was obviously angry with her for causing him to remember the pain of his lost love, so why should he care if she came to look over his dogs? But to her surprise, a slow smile crept over his face.

"You are welcome at any time, Miss Browne." He turned and rode away, the mud flying beneath his horse's hooves.

Nancy rode slowly home, pondering what had happened in the little stone kitchen and wondering if she should mention it to Eleanor or Lady Chetwynd. No, she thought. She could never make them understand and would only be embarrassed by it. Besides, they would doubtless tell her she

had behaved with impropriety, which word, she realized
now, was of no use at all in describing half the things that
might happen to one in the company of a gentleman.

CHAPTER SEVEN

As EVENTS FELL OUT, Nancy did not find the time to visit Marbelmeade as soon as she wished. Sir Reginald's rheumatic pains grew worse, and his ill temper at being deprived of his excellent health set the household on edge. Nancy had her hands full attending to her great-uncle, amusing him as best she could, with no help from the others, for Sir Reginald could not bear his children or grandchildren, particularly when he was ill.

Lady Verena, frustrated because Lord Selbridge had shown little interest in either her or her daughter, took out her annoyance on Eleanor. Their quarrels were frequent and, though Nancy did not know their cause, they spoiled what little attention and instruction she hoped to get from her cousins during the brief periods she was not attending to Sir Reginald.

Fortunately the other gentlemen of the family gave Nancy no trouble during this difficult time. Gervaise was contentedly at Marbelmeade, and Osbert spent much time searching the Selbridge grounds and corresponding with his antiquarian friends, even taking the amazing step of going into London for a few days to consult other experts. To Nancy's delight, he often slipped away to the rectory to see Caroline Phillips.

Though the household now ran smoothly and all the servants were performing their tasks with almost their old dedication, Nancy fell into bed each night weary and sad, convinced that she had made herself too useful at Ellwood and would never see London or meet eligible gentlemen.

There was one development in particular that made Nancy believe Lady Verena might even consider cancelling her London journey in the spring. Sir Francis Garrard had been calling assiduously at Ellwood for the past fortnight, and although Nancy always chatted with him briefly on the progress of his freckle lotion, she knew that he came to see Eleanor—and that Eleanor had begun to welcome his visits.

Of course, Lady Verena would not consider Sir Francis, baronet though he was, a suitable husband for Eleanor, unless he became a great deal richer, but there was always the chance that Sir Francis would succeed in his undertaking and convince Lady Verena to allow him to become betrothed to her daughter. Of Sir Reginald's opinion Nancy could not be sure. He would be delighted to have Eleanor married, but she doubted he would be pleased to have her marry a penniless baronet to whom he had taken an instant dislike.

But even if all these obstacles were overcome, what, Nancy wondered, would become of herself? She would be deprived of her only chance to be presented to Society and would no doubt end her days as a drudge for the Drakes' family. Though she loved Ellwood, to live this way forever was not a pleasant thought. She longed to be her own mistress, and marriage to a good man of independent fortune was the best route.

As for those ridiculous thoughts she had entertained about Lord Selbridge, she had better forget them, and at once. If he had not fallen in love by now with the beautiful and elegant Eleanor and was still nursing a broken heart for another, how could she ever expect him to feel anything for plain Miss Nancy Browne, whom he had once mistaken for a housekeeper?

At last Sir Reginald's condition improved, almost a fortnight after Nancy and Selbridge had sought shelter in the old gatehouse. Nancy had more leisure time. Lady Verena had begun to talk of London fashions once more and had even offered to take Nancy to her dressmaker and order her two new gowns, at Sir Reginald's expense. The atmosphere at Ellwood had brightened, and one morning Nancy decided to ask Eleanor if she would accompany her to Marbelmeade, for she still did not wish to go alone. Before she had a chance to speak to her cousin, a visitor was announced.

Nancy's heart leaped, for she had been hoping for a call from Lord Selbridge, but it was only Sir Francis Garrard. He was shown into the morning-room, where Nancy was labouring alone over some Berlin embroidery, for the other two ladies, bored with their mother-daughter quarrels, had gone up to torment Sir Reginald about giving a dinner party.

Nancy saw at once that something had happened, for Francis's face was flushed and his eyes glittered.

"It is done! The formula is complete, Miss Browne!"

Nancy congratulated him warmly, and he pressed a little blue glass bottle sealed with a cork into her hands. "Please apply it every evening. In a few days we should begin to see results."

"I shall be happy to do so, Sir Francis. And I will not say anything to the others yet, if you do not wish it," she offered.

Sir Francis looked at her gratefully. "Lady Verena and Sir Reginald must not know yet. They might not understand. But Eleanor—I mean, Miss Chetwynd—knows all about it." He looked very conscious as he uttered Eleanor's name. "I must confide in you, Miss Browne..." he said after a moment's hesitation.

"Of course," Nancy murmured, wondering to what she owed the blessing of having escaped these confidences before.

Francis paced a little, then turned to face her again, looking unusually humble. "I have hopes... that is, Miss Chetwynd has given me the encouragement to believe that one day..."

The ordinarily confident Francis seemed as shy as a schoolboy. She hastened to rescue him. "Eleanor has not spoken to me of it, and I wish you well, Sir Francis. Of course, there may be opposition from the family on grounds of fortune, but if your invention is successful..."

Francis was glowing again. "It *shall* be, Miss Browne. I was ambitious for myself before, but now there is even more reason to strive for success."

Just then Eleanor glided into the room. For once, Nancy was sure her cousin had not been eavesdropping, for she greeted Francis with her usual reserve.

"How do you do, Sir Francis?" She held out her slim white hand. He took it and pressed it to his heart, and she made a swift sign in Nancy's direction, but he ignored her.

"This is the hour of truth, my dear. I have completed the formula, and Miss Browne is going to be so good as to put it to the test for me. I... I have told her about us."

Eleanor's most forbidding frown was gathering, and out of sympathy for Francis, Nancy forestalled a scene by embracing her cousin and wishing her happiness, adding praise for Francis's hard work.

"And, of course, my dear Eleanor, not a word of this will pass from me to your mama or Uncle Reginald. I quite understand the need for secrecy." Eleanor smiled.

But when she had left the two alone, promising to faithfully apply Francis's concoction every evening, Nancy knew that she was seeing the beginning of the end of her dream.

Obviously Eleanor's cool, reserved heart had been touched, perhaps because Francis and she were so much alike. Now Eleanor would no longer need to be presented to Society, and Miss Browne would end her days a spinster.

To distract herself from these gloomy thoughts, Nancy knocked on the door of Osbert's study. He had only returned from London late last night, and she had not yet heard the results of his research. To her gratification, he was genuinely happy to see her. It reminded her that, despite everything, her family at Ellwood had come to rely on her. Perhaps she would learn to be satisfied with that. She ignored the sudden lump in her throat.

"I have found the spot on Selbridge's land where we must dig," Osbert informed her, "and my friends at the Antiquarian Club all assure me that it is very likely that the ruins written about in that diary so long ago really are Roman. In fact, two gentlemen are coming next week to witness our expedition."

"Next week! You do not allow us much time, Osbert, to make up our picnic party. But I do not think that anyone we planned to invite is engaged for next week," Nancy said.

Osbert looked blank. "Picnic? Oh, yes. I'm sure Caro—I mean, Miss Phillips will be happy to be one of the party."

Nancy was pleased at the telltale redness in his cheeks. "Let's go and tell her now...that is, if you are not busy," she suggested. "I have been so occupied with Uncle Reginald that I have neglected them, and I am sure Miss Phillips would like to hear about what you learned in London. And Mrs. Phillips and I must confer about the picnic."

"Very well," said Osbert. He tried to hide his eagerness by shuffling through the papers on his desk. "There are some things I should like to ask Miss Phillips about her father's work in this field. Oh, and Nancy, you need not mind about the picnic. Selbridge is seeing to it, remember?"

"Yes, of course," Nancy replied, unhappy at being reminded of him. If only she would not make a fool of herself next week in his lordship's company.

The object of Nancy's anxieties was at that moment engaged in a war of words with Gervaise. His lordship had been pleased with Mr. Chetwynd lately, and the boy had proven useful in deflecting his Cousin Felicity's wilder moods.

But recently he had noticed that Mr. Chetwynd had a stiff, offended air and was uncustomarily dignified in his presence. He had shrugged it off, but finally Mr. Worthington advised him that something was wrong. "You should speak to the young man, my Lord. Something is troubling him, and it is affecting his work. He won't talk to me about it, and he seems to be nursing some sort of grievance against you."

Jack had laughed. "Grievance! How, pray, have I offended the young miscreant? By not giving him leave to lead as many farm animals as he pleases through my mother's formal gardens? Still, I shall speak with him."

In the end it had not proven necessary. Gervaise had arrived early as usual that morning and as had become his habit, partook of breakfast with the earl and his cousins. During this meal he and Felicity kept up a discreet flirtation.

As the earl left the room, he gave Felicity a pat and dropped his brief, customary kiss on her forehead. Formerly she had made a pretty moue, but lately, Jack noticed, she had been shrugging off his hand, and this morning her eyes had filled with tears.

"Why, Felicity, what have I done to distress you, child?" Jack had asked in genuine concern.

Two chairs were pushed back from the table with great energy. One was Felicity's, and with a muffled cry she ran from the room. The other was Gervaise Chetwynd's, but he, though he looked after Miss Garrard with his heart in his eyes, did not retreat. Instead he marched over to Jack.

"I must request, my Lord, that you do not continue to insult Miss Garrard in this way, or you shall have me to reckon with."

"What the devil do you mean, Chetwynd?" Jack was mystified and annoyed.

"I am referring, my Lord," said Gervaise, with all the dignity he could assume, "to your cruel habit of treating Miss Chetwynd like a child."

"But she is," asserted Jack. "An engaging, naughty child, but you can hardly accuse me of any cruelty toward her."

Gervaise's fair skin grew mottled with anger, and the earl was completely taken aback. "I insist, my Lord, that you take back those words. Miss Garrard is a *young lady*."

Light began to dawn in Jack's bewildered brain. He asked, "And if I refuse, sir?"

Gervaise swallowed audibly, but faced bravely up to his opponent. "I shall be forced...that is...I shall request that you name your friends, my Lord. I cannot continue to permit that darling...I mean a lady of Miss Garrard's beauty and charm...you must see, she is no longer a child!" On which words Gervaise's voice broke.

With truly heroic restraint Jack managed to keep from smiling at the young man's look of mortification.

"Oh, my God," Gervaise muttered, turning away and burying his face in his hands. "I'm nothing but a fool, but I beg you will forgive me, my Lord. I spoke out of turn."

"No, no, not at all, Mr. Chetwynd," said the earl, quite prepared to be lenient. Could it be that Chetwynd would take Felicity off his hands? There was the lack of fortune on both sides, but that matter could be dealt with. "We shall forget that this conversation ever happened," he said, testing the waters.

"That is just what I cannot do, my Lord," said Gervaise, much to the earl's gratification.

The young man raised a flushed but determined face to him. "Miss Garrard is an angel, and though I have no right to . . . that is, I could not help but notice that you return her admiration for you with only the most perfunctory attention. She is worthy of more!"

Selbridge smiled. "Do you wish, then, that I would give it more serious attention?"

"No! I mean . . . dash it all, sir, I'm in love with her, and to see her hanging upon your sleeve is more than a man can bear."

"Do sit down, Chetwynd, and have some more coffee, and I will tell you something in confidence."

These intriguing words, mildly spoken, relieved Gervaise of any apprehension he might have had of having offended his employer. He willingly sat down, poured more coffee, flattered at being taken into the earl's confidence.

"Firstly, I am not at all averse to your paying your addresses to Felicity. And I am prepared to do something handsome for her upon her marriage."

Gervaise nearly leaped from his chair at these words, ready to go and throw his heart at Felicity's feet, but Selbridge was still speaking. "You need not fear that I will endeavour to strengthen her affection for me. I have come to believe that my heart is engaged elsewhere."

"Is it the lady in London, sir? The one you were engaged to?" asked Gervaise eagerly, quite forgetting himself in the intimacy of this man-to-man discussion.

Selbridge sighed. "Does everyone in the county know of that? I suppose it is too much to ask that a man be accorded a little privacy. No, young man, it is not she. I did behave like a mooncalf for a bit, but that is over. There is another lady, in fact, a lady at Ellwood, who occupies my thoughts now, though I fear that I do not occupy an equal place in hers. I see you are surprised. No doubt you thought my choice would fall elsewhere, and I must admit it surprises even me, but so far I have had little encouragement to proceed. I ask that you keep this to yourself. I would not wish the lady to be distressed, should she find herself unable to return my regard.''

Gervaise, understanding the earl immediately, swore several oaths that he would divulge this fascinating story to no one.

"And I must ask another favour of you, Chetwynd."

"Anything, sir!"

"Do not alarm Felicity with your ardor. I believe she likes you better than any gentleman alive, with the possible exception of myself," he said wryly, "but go slowly. She may not yet have considered you in the light of a serious suitor."

"Of course," Gervaise assured him. "You need not fear for Miss Garrard's happiness."

With that, Selbridge had dismissed him to his work and mused over whether he had been right in giving away his secret to such a puppy as Gervaise Chetwynd. But he could think of no better way to obtain some peace.

Perhaps Gervaise, without revealing what he was about, could put in a good word for him with his cousin Miss Browne. She was so strong and practical, yet so shy and easily alarmed! Jack had cursed himself for having frightened her at the gatehouse that rainy morning, but the intimacy of their predicament and the warmth of his feelings for her had induced him to show his hand too soon, and he had prudently stayed away from Ellwood since.

To his amazement, that very afternoon Lady Verena's barouche, the one carriage that had been saved from her husband's bankruptcy, pulled up before his door and disgorged Miss Browne and Mrs. Phillips.

Selbridge's heart was light as he rang and instructed that the guests be shown into the drawing-room and that refreshments be brought, while he speedily retired to his chamber to change.

When he entered the drawing-room some minutes later, looking, in his own opinion, much more the thing, Jack's gaze immediately flew to Miss Browne, who seemed perfectly at ease. There was nothing in her greeting to him to show that she even recalled what had passed between them a fortnight ago in the rain. He restrained a sigh of disappointment, then sharply told himself not to be a fool, and greeted her with warmth. He was rewarded by a shy smile.

"We are a deputation, my dear sir," Mrs. Phillips said. "Mr. Drakes would like to set a day to dig for the ruins, and we should like to organize the picnic."

"Osbert has located the exact spot," Nancy added, "and he would like your permission to bring his men to dig there next Thursday morning. The guests can come later to view his finds and enjoy their picnic."

"A very good plan, Miss Browne, but then it is no more than I have come to expect from you."

Mrs. Phillips looked significantly at her companion at this compliment, but Nancy avoided her gaze, and while they partook of Selbridge's refreshments, the matter of the picnic was arranged.

Nancy had been anxious but pleased when, at the rectory, Mrs. Phillips had whispered that they should leave Osbert and Caroline alone in the rector's study, under his indulgent eye, while they took a drive to Marbelmeade to arrange the next week's antiquarian diversion.

Nancy had been struggling to hide the fluttering in her breast from the moment Selbridge had walked into the room. Although she was a little overwhelmed by his almost exuberant vitality, she considered that she had succeeded very well so far.

But when he settled himself on the chair next to hers, and his brown curly head was bent close to her face as he pressed another little cake upon her, Nancy was flustered and utterly undone. She refused the cake and hastily rested her cup and saucer on her knee, as they had begun to shake most alarmingly. But what sounded like an enormous clatter to her went apparently unnoticed by the earl, who was looking at her face and not her trembling hands.

"I see you have not forgotten your promise after all, Miss Browne," Lord Selbridge said. "When you have finished, I should be honoured if you will allow me to show you over Marbelmeade."

At the warmth of his words, joy leaped in Nancy's heart, swiftly repressed by common sense. "I would be delighted," she said calmly, but she could not face the prospect of being alone with him with any assurance. "Perhaps Mrs. Phillips would join us," she suggested.

Selbridge looked at her curiously for a moment, then exchanged a swift glance with the rector's wife, who said immediately, "Oh, but you recall, my dear Miss Browne, I came with you especially to see Lord Selbridge's housekeeper about a receipt she wanted." Unmoved by Nancy's pleading look, Mrs. Phillips rose and excused herself. "I know you will enjoy seeing Marbelmeade, my dear."

Nancy gathered her courage and took the earl's arm. At first she felt anxious about her behaviour to enjoy the tour of dairy, stables, barn and hothouses, but Lord Selbridge's obvious enjoyment of his estate quickly melted her reserve.

Soon Miss Browne was asking question after question, and Jack did his best to answer them to her satisfaction, pleased with her intelligent interest.

The highlight of the tour was when his lordship bade her step into his kennel yard, and there she forgot the last of her anxiety in his presence in her delight at all the healthy, energetic canines.

Jack watched her with appreciation as a droopy-eared giant of a dog, who considered himself king of the kennel, approached her at a gallop, obviously intending to throw himself upon Miss Browne in an ecstasy of welcome. Nancy stood her ground, commanded firmly "Down!" and in a moment the erstwhile monarch was a crouching supplicant at her feet.

Selbridge listened in appreciation as Miss Browne cooed "What a good dog, what a handsome fellow!" The canine, although already aware of his superiority to others of his species, preened, if a dog could be said to do so, and the earl exchanged a look of amusement with his guest.

The other inhabitants of the yard came in for their share of attention and praise, but finally Jack extricated Miss Browne from her canine admirers. "I want you to see something." He took her inside the kennel where a new family of puppies was crawling over its dame, a descendant of the much-indulged Griselda.

"Oh, the darlings!" cried Nancy, and knelt on the straw, heedless of her gown. The mother appeared not at all concerned and went on washing her brood, knocking even the biggest one over sideways with a strong swipe of her tongue. This pup, cream with brown markings, staggered drunkenly to his feet again, and waddled over to Nancy's outstretched hand.

He licked it, looked up at her with liquid brown eyes, and Selbridge wished at that instant that he could as easily win Miss Browne's elusive heart.

"Do you like him?"

"Oh, yes!" Nancy scratched the little fellow behind the ears, and he wagged his tail and tried to box with her fingers, finally capturing her forefinger triumphantly in his infant jaw.

"He is yours, if you want him."

Nancy looked up at him in amazement. "I couldn't, my Lord! By the looks of him he is the best of the litter! Why, to give away such a dog—"

"But I want you to have him—I've plenty of other dogs. You and he seem to have taken to one another instantly. Please accept him as a token of my...my respect and liking for you, Miss Browne." Stronger words than that he dared not use, but he was rewarded by the sight of a peachy blush.

She rose, clutching the puppy to her. "I...I do not know how to thank you, my Lord. I shall take very good care of him, you may be sure." She bent her head to the puppy, who licked her nose.

"I have no doubts about it," the earl said softly, smiling at the pretty picture made by auburn curls escaping from beneath her bonnet and resting on the puppy's cream-coloured coat.

Selbridge gave Nancy his arm as she clutched the puppy with her other hand, and they departed the kennels. "What will you call him?"

Nancy looked thoughtfully down at the little creature, who had immediately taken her loose bonnet ribbon between his little teeth and proceeded to gnaw at it.

"Oh! This behaviour will not do at all, sir," she said, taking the ribbon from him. "I shall call him Mischief, my Lord," said Nancy with a smile.

"Then he will make an excellent companion for Trouble, that adventurous kitten," replied Selbridge. His eyes met

Nancy's, and he was relieved to note that there was not a trace of shyness in them.

At that moment Mrs. Phillips emerged from the house, and Jack, despite the affection he had for that lady, could cheerfully have told her to go to the devil.

She looked at the earl apologetically. "James will be wondering what has become of me, I'm afraid, and we must not leave my sister-in-law alone so long to entertain Mr. Drakes."

Jack pitied the poor creature, for he thought Drakes a dull fellow. "I'm grateful to you, my dear, for coming with Miss Browne today," he told Mrs. Phillips.

Then he turned to Nancy, who was occupied with halting Mischief's depredations on her costume, but to Selbridge's disappointment, she did not do more than cast a swift glance up at him as she thanked him again. He was tempted to press her to meet him the next morning on horseback, but when he kept her hand lingeringly, she seemed agitated and hastily withdrew it, so he reluctantly decided that he must move more slowly.

Gervaise Chetwynd, meanwhile, had gone home to Ellwood full of self-importance. One of the most prominent landowners in the country had confided a most delicate matter. Although he could not precisely understand the cause of the earl's sudden affection for Eleanor, his opinion of his sister had never been so high, and he itched to tell her and their mother about their good fortune. Why, what would not the earl do for him if he became his lordship's brother-in-law? And had he not already all but promised to give Miss Garrard a handsome dowry and approved him as a suitor? How thrilled his mama would be!

He proudly kept the secret for two whole days, but at last, after his mother had asked him for the tenth time if he needed a physic and his sister had said witheringly that working for Lord Selbridge had swelled his head, he was provoked beyond endurance.

"I'm cleverer than you give me credit for, Miss Nell. I am in possession of some information I'll vow you'd give a great deal to hear."

The Chetwynds were alone after dinner one evening. Osbert had, to their surprise, dined with the Phillips family and had not yet returned. Nancy was with Sir Reginald, who eschewed his daughter's and grandchildren's company and had spirited his great-niece away to play chess.

"Oh, and what might that be, sir?" Eleanor looked up at him, head tilted, eyes half shut and mouth pursed.

Gervaise snorted, unimpressed. "You'd never guess, and it would serve you right if I let you miss your great opportunity. With that sour face, he'll be frightened away before long."

Both Lady Verena and her daughter were alert now. "Who will be frightened away, Gervaise? Do not talk in riddles. And your sister has not a sour face; it is very lovely—that sweet expression they taught her at the academy."

"As you are not interested, I suppose I had better not break my promise after all. I may not speak of it, you know, to anyone," said Gervaise with lofty indifference.

Eleanor let her sewing drop and glided over to her brother. "But it is too late, brother dear," she murmured. "You have already spoken of it, and since it apparently concerns me, I certainly have a right to know."

"Very well, then," Gervaise said carelessly, "it is Selbridge. He has taken a fancy to you, and only waits for your encouragement to speak."

"Selbridge!" Lady Verena, with more energy than her daughter, left her chair and went to hug her honoured child.

"I cannot believe it! Why, I thought I knew the signs, and there were none of them in his behaviour."

Eleanor resumed her chair and calmly picked up her work again. Her face, however, was creased in a frown of puzzlement. "I confess, Mama, that I am surprised, as well. I did exactly as you told me, and he did not appear to take the bait."

"Nonsense, my dear! That is just his gentlemanly way of trying not to frighten you with his ardor! Now, my love, you must listen to me." And from then until the tea was brought in, Lady Verena instructed her daughter in the intricacies of bringing on a hesitant suitor, while Gervaise began to regret that he had said anything.

"It is too bad, my love, that you did not get rid of that Sir Francis Garrard and go with Nancy to Marbelmeade today," Lady Verena said as they were preparing to retire for the night. "Not, of course, that there is any danger in dear Nancy seeing Selbridge. He would not think of her, knowing that you might be his. In fact, I wonder if he did not mean that puppy for you but was too unsure of himself to give it to you. You have been neglectful of late, and now you must see to it that he receives the encouragement he wants."

"But, Mama, I am not...Selbridge is well enough, I suppose, but he is hardly exciting, and seems quite content these days to stay at home with his horses and dogs. That is not the kind of life I envisioned for myself. Nancy is certainly welcome to the dirty little animal. I should be insulted to think a gentleman would intend such a gift for me!"

"Be silent, you foolish girl! What have I done to deserve such a daughter?" Lady Verena asked no one in particular. "When you and he are married you may easily get him to do just as you please. He has a house in Town, you know, and his mama, though a little stern, would be happy to see him married. In any case, I suppose there is a residence where she can be sent to be out of your way.''

Thus Lady Verena settled the future of the earl, his prospective countess and the unfortunate dowager.

Eleanor began to protest, then bit her lip. ''Good night, Mama.'' She took her candle and climbed the stairs to her chamber, where she thought very hard about her dilemma. She had an impulse to confide in Nancy, but pride and reserve held her back. Flattering as it was to be chosen the bride of an earl, Lord Selbridge was not the sort of man she could admire, except for his title and fortune. Were it not for the handsome and charming Sir Francis Garrard, she might have been content as Countess of Selbridge, after an appropriately glittering Season, of course, but now she could not face the prospect of marrying her neighbour with any joy.

CHAPTER EIGHT

THE LONG-AWAITED PICNIC and antiquaries' expedition to Selbridge's northwest meadow fell on a day blessed with perfect summer weather. In fact, Selbridge, seeing the sunshine, regretted having committed himself and wished he could spend the time coursing instead, as his dogs were ripe for exercise and the hares on his property had become numerous. But he had given his promise and so gave orders for the food and wine to be sent on a cart to the meadow in time for the arrival of the guests at one o'clock, then went to his study to write some letters.

Searching one of the overstuffed drawers of his desk, Jack came upon a tiny bundle of papers tied with a ribbon. At the sight of it his heart quickened with sweet memory. But when he untied the bundle and re-read the little notes from the lady who had once been everything to him, he felt nothing. The notes, of course, were innocent of any of the phrases of love, being simple invitations or replies to his own communications, but formerly even the sight of the elegant hand of his beloved could make the passion rise in Selbridge's breast. They held no such power over him now.

Now another's charm and sweetness held his heart in thrall, though she remained unaware of it. He crushed the notes in his hands, preparing to discard them, and decided that today he must begin to let Miss Nancy Browne know he admired her. But he stopped crumpling the papers, smoothed them out and put them carefully away. Although his former passion had died, he could not treat these fragile relics so roughly. Had it not been for his despair over losing Miss Wentworth's hand he might never have come to Mar-belmeade and met Miss Browne.

That afternoon at Ellwood Park, Nancy paced agitatedly about her room, picking up gowns and holding them up to herself, then tossing them aside. Her limited wardrobe had since been supplemented by castoffs from Lady Chetwynd and Eleanor, but none pleased her today.

She knew she was wasting time and would no doubt be guilty of making the Ellwood ladies late for the picnic, but she struggled out of the last gown she had donned, an old embroidered white muslin of Eleanor's and cast the offending garment from her. Just then the door opened and the former owner of the dress entered, herself attired very properly but prettily in another such white muslin.

"What is the matter, Nancy? Mama and I have been ready for ages, and we have already given orders for the carriage to be brought round." She looked with disapproval upon the disordered room and set to work shaking out the scattered gowns and folding them neatly.

"You must help me, Eleanor," wailed Nancy, quite startling her cousin with this unusual fit of nerves. "Everything I put on looks dreadful, and I am quite beside myself."

Eleanor, eager to see Francis, who had promised to be at the picnic, cast a swift and almost professional eye over the garments remaining. She held up an ecru gown of fine jaconet adorned with green floss trimming. "This was one of Mama's last year, but she has grown too plump for it. It will do nicely."

"But I thought . . . you and Cousin Verena have always said that white muslin is most suitable for a young lady, especially in summer."

"You look dreadful in white," said Eleanor with un-characteristic bluntness, helping her cousin into the dis-puted ecru gown. "And the ecru gown is perfectly suitable. We are only in the country, you know."

Bonneted in chip straw with moss-green ribbons, gloved in beige kid and shod in jean half-boots, Nancy felt pleased, and then was hustled out of the room by Eleanor, who stopped at her own room to fetch a parasol to lend her cousin. The two young ladies then hurried down the stairs, Nancy trying her best to imitate Eleanor's graceful quick-ness, but only feeling clumsy.

In the light streaming in the tall windows of the hall, Eleanor stopped and looked more closely at Nancy. "Wait! have you been using...that is, Francis said that you would..."

"Yes, every night," said Nancy. "I do not know if it is my imagination but the freckles do not seem so numerous or so noticeable."

"It is not your imagination at all," said Eleanor in de-light and wonderment, examining her cousin's fair skin, which was decidedly less freckled. "I cannot wait until Francis sees this! Our fortune will be made!"

She took Nancy's arm and all but dragged her out to the carriage, where her mother and grandfather were waiting in great impatience.

To everyone's surprise, Sir Reginald had consented to at-tend the pastoral frolic. He had always made very clear his dislike of such entertainments and had often ridiculed his son's antiquarian preoccupations. Nancy, however, who thought such an outing would be good for her great-uncle, had carefully prepared the ground. By emphasizing Lord Selbridge's interest in Osbert's work, she had managed to bring the old man to a state of intense curiosity and secret pride that his son could have made such an interesting discovery.

Now he shouted, "Ha! I suppose it's Miss Eleanor we have to thank for this delay. Come now, let us waste no more time. Bad enough I must go gamboling about the meadows at my age."

Nancy and Eleanor were swiftly helped into the carriage by a groom, and the former went to work at once to assure Sir Reginald that the delay was entirely her fault.

"Please, Uncle Reginald, I beg you not to be cross with Eleanor. It is I who have kept you waiting, and she was only kind enough to help me choose a gown."

Eleanor was not the only young lady Nancy had studied. Miss Felicity Garrard's kitten-like airs now stood her in good stead. She tilted her head and smiled up at Sir Reginald. "I only wanted to do you credit, sir. I hope you like it."

"Very nice, very nice indeed," he replied, softened. "But you shall never convince me, young lady, that it is your old Uncle you are rigged out to impress today. However I am not totally ignorant of who the lucky fellow is, you know."

At this, all Nancy's confidence in her appearance dropped from her. "Why, there is no one..." she faltered, and noted to her shame that Lady Chetwynd and Eleanor were looking at her with interest. Was it so plain that Lord Selbridge was her object?

Sir Reginald gave his gravelly laugh. "Ha! I wish you a great deal of luck, my dear. If any girl can induce the fellow I'm thinking of to notice a fine bonnet and a pretty gown, that girl is you, Miss Nan. I only hope he is not too busy to notice you today."

Nancy's discomfort increased immeasurably. There was no doubt he was speaking of Selbridge.

"What nonsense, Papa," said Lady Chetwynd, apparently coming to the identical conclusion. "Nancy is a delightful girl, and we are very fond of her, but pray do not be giving her ideas above her station."

"But I assure you, I have never intended . . . indeed, I am sure that he . . . no gentleman has ever thought of me in that way," was as much as Nancy could say. Her face grew heated, and she was sure that she had turned an unflattering shade of red.

Sir Reginald patted her hand and chuckled. "Modesty. Becoming in a girl of your age." He scowled at his granddaughter. "Not that phony stuff you call modesty, miss."

Eleanor ignored him, and he turned to Nancy again. "Now, no nonsense about your knowing your station, girl. You're as well born as any young lady in the county, never mind that you've no fortune. And you have done so much for Ellwood—more than this lazy daughter of mine and this arrogant chit, your cousin."

This harangue so insulted Lady Chetwynd that she burst into tears, while Eleanor sat in offended silence, and Nancy suffered a most uncomfortable journey to the meadow. She only hoped that her cousins would not hate her for somehow having given Sir Reginald the idea that she wished to impress Lord Selbridge. She knew very well that they considered him their joint property.

When at last they arrived, they found the cloths spread and baskets and hampers full of food and wine awaiting them, with Selbridge's servants ready to attend them.

The party from the rectory was already there, and Nancy thankfully hurried over to Mrs. Phillips and Caroline, who were watching from a safe distance as Osbert's diggers, observed by two unfamiliar gentlemen, presumably London antiquaries, tossed up the last shovelfuls of earth.

The labourers were so deep in the ground that all one could see was the flying dirt. Occasionally a cry was heard as some find was made and carefully hauled over the side of the trench. There lay several dirt-encrusted objects which might, for all anyone knew, have been of extreme antiquity, but as they were irregularly shaped and their surfaces completely obscured, it was impossible to tell.

At last the digging ended. "They have reached bottom!" Osbert exclaimed, approaching the ladies. "You will not believe what we have found—quite a pile of artifacts—they shall be cleaned by my friends from London who are experienced in these matters, and after lunch we shall examine them carefully."

"Oh, Osbert—I mean, Mr. Drakes—how thrilling it is!" declared Caroline Phillips, colour suffusing her face. Osbert turned to her in appreciation, and Nancy looked on with pleasure.

Eleanor, meanwhile, had glided unobtrusively over to Sir Francis Garrard and under cover of her tilted parasol informed him of the success of his freckle lotion. His joy was extreme, but she managed to calm him before they wandered with studied casualness over to Nancy and took her away from the others.

"By heaven, you are right, my love!" cried Francis, examining Miss Browne's skin in the sunlight. "They are disappearing, and so quickly, too. Do you realize what this means?"

Eleanor smiled. "Of course. It means that you must now begin to manufacture the stuff in quantity, advertise in the newspapers and ladies' magazines and sell it."

Francis blanched. "I know that I promised myself I would do whatever I must, but...I beg you will understand when I tell you I shrink from so exposing myself. A gentleman to put the work of his hands up for sale to the vulgar public!''

Eleanor sniffed. ''What a lot of nonsense you talk, Francis. No one need know that you are the inventor and seller of the lotion.''

''But, Eleanor—''

''I will not accept such a flimsy excuse, sir. If all your protestations of affection for me come to this…shirking of your duty, then I shall consider myself unbound by any promises I might have given you.'' Her voice was tearful at the end of this speech, and for once Nancy believed that her cousin's emotion was genuine.

Eleanor turned and walked off toward the picnic party, and Francis looked at Nancy in dismay. ''What have I done? How can I make it up to her? She will not marry me unless I make my fortune, but I fear I did not think of all the consequences that might beset me if I actually went into this business seriously.''

''But Eleanor is correct, you know,'' said Nancy thoughtfully. ''No one, after all, need know that the inventor of the lotion is Sir Francis Garrard. You need not even manufacture it yourself. I am sure some women in the village would be glad of the work, once someone showed them how to do it, and the advertisements needn't say more than that it is the invention of a gentleman.''

''You are right,'' said Francis, much heartened. ''But I cannot myself go down to the village and show the ladies how it is to be done. The story would reach Jack in no time, and I am sure he would not be pleased, nor would my Aunt Margaret, who is a stickler for propriety.''

''I shall do it,'' offered Nancy.

Francis was about to say that he could not allow Miss Browne to take such a burden on herself, but as he saw no other way to accomplish his goal, he swiftly agreed to everything she proposed. Then they saw that the guests were gathering round the food and hurried to join them.

Jack had been annoyed to find Miss Browne engaged in such long conversation with his cousin, especially as Lady Chetwynd had, in the interval, summoned her recalcitrant daughter and practically forced her on his attention. But to his relief, after a show of flirtation that was apparently strictly for her mother's sake, they were left alone and Miss Chetwynd lapsed into blessed silence.

Since his companion appeared disinclined to discuss the weather or her uncle's interesting discoveries, Jack decided he would talk about what most pleased him. "Miss Browne is looking very well today, is she not?" he said.

Eleanor looked with quickly veiled surprise. "Indeed. She seemed anxious about her appearance today. Grandpapa teased her about wanting to impress someone."

This fascinating tidbit was all Jack managed to elicit, for the guests were all gathering about to be fed, and he excused himself to give a few last orders to his servants. Mrs. Phillips kindly acted as hostess, and soon everyone was seated, and at last Selbridge was free to speak to Miss Browne.

"How is the puppy? I hope he is not living up to his name."

"No, indeed, sir. In fact, Mischief is a very good dog, but I am afraid he will obey only me."

"Wise creature," said Selbridge. "In my opinion there is no one else at Ellwood, with the exception of Sir Reginald, perhaps, who is worthy of attention."

Nancy was discomfited but pleased. She rattled on, "Lady Chetwynd is rather disgusted because my uncle allows me to keep the dog in the house, and the others only ignore the little fellow. But so far he has not made any...mischief indoors.'' By then her face was flaming, and she was looking down at the ground.

"Won't you look at me, Miss Browne?'' asked Jack softly. "Surely I am not so very horrid.''

"Oh, no, Lord Selbridge!'' cried Nancy, looking up and relieved to see a smile on his face.

"My goodness, Miss Browne,'' said Jack quite without thinking. "Where have all your freckles gone?''

"Freckles?''

Jack instantly perceived that he had affronted her by mentioning them and cursed himself. "I am sorry, truly I did not mean to be offensive, but—'' he looked wistfully at her "—I thought them quite charming, and I cannot pretend that you did not once have many and now have very few.''

Nancy's amazement at his declaring an admiration for nasty things like freckles was coupled with an insight that this moment was an opportunity to help Sir Francis and Eleanor. She swallowed her pride and hid her pleasure in the odd compliment to ponder over later. "It is true, the freckles are disappearing, and if I may confide in you—''

"Of course!'' said Jack immediately. He looked about. They were in the midst of a large group, for Mrs. Phillips had, with his permission, invited some other young people of the neighbourhood to the picnic, and he knew if he remained seated by Miss Browne for much longer it would be remarked on and she would feel uncomfortable. "If you are finished, will you come for a stroll with me? Then we may speak without reserve.''

Nancy, who had hardly been able to eat a bite of the delicious food, willingly rose and allowed Selbridge to take her arm. In a few moments they were walking under the trees that edged the meadow, out of hearing of the antiquarians and picnickers both.

Gathering her courage, Nancy told Lord Selbridge all about Sir Francis's invention and her own part in it. She did not add anything about Francis's plans to marry Eleanor, for she thought that this secret was not hers to tell. She only needed Jack's assurance that he would support Francis in his undertaking.

"You see, my lord, your cousin is afraid to begin selling large quantities of the lotion, for fear the world would very soon discover he was its inventor and he would be shunned by polite society. I have conceived a plan that would prevent this."

Selbridge listened in wonder and appreciation to her revelations and ended by heartily approving a plan in which Francis would have the stuff made by some village women and engage someone to bring it to market without revealing his identity.

"And you, Miss Browne," he added, "should be commended for volunteering your services to my cowardly cousin. Although I do not think it wise for you to be the one to teach the village women how to make the potion."

"I do not think Sir Francis cowardly at all, my Lord. He is very brave to risk his reputation. And the village women will not think it at all odd, for I deal with them frequently. Some of them do sewing for the household at Ellwood, and many of their children or husbands have worked for Sir Reginald at one time or another. I have learned that the late Lady Drakes was very interested in herbal remedies and often made them herself, so they will think that I am just carrying on her work."

"You are a genius, Miss Browne!" said Jack. By now they had wandered back to where the digging had just ended and the London antiquarians were still cleaning the artifacts, assisted by Osbert and overseen by Sir Reginald, who was getting in everyone's way and thoroughly enjoying himself.

Jack stopped and drew Miss Browne aside before they got any closer. Now that she had confided her little secret, this was undoubtedly his moment to hint at his feelings. "My dear Miss Browne, I must speak to you about another matter," he began. But he was too late. Sir Reginald had left the site of the abandoned well and strode purposefully over to them.

"It appears my son Osbert isn't as much of a fool as I once thought, Selbridge," he said. "And I have Miss Nan here to thank for it. She's the one who encouraged him to come out of his room. Do you know that my boy has actually dined out twice, been to London and even spoken to some neighbours today?"

Jack agreed that the change in Mr. Drakes was noticeable, but when he turned to smile at Nancy, she was gone.

"Just as well she has slipped away, Selbridge," said Sir Reginald, taking the younger man's arm in his and continuing his walk, striking out with his stick at any clump of grass or twig foolish enough to put itself in his way. "I wanted you to be the first to know. Fact is, I think my boy Osbert is sweet on his cousin, and that's why she's been able to make him behave like a man. Now I know that the girl has no fortune and her birth is only respectable, but she's good as gold, true as they come and there's no one I'd like better for a daughter-in-law. The match has my approval, and that's all anyone needs to know, if they should ask you, my Lord. I'm sure, seeing as how you appreciate Miss Browne almost as much as I do, that you'll agree."

Jack was thunderstruck. It had not occurred to him that matters had gone that way between Miss Browne and Osbert Drakes, yet there was proud Sir Reginald giving his approval.

Sir Reginald was waiting for his reply, so Jack said he hoped the young people would be very happy. But his heart was not in it, and Sir Reginald saw this.

"I know that the Drakes have always married above themselves, rather than below," the old man said, misinterpreting Jack's hesitation. "Why, my late wife was an earl's daughter herself. But that girl Nancy is a treasure, and I hope she and Osbert will speed this courtship along, so Verena won't take her to London in the spring."

"When . . . when do you expect that the betrothal will be announced, sir?" asked Jack, after assuring the old man once more that he did not think any less of Miss Browne for not being wealthy or particularly well-born, which he could do with absolute truth.

Sir Reginald squinted, for they had emerged from the trees into the meadow again and the sun was strong. "Oh, I would not be surprised if Osbert told me of his intentions in a fortnight or so. Probably has to muster his courage." The old man gave his harsh chuckle. "Perhaps I should move things along for him. There," he directed Jack's attention to the excavation, where the guests were now crowded outside the paling to view the objects. Nancy was at Osbert's side, listening appreciatively as he explained the findings. "I'm sure she must be very fond of him, or she wouldn't spend so much time with him. Then again, she is a practical little thing and must know that she might wait a long time before she could do better than Osbert."

These reflections cast Selbridge into a deep gloom. He watched at a distance as all Sir Reginald had told him was illustrated before his eyes. Nancy was at her cousin's elbow, encouraging him to talk to people, sharing in the pride of his achievement, and left Osbert only when she was able to encourage the shy Caroline Phillips to take her place.

Even the discovery that a particularly large clump of artifacts all but cemented together by time and dirt and expected to be of immense value were only some broken wine bottles no more than a hundred years old, did not cheer Lord Selbridge. The Roman bricks and pottery shards that everyone pored over excitedly were only old clay to him, and the thought that Roman chariots had once thundered over his lands stirred him no more than the thought of the London mail passing by every evening.

Miss Browne's future was assured, and her seeming reluctance to accept his compliments thoroughly explained by Sir Reginald's revelations. For a man to have to suffer two disappointments in love within such a short time was manifestly unfair, but this time, Jack vowed, he would not be so foolish as to pretend that solitude and reflection were the cure.

Society might be irksome to him at first, and though any attempts he made at entertaining must, of necessity include the family from Ellwood, he would bear up under the temptation of Miss Browne's presence, especially if he saw her truly and happily in love with Osbert, who, of course, did not deserve her, but was a very lucky dog.

After everyone had eaten and drunk and gazed their fill on the artifacts, the picnic party broke up, and Selbridge returned home to a quiet Marbelmeade, Francis and Felicity having gone to Ellwood for tea, Gervaise with them. Jack walked in the garden alone.

Finally he came to a decision. No more solitude. Let Marbelmeade be filled with guests and laughter. That very evening he sat down and wrote invitations to ten of his most lively friends, ladies and gentlemen, to a week of country pleasures. After thinking long and hard he penned another note to Lady Chetwynd, asking her to act as hostess at the large dinner party and ball he planned to give, for he could think of no one else to ask, Felicity being too young, and the incomparable Mrs. Phillips being, unfortunately, of too low a rank and frankly of too much value to her husband to deputize for the absent countess.

As for Francis, Jack trusted Miss Browne to look after his cousin's interests better than he could, and though he did not altogether approve of the scheme of manufacturing this cosmetic lotion which had deprived him of the pleasure of Miss Browne's freckles, it could do no real harm and might bring his cousin some independence.

For himself, Jack asked nothing more than congenial company and to forget his troubles in the many duties of hosting a lively party of fashionable ladies and gentlemen.

However, if he had been completely honest with himself, Jack would have admitted another desire. In the corner of his heart there was a hope that Miss Nancy Browne would be so impressed by the glamour and high style of his entertainments that she would completely forget Osbert Drakes and his dreary Roman ruins.

CHAPTER NINE

NANCY SOON FOUND HERSELF busier than she had been since her arrival at Ellwood Park, thanks to Francis Garrard's new enterprise. She still enjoyed the beneficial effects of his invention, which she had suggested be named Whisper Balm, to reflect the sensitive nature of its purpose and its soothing effect upon the skin, and had carried out her plans to help him manufacture it.

It had been a fairly simply matter to hire some of the village women to mix the miraculous potion, for they assumed, as she had predicted, that Miss Browne was simply following an old receipt left by the late Lady Drakes and wished to lay in a household store of what she told them was a skin remedy. Fortunately the quantities needed were not yet so large as to cause comment.

Francis, with much encouragement from Nancy and from Miss Chetwynd, who had decided to forgive him now that he had given proof of a desire to improve his fortunes, was able to send an order to a London apothecary for some of the necessary ingredients, and Nancy took it upon herself to gather the rest of them—herbs—which grew nearby, until Eleanor told her sharply, "Nancy, you will be freckled again before you know it. You spend far too much time in the sun."

Nancy, though hugging to herself the secret that Lord Selbridge had regretted the passing of her freckles, did not at all desire a return of them, so she reluctantly passed her herb-gathering task to someone else.

Francis finally informed his sister of the nature of his great plan, and Felicity was so happy that she readily agreed to take over the herb-gathering herself in order that her brother's most prominent advertisement, Miss Browne, should not be lost to the cause.

"What a kind brother you are, my dear Francis! And to think that I once thought you had gone mad!" She laughed merrily at this recollection, and her brother could not help but grin.

He then informed his sister of his secret betrothal to Miss Chetwynd, which news she received with somewhat less rejoicing, for the two young ladies had not become friends.

"Of course, she has no fortune," said Miss Garrard of her future sister-in-law, "but she is very pretty. And at least if she is betrothed to you one may hope that she will no longer flirt so brazenly with poor Jack."

Francis denied that his betrothed had ever flirted with their cousin and said, "You flirt outrageously with him yourself, only he is too kind to show how it annoys him. Best leave Jack alone and put your charm to better use. Mr. Chetwynd, for example, appears to have conceived a tendre for you. I cannot understand it myself, but then each man must choose his own poison."

Felicity frowned at his metaphor, but coloured becomingly. "I shall ask him to accompany me on the herb-gathering expeditions," she mused. "I could wear my leg-horn bonnet with the yellow silk roses, and my primrose morning dress with the embroidered bodice...perhaps even an apron..." She cocked her head and contemplated the charming rustic vision she would make, treading lightly across the meadows with the handsome Gervaise Chetwynd at her side.

"I am sure he will think you very fetching," Francis said, "but it will not be all fun, you know. If you wish to help me there is something else you must do. As you know, Jack has invited some of his London friends here, and they will arrive in about a fortnight. I want you to spread the word among the ladies in the party that you have discovered a wondrous lotion that leaves your skin as white and smooth as a baby's." He chuckled at the look of dismay on his sister's face.

"Word of mouth is the best advertisement, you know, and these fashionable ladies will take the word back to their friends that 'Whisper Balm is a little bottle of miracles for ladies troubled with freckling and browning of the skin.' That is the notice going into the ladies' magazines. Do you like it?"

"It makes your invention sound most enticing," Felicity said. "But I haven't a single freckle, so how can I recommend it to Jack's guests?"

"That need not stop you. Simply tell them it works. It worked for Miss Browne, you know, so you will be perfectly truthful. Besides, the ladies have never seen you. They will not know if you were ever freckled or not."

Felicity was moved by this line of reasoning and agreed to do her part to improve the family fortunes. As they turned back toward the house, she said, "I know the advertisements are necessary, Francis, but how have you arranged to remain incognito? What is to stop the man who is to deliver Whisper Balm to the shops from revealing your identity?"

Francis gave his sister a crafty wink. "The fellow will know better than that. He is to leave my name out of the transactions in return for being the exclusive agent for Whisper Balm. He was a travelling merchant passing through the village and knows nothing about me. Miss

Browne happened to see him one day when she was shopping and helped me arrange it."

Felicity sniffed. "It seems you owe a great deal to Miss Browne. Her name is constantly on your lips. You are as bad as Jack and that old Sir Reginald Drakes. *They* seem to think her nothing short of miraculous. And there is another thing you have not told me, Francis. Wherever did you find the money to fund this manufacture and advertising?"

Her brother flushed with discomfort, and she looked at him sharply. "You have not gone on tick, have you? Or taken a mortgage on Birchley? It is all we have in the world!"

"Of course not. I would not squander our birthright nor would I get into the hands of the moneylenders. I got the money from Jack."

"From Jack! I hardly thought he would lend you any more!"

Francis evaded her gaze and opened the gate for her to reenter the garden. "Well, it was actually Miss Browne who—"

"Oh, that Miss Browne! I am excessively weary of hearing her name. Pray do not begin singing her praises to me again."

Her brother meekly complied.

Only a week had passed since the successful picnic, but to Nancy it was as though her summer had ended. Her days had been filled with supervising the housekeeping at Ellwood and acting as an intermediary for Sir Francis's business venture, and she'd had little time to sit and practise her needlework or pianoforte or to read the latest poetry and novels with Eleanor and Lady Chetwynd.

Her Cousin Verena had, however, redeemed her promise to take her to the dressmaker, and one day they went into St.

Albans to the modiste patronized by the Chetwynd ladies.
Nancy thought the cost of the gowns exorbitant, but did not
protest. She marveled at the stylishness of her new gowns
and the richness of the fabrics, as she had formerly worn
only the cheapest and most sturdy of materials.

Now being made for her were four gowns, two for day
and two for evening, which was an unexpected bit of generosity from Sir Reginald, disguised as a scold to his
daughter for being such a cheeseparer in regard to his niece.
He had flung a purse at her feet and ordered, "See to it that
this young lady is rigged out as fine as that simpering chit of
yours. You shall hear from me if she is not!"

Lady Verena had shed no tears over this, as she loved ordering gowns, whether for herself or someone else. "Papa
will be astonished when he sees you in your new clothes, and
he will not regret his generosity. We shall use every penny of
this, my love," she had said, shaking the purse, which made
a satisfying clink and rattle. "And you shall be attired à la
mode within no time at all. Just in time, too, for Selbridge
has invited a large party to Marbelmeade and has asked me
very prettily to be hostess for him. I am sure it is a sign that
dear Selbridge thinks of us as part of the family," she said
smugly.

At this news Nancy had been stricken with fear. Even
properly dressed, how could she maintain the illusion of
grace and breeding before a crowd of London fashion-
ables? Even the sight of herself in the fashionable new
gowns did not calm her.

In her spare moments, she encouraged Osbert to leave his
study. Flushed as he was with his recent successful discovery and the congratulatory letters that had poured in, this
was not too difficult to do, and once or twice he even sought
her out and asked her if she wished to drive with him to the
rectory, which had become his favourite haunt.

He and Caroline Phillips spent many hours together, unknown to any but Nancy and Mrs. Phillips, but to the dismay of these two matchmakers, no betrothal seemed imminent. They conferred and decided to let nature take its course, for it was obvious to them that Osbert and Caroline were made for one another.

Nancy grew fonder every day of her crusty great-uncle and was pleased to see that the success of the picnic and antiquarian expedition had put Sir Reginald in good humour. He had not made his daughter cry once in the ensuing week, and if he ignored his grandchildren, at least he did not insult them. He did not fly into a rage when Nancy beat him at chess, and even said some complimentary things about his son's scholarship.

Nancy was delighted. "I was wondering, sir, when you would realize that Osbert is a very learned, clever man. He just needs a little encouragement. How happy he would be if he thought you were proud of him."

Sir Reginald smiled in a way Nancy had never seen him smile before. "I would be proud of him, my dear, for your sake."

"What do you mean, sir?" she asked, startled.

"Now, don't come over all innocence on me, my girl. I've got eyes, haven't I? When the boy comes to me and tells me he wants to marry you, you'll have the finest wedding that's been seen in the county for years."

Nancy was stunned and horrified. It had been Osbert, then, and not Selbridge, to whom Uncle Reginald had been referring on the day of the picnic!

She could not even enjoy knowing that she had not, fortunately, publicly exposed her feelings for Lord Selbridge. Something must be done about this misunderstanding. Thinking quickly, she realized that disabusing Sir Reginald at once of his extraordinary notion would never do. First she must confer with Osbert. Perhaps this news would encourage him to speed his courtship of Caroline Phillips.

"Well, Uncle, Osbert has said nothing to me, and he may never do so, so pray do not order a wedding-breakfast just yet," she said as carelessly as she could.

Sir Reginald only winked at her. "Time enough, my dear, unless you are still set on doing the Season with Verena. Take my word for it, nothing but fortune hunters, rakes and gamesters to be found in Town. You want a solid county man, one with an old name and good lands. Someone like Osbert. There, there," he added, for Nancy was by now quite flushed, "I did not mean to distress you, my dear. I won't say anything to Osbert, but he has always been shy."

In her bed that night, Nancy worried over her great-uncle's misapprehension and slept wretchedly because of it. She vowed that she would speak to Osbert at the earliest opportunity.

That next day was Sunday, and due to church services and the fact that Osbert locked himself in his study for most of the morning almost as he had before her arrival, Nancy could not get a word alone with him until late in the day. Sir Reginald had invited the rectory party to dine at Ellwood, which was the only social duty, aside from calling at Marbelmeade, he regularly performed.

At dinner, though she had arranged that Caroline be seated at Osbert's side, Nancy noted that Caroline was painfully shy and Osbert sat in embarrassed silence.

When the ladies retired to the drawing-room, Nancy tried to encourage Caroline to be more forthcoming with Osbert, but the young woman declared she could not, as the gentleman gave her no encouragement.

Nancy tried to assure her otherwise, but before they could discuss the matter further, the gentlemen came in.

Nancy invited Osbert's company with a look that, though mild and welcoming, was a command. But before he arrived at her side Caroline Phillips had slipped quietly away to shelter next to her sister-in-law.

Nancy looked at her with annoyance, then said to Osbert, "I suppose it's just as well. I wished particularly to speak to you about Caroline."

"About Caro—Miss Phillips?" Osbert shifted warily and avoided his cousin's gaze.

From across the room Sir Reginald, deep in conversation with Mr. Phillips, looked up at them and gave his son and great-niece a nod of approval.

Nancy sighed and looked away. "Yes, and do not pretend you do not understand me. If you do not speak soon, Osbert, you may be suspected of toying with her affection."

"I! Good gracious, Nancy, that is absurd. Why, I have done nothing—"

"No, and it is high time you did, sir." She lowered her voice. "Your father has spoken to me, Osbert. It appears he believes that we...that you and I...oh, he has the nonsensical idea that you wish to marry me."

Osbert appeared incapable of speech for a very long minute, staring at her with frightened hazel eyes, like a captive a..imal. Finally he closed his mouth and blinked. "I hope you did not deny it, Nancy," he said anxiously.

Nancy was taken aback. "Why? Surely you do not wish to marry me."

"No! That is, I should be honoured, of course, but..." He shook his head. "Oh, it is no use. It is Caroline I love, but now that Father has gotten this maggot into his head, how can I oppose him? You do not know what he is like, Nancy, when his anger is aroused."

"I wish you will not be so idiotic, Osbert," replied Nancy, losing all patience. "Uncle Reginald is always angry about something, and I pay him no heed at all. That is why he and I get along so well. You must learn to do the same."

Osbert insisted that this was impossible. "He would eat me alive," he said solemnly. "Right now he tolerates me and my ways. Why, if I were refuse to marry you and tell him I want Caroline for my bride, I would never have another moment's peace."

Nancy kept hold of her temper. "You need not start trembling now, Osbert. I have neither denied nor confirmed his supposition, and I have said nothing to him about Caroline. That is for you to do."

"I...I could not do it. He will say she is not good enough, though she is a delightful creature. She has no fortune, and though I esteem her father's memory greatly, he was not of good birth and Father will despise her for it."

"Then you must stop seeing Caroline altogether," said Nancy firmly, experimenting with harsher tactics.

"Oh...how could I? I should be miserable if I did not see her," he declared, and Nancy was encouraged.

"You must, since you will not marry her. I do not think it fair to visit the young lady so often without making a declaration of your intentions. Are you or are you not in love with the girl?" she demanded in a voice that lost nothing of its authority for being pitched to a whisper.

Osbert blinked nervously. "Of course. B-but I do not think I am prepared for the responsibilities which such a declaration would inevitably—"

"Stuff!" said Nancy. "You are simply afraid."

"Very well, yes, I am afraid of making a cake of myself and of angering my father."

"Coward!" Nancy whispered.

Beads of sweat had broken out on Osbert's broad forehead. "I...I will think about it. Give me some time, Nancy, I beg of you. Pray say nothing to Father or to Caroline. I must work up my courage, for you are right, I am a puling, mewling coward where Father is concerned."

"Very well. I shall give you time. But when your father brings it up again, you must act," said Nancy firmly.

Osbert promised to do so, but Nancy was not sanguine about the results. In the end, she supposed she herself would have to tell Sir Reginald the truth, and though he did not frighten her, she did not look forward to it. It was his son's timidity and not his choice of a bride that would certainly enrage him.

The first intimation anyone had that something had gone awry in the scheme to sell Whisper Balm came when Sir Francis Garrard went into the village on the morning his cousin's London guests were expected to arrive. He wished to see for himself if the local shop, the first to carry his potion, had sold any of it.

Naturally the proprietor could not know that the inventor of Whisper Balm was this tall, fair young aristocrat who strolled in attired in buff pantaloons, striped waistcoat, crisp neckcloth and exquisitely fitted coat. Neither could the other customers, so he would be quite safe, Francis assured himself.

Browsing about the shop, for it would never do, he felt, to head straight for his object, he affected to be interested in the price of some handkerchiefs and eau-de-cologne, moving ever closer to the shelf where a display of Whisper Balm, in its pretty blue bottles, beckoned. However by the time he had purchased a bottle of cologne, he noticed a small crowd of villagers milling about, murmuring and staring.

As yet innocent that he might be the cause of their interest, he began to count the bottles of Whisper Balm unobtrusively while his purchase was being wrapped. "Two dozen..." he muttered beneath his breath. "The shopkeeper took four dozen last week..." His calculation was coming to a joyful conclusion, but when he turned back to retrieve his wrapped package, he was dismayed to find that the shopkeeper, bowing and beaming, had brushed aside his attendant and was himself handing him the package.

"Yes, Sir Francis, it has done very well, as you see. All the ladies hereabouts are using it, even their maids and the farmers' wives—everyone is quite enthused about Whisper Balm." He gave a hearty laugh. "Though the whisper has risen to a cry, as one might say, heh, heh..."

Horrified, Francis simply stared at the man. Here was disaster, indeed! At the shopkeeper's words the other customers felt free to approach him, and one after another offered him their congratulations.

He replied politely but numbly to these attentions, and eventually made his way out of the store in a fit of panic, clutching his purchase and wishing it were a loaded pistol, for he saw no other remedy at that moment than to put a period to his existence.

"The scoundrel!" were the first words he spoke to Nancy not long after, for he had whipped up his horse and driven his cousin's curricle straight to Ellwood.

"The audacity of the fellow to reveal my identity when he was instructed to do no such thing! The gallows would be too good for him!"

Fortunately on the ride from the village to Ellwood, Sir Francis had relieved his feelings with curses and other epithets unsuitable to a lady's ear and could confine himself to this heated but not unseemly language.

Nancy, however, would not have minded hearing something stronger, for she felt that she as well as Sir Francis had been taken in by the merchant with whom they had arranged to distribute Whisper Balm. After her first flush of anger, she sat down, gave Sir Francis some wine and tried to think calmly of a solution.

Fortunately she was alone when Sir Francis arrived, Eleanor and Lady Chetwynd having gone to St. Albans to shop, promising to bring back Nancy's finished gowns with them. Sir Reginald was engaged with his estate agent, and Gervaise was, as usual, at Marbelmeade.

To the distraught Sir Francis, Nancy said, "I fear we have no way to stop him. He is already in London selling it to the shops. We can only hope that he was simply tempted to impress the local people by identifying you. In London, where you are not well known, he would have no such inducement," she said.

Francis had already begun his second glass of wine and was somewhat calmer. "Perhaps, but I am not entirely unknown in Town. Jack sponsored me for his club, and I am acquainted with several gentlemen who frequent fashionable circles."

Suddenly he choked on his wine, hastily put down his glass and leaped up. "Jack's guests! I had almost forgotten, but the first of them will arrive this afternoon. If word of my folly has reached Town, they are sure to bring it with them, and both Jack and I will be mortified." He laughed bitterly. "An earl and a baronet engaged in trade, selling ridiculous potions to ladies. We shall be laughed out of our club."

Nancy frowned. "Sit down, Sir Francis. I do not wish to be inhospitable but I think you should take no more wine. Lord Selbridge's name need not be connected with any disgrace you might suffer, and you must not make light of your accomplishment. Whisper Balm is quite efficacious. I am proof of that.''

Indeed, Miss Browne's golden-tinted skin was innocent of all but a light dusting of freckles across her nose. Francis steadied himself. ''You are right, of course. And I am assuming that everyone in London knows already.'' His expression brightened. ''Why, even if that untrustworthy merchant of ours is giving away my secret, Jack's friends may not have heard anything yet.''

''It is entirely possible,'' said Nancy. ''And I have every confidence in Lord Selbridge. He will not desert you.''

This soon restored Francis to his customary bold assurance, and he promised to prepare his cousin for any unpleasantness that might arise. ''You are right. Jack will know how to deal with it,'' he said. ''And perhaps it is not so dreadful after all. I will be considered to have disgraced my rank, but if everyone knows that I am the inventor of Whisper Balm, I shall no doubt become even richer that I had hoped, and Eleanor will be most happy.''

Nancy forbore to disturb his complacency by reminding him that he had first to discover if Lord Selbridge's guests knew of his disgrace. When no frantic note arrived from Sir Francis, she assumed that the first arrivals, at least, had heard nothing, and hoped that the rest of the party would be equally ignorant. The first occasion at which this hope could be tested was two days hence, when everyone of consequence in the neighbourhood was invited to dine formally at Marbelmeade.

Meanwhile, Felicity and her brother were delighted with the first four arrivals—a married couple and a single gentleman and his sister—whose presence added considerable interest to what had promised to be a dull summer.

''Poor Jack is always so busy,'' Felicity confided to one of the London ladies that evening after dinner, ''that Francis and I have often been left to our own devices. How happy we were when he decided to invite his friends."

"Yes, we all know that dear Selbridge suffered greatly last Season," replied the guest, and proceeded to detail Lord Selbridge's crushing love affair of the season before.

Despite her great interest, Felicity did not forget her promise to her brother. She decided that the two ladies from London, though not heavily freckled, could use some improvement in their complexions, and so she skillfully directed the conversation toward the hazards of the summer sun to the skin.

"Indeed, I have been so bored here some mornings that I find myself spending hours in the garden. If it were not for a particular secret of mine," she said with a sly smile, "I should be most afraid of the sun's effects."

Both ladies looked interested and immediately said that they would never have guessed that Felicity spent much time in the sun, so very white was her skin.

She appeared to have no intentions of revealing her secret, and naturally the ladies were intrigued and pressed her to go on.

"It is Whisper Balm, of course," Felicity said.

"Whisper Balm?" asked the older of the two ladies. "Why, I have never heard of it."

Felicity looked crafty. "I daresay the secret will soon spread to Town. Indeed, I cannot in all justice keep it to myself. There are so many fellow sufferers, you know."

The ladies, conscious that their own complexions did not show to advantage beside Felicity's, were immediately snared, and Miss Garrard cleverly allowed herself to be persuaded to discuss how one might go about procuring a bottle of the lotion.

She reported her success the next day to her brother, and he was so relieved that his good name was apparently still

safe that he rushed over to Ellwood to give the news to
Eleanor and Nancy.

Sir Francis's beloved and Miss Browne received this news
with delight and relief, though Nancy was not entirely sanguine about the chances of his commercial activities remaining a secret. There were other guests yet to arrive
during the next two days, and the following morning she
and Eleanor had a small fright when Miss Garrard, accom-
panied by a now augmented party of female guests from
Marbelmeade, came to pay a call on the ladies of Ellwood.

However, it was soon apparent that Sir Francis's reputation as a baronet and gentleman was still safe, for Felicity
was unworried and the London visitors behaved charmingly to Nancy and Eleanor. To her surprise, Nancy was able
to forget her feelings of unpreparedness for such society and
joined in the conversation.

Eleanor did her part in the promotion of Whisper Balm,
to the horror of Lady Verena. Nancy was amused both at
her aunt's dismayed expression and at Eleanor's heretofore
unknown talent for exaggeration.

"Yes, indeed," Miss Chetwynd was saying with the
greatest sincerity to one of the newly arrived London ladies, "I assure you I was the brownest thing imaginable before Felicity told me of her discovery. I could not so much
as step outdoors without spoiling my complexion. But
now..." She lifted her chin and turned her head a bit, so that
the awestruck ladies could witness her miraculously fair
skin.

"Why, Eleanor, how can you—" began Lady Verena,
who had never heard of Whisper Balm and could not imagine why her lovely daughter should suddenly pretend to
any imperfection of face or figure.

"You may be certain," Nancy interrupted hastily, offering her own visage for the ladies' edification, "that I was

covered with freckles until Eleanor lent me some of her Whisper Balm. It was most distressing, and Cousin Verena despaired of ever seeing me rid of them, did you not, Verena?''

Lady Chetwynd, though still confused, was easily distracted. "Indeed, my dear Nancy, they were frightful, but they do seem to have almost disappeared." She stared at Nancy in wonder. "I suppose that Whisper Balm of Eleanor's does work. Though I still fail to see why—''

Eleanor swiftly changed the subject to the Earl of Selbridge. Her ladyship gave herself up to the enjoyment of hinting delicately at his admiration of her daughter and preening before the ladies because he had asked her to deputize for his mother at his formal dinners and ball, the first of which was that evening. Nancy was half-anxious and half-eager to test herself at these affairs.

Although the family at Ellwood lately had been included in several entertainments given by neighbours and Nancy now felt more confident of her ability to conduct herself creditably in Society, a formal dinner at Marbelmeade still loomed as an ordeal, not the less because the earl himself was the object of impossible hopes and ill-suppressed dreams.

Nervously she made herself ready for dinner, putting on one of her new evening dresses, a gown of cream-coloured net over a topaz satin slip, with a wide lace flounce at the hem and more lace under the bosom. The neckline was the lowest she had ever worn, but Lady Chetwynd assured her it was quite the thing. She wore her mother's pearls, her only jewels, and Eleanor had lent her a light evening shawl. Her hair, curled and drawn back, was fastened with a wide topaz satin ribbon adorned with clusters of flowers. She regarded this vision in the looking glass with disbelief.

Even Lady Chetwynd and Eleanor, usually quick to be jealous of any female beauty but their own, were lavish in their praise of Nancy's appearance, and when she came downstairs, Sir Reginald pinched her cheek and nudged Osbert, who obediently complimented his cousin.

Nancy thanked them. "But I am still a trifle anxious about meeting all those fashionable people. I am sure I will not know what to say to them," she said as they drove to Marbelmeade.

"Nonsense, my girl. You are as good as any of 'em," said Sir Reginald. "Hold your head up and don't be afraid. Osbert isn't afraid of them, are you?" he demanded suddenly of his son, who sat in great discomfort between Nancy and his sister.

"No, sir. Not at all," Osbert replied with absolute truth. The thought of the evening ahead bored him, but it certainly did not frighten him. The only fear in his heart was lest his father observe how besotted he was with Caroline Phillips.

Lady Chetwynd smiled at Nancy. "You have nothing to fear, my dear. Simply follow my lead. Eleanor and I are used to being among people of fashion, are we not, my love?"

Eleanor's reply was absentminded. She had no thought but for Francis. The misfortune that had occurred in the village preyed on her mind, and though so far the London guests seemed entirely ignorant of her beloved's activities, she was rapidly becoming anxious about the latest arrivals. These fashionable Londoners would have no scruples about making her betrothed a laughingstock, she was certain.

And when they had been set down at Marbelmeade, sonorously announced by Jenkins and welcomed by Lord Selbridge, it appeared that their worst suspicions had been confirmed. The earl took Nancy and Eleanor aside while Francis stiffly performed the introductions of the other members of the Ellwood party to six elegantly dressed strangers who, along with all the other guests, were gracefully disposed about his lordship's drawing-room.

"You must go to poor Francis, Miss Chetwynd," said Lord Selbridge. "Lord and Lady Widhurst, who arrived today, have heard all about the 'gentleman' who invented Whisper Balm, and by now everyone knows. Poor Francis!" Selbridge was more ill at ease than Nancy had ever seen him. "In addition, that merchant fellow had the infernal impudence to reveal not only the inventor's name but the fact that he is a relation of mine!"

Nancy forced herself to speak through a constricted throat. Whatever respect Lord Selbridge might have had for her must have disappeared by now, for he knew that it was she who had egged on his cousin in his scheme. "I was afraid of that very thing, my Lord, and I am so dreadfully sorry," she said. "I know it is mostly my fault. I should never have interfered."

"Pray do not distress yourself, Miss Browne," Selbridge said with a quick smile of reassurance. "You were only trying to help my cousin and could not know that the merchant would broadcast his identity all over town."

Eleanor was fidgeting, twisting her gloved hands. "Oh, please, Lord Selbridge, we must go home at once. I do not care if the dull people in this neighbourhood know about Francis, but how can we ever face your London friends now?"

Nancy lost patience with her cousin. "Do not be so silly, Eleanor. They know nothing of our connection with Whisper Balm, except that we have used it. And besides, we are not the ones who will suffer most from their scorn. Pray think of Francis, and not of yourself for once."

Selbridge added his weight to this, looking at Nancy with approval. "Miss Browne is right. Fortunately, my friends are treating the matter as a joke, but poor Francis has had to endure much teasing on the subject. Pray do what you can to distract them from him.''

Eleanor had taken Nancy's reproof surprisingly well. Now she arranged her features in an expression of determination. ''I shall gladly do my part. If you will introduce me, my Lord, I will do my best to engage your friends in conversation and discourage the subject of Francis's disgrace.''

By this time Nancy was so anxious for Francis that she did not have time to be anxious for herself. During the introductions she felt a reassuring pressure; Lord Selbridge was holding her arm, and he made her known to his newly arrived friends as if conferring some great favour upon them.

She already knew that they were not such frightening creatures after all. The ladies were all well-dressed and lively, and though one of them was extremely handsome, the rest were not as lovely as Eleanor. The gentlemen seemed amiable enough, and one or two of them even gave her glances of admiration. All of them spoke very wittily about matters of no great importance, so there was no need for her to say anything, except to reply briefly when her opinion was called on. As a yes or no usually sufficed, she experienced no great difficulty. The ladies she had already met were very kind to her, and soon she felt comfortable.

But Nancy felt Lord Selbridge's gaze upon her more than once as she mingled with his friends, and once when she caught his eye he smiled encouragingly. Why, it was as though he was watching her to see how she would behave, and the idea unnerved her. She allowed Eleanor and Felicity to vie for the attention of the fashionable strangers, and soon slipped away to sit beside Mrs. Phillips, where she could comfortably observe the glittering scene while sipping sherry.

Though Francis and Eleanor seemed to be bearing up well, it was not long before once again one of Selbridge's London friends made a remark about the young baronet's commercial enterprise. The guests were just sorting themselves into couples to go into the dining room. "I see the famous Sir Francis Garrard is to take you in to dinner, my dear," said a jovial gentleman to his wife. "Take care he does not attempt to sell you some of that miraculous balm of his."

Francis reddened, the other guests laughed, and Nancy saw Eleanor give her betrothed an encouraging glance, at which he bowed deeply to the lady awaiting his escort and offered her his arm. "I assure you, sir, your lady is in no need of any balm I could devise. Nature has left no room for improvement."

The lady smiled up at him and no further comments followed. Nancy's eyes searched for Lord Selbridge, and she exchanged a smile of relief with him across the room. Mr. Phillips then offered her his arm, and she and the rector proceeded to the dining room, almost at the end of a long line of couples.

Selbridge wished that she could be heading the line with him, but one of the London ladies was of very high rank, so he had to lead her in himself. Nancy, alas, was one of the lowest in rank. How these details irked him, when he wished for nothing more than to take Miss Browne on his arm and proclaim to everyone that she would be his next countess. At least he had been able to put the dull Osbert next to Caroline Phillips. Though her brother was his great friend, and Miss Browne appeared to dote on her, he could not admire a young lady who blushed so often and said so little. She and Mr. Drakes could bore one another as much as they pleased, he thought with satisfaction.

There were forty to dinner altogether, and the vast, un-used state dining room had been opened, aired and pol-ished. Jack had found himself more enthusiastic at the prospect of grand entertaining than he had thought he would be. At first the idea of company had come to him only as a way to ward off his gloomy thoughts about his second failure in love, but now he found he enjoyed watch-ing Miss Browne as she took in the splendour of it all.

He kept up a steady conversation with his dinner com-panions during the long and elaborate meal, while keeping an eye on his guests' comfort as well. To his surprise, Lady Verena was an excellent hostess. He had been afraid that his request might have put her above herself and brought her to think he had some matrimonial intentions toward her, but she had not flirted with him for some time, though she had not stopped urging Eleanor on him. Indeed, her attitude toward him, though still proprietary, was more like that of a prospective mother-in-law, and he knew that he was in for some teasing from his friends.

Eleanor seemed to have lost the lust for the chase and had troubled him very little, except when her mother was watching. This he attributed to her obvious interest in his Cousin Francis. Though no one had told him anything spe-cific, it was quite plain that there was some kind of ar-rangement between them and that Miss Browne approved. But for that, he might have thought Francis was making a mistake, but he trusted Miss Browne's judgement. He won-dered if Lady Chetwynd and Sir Reginald were aware of it.

But it was Nancy he could not keep out of his mind. To-night she was lovelier than she had ever been, and her eyes were like stars. Completely unaware that she might actually be the object of Selbridge's thoughts, Nancy envied the beautiful lady at the earl's side, continued her conversation with Mr. Phillips and cast occasional swift glances down the long table at the earl, wondering what it was that the lady was saying to him to make him smile and laugh so much. When he bent his head to speak earnestly to his fair companion, Nancy's fingers tightened on the stem of her glass.

"Gently, Miss Browne," Mr. Phillips said to her in a soft voice. "The countess might be disturbed if you broke one of her set of matching French crystal."

"Oh! I did not realize..." Nancy set the glass down carefully. "Thank you, sir. I do not know what I was thinking of."

Mr. Phillips merely smiled and drank his own wine. After a moment he said, "That lovely lady next to Selbridge is an old friend of his."

"Oh?" Nancy tried to appear nonchalant, but a fork dropped from her hand to the white damask cloth.

The rector did not appear to notice. "Yes, and she is married to one of his best friends—that very tall gentleman to Lady Chetwynd's right."

"Oh. She is...very lovely." Insane relief flooded Nancy's brain. As if it mattered, she told herself, viciously attacking the food she had hitherto ignored. She forced herself to turn to Francis, who sat at her other side, and talk to him reassuringly until Lady Chetwynd rose and the ladies followed her from the room.

In the drawing-room, Eleanor came to her at once. "Grandpapa will certainly have heard the story from those London gentlemen by now," she whispered, "and he will be furious when Francis offers for me. Please, Nancy, you must break the news of our betrothal to him for us."

"I do not know if that is wise, Eleanor," she replied, thinking of the ordeal ahead of her when she must tell her great-uncle about Osbert and Caroline. "He might not have objected too much if you married Francis before this news was announced, but now...I cannot promise, but if I find

him in the right humour I will tell him. You and Francis will
have to wait, anyway, until you see how well Whisper Balm
does. It will not do to assume it will make your fortune, you
know.''

Then they joined the other ladies, whom Nancy found, to
her pleasure, kind and interesting. How different were their
manners from Eleanor's affected ways! Nancy began to see
that she had been taking her lessons from a poor teacher.

Still, the conversation did seem to centre on Selbridge,
and Nancy found it difficult to keep pretending that the very
sound of his name did not arouse a thrill in her heart.

When the men joined them, the older people broke up
into card tables while the younger ones drifted into musical
or conversational groups. Selbridge, as host, found himself
tied to a card table and not enjoying himself at all. He con-
soled himself with listening intently to the musical perfor-
mances of his young guests, and was delighted at the
charming duet Miss Browne performed with Osbert. To give
the dull fellow credit, he had an excellent voice, Jack mused,
one not so evident when he sang with that little Miss Phillips, but with Nancy... He let his attention drift again and
again to Miss Browne, her lovely lips opened in song, her
pure contralto filling that little corner of the room most
pleasantly. Several times he had to be called back to attend
to the cards. By the end of the game, he had come to a decision. Osbert Drakes or no Osbert Drakes, he must speak
to her tonight.

Surely it was not too late to let her know she had captured his heart, and beg her to at least consider his offer,
before tying herself to Osbert Drakes. He could not believe
she loved the man. It must be, as Sir Reginald had said, that
she thought there was no other chance for her. Foolish little Nancy!

If his guests noticed that Lord Selbridge's attention was drifting, that he often wore a rather silly smile on his face, none of them were so ill-bred as to mention it. Nancy noticed, because no matter what her intentions she could not help fixing her gaze on him now and again, but could not account for it. At last he got up from the card table and made his way across the room. At that moment a servant interrupted his progress with a whispered message. His lordship's features betrayed amazement and dismay. As she saw him leave the room hastily, Nancy wondered what could be the matter.

In the hall, Selbridge was faced with an elderly apparition at his door, surrounded by servants burdened with boxes and trunks. "Mama! Whatever are you doing here? I thought you were quite settled at Brighton!"

"Thank you, my dear, I am quite well," said the countess crisply. "As usual, you are an attentive and loving son."

Jack hastily apologized and planted a filial salute upon her cheek. "I did not mean to be rude, Mama, but you startled me. Is anything wrong? You did not mention this in your last letter—"

"I have not written to you since you last wrote to me, my boy, which was over a fortnight ago. However, since then I have heard some news which demands my presence here. Where is your Cousin Francis Garrard?"

Jack at once grasped the situation. "Why, he is . . . but surely you do not wish to see him now? Come, you have had a long journey and must go to your room. It is tiresome, but I have a small house party—some guests from town, and most of the neighbourhood have been to dinner and are in the drawing-room. They would bore you. Time enough to talk tomorrow."

Lady Selbridge, who was indeed weary, was easily persuaded. Jack was about to heave a sigh of relief and run to tell Francis that he must leave Marbelmeade or face his aunt's wrath, when his mother, who was progressing slowly up the stairs, turned around.

"Did you say guests, Jack? Was it for this that you all but sent me into exile at Brighton? Hmph! You and I will have a long talk tomorrow, sir."

"I am sorry, Mama. I had intended, as I told you, to spend the summer alone, but circumstances—"

Her ladyship sighed. "Never mind."

When she was out of sight, Jack hurried into the drawing-room. There he deftly and unobtrusively detached Francis and Miss Browne from the party. Just when he had planned an interesting tête-à-tête with the lady, he was forced to ask for her help again, Jack thought in irritation. He led his curious companions to an anteroom.

"Francis," he said, "we must hide you. My mother has returned, and it can be for only one reason. News of your activities has somehow travelled to Brighton."

Francis blanched. "Is Aunt Margaret very angry?"

"No, she did not seem so. Just . . . determined."

Francis shivered. "I will leave. Tell her that I've gone back to Birchley for the rest of the summer."

"Nonsense," said Jack. "She knows your circumstances. Mama has an amazing memory for details. I have managed to put her off for tonight, but she knows you are here, and she will not rest tomorrow unless I bring you into her presence. We must hide you at Ellwood."

He turned to Nancy. "You would not mind arranging it, would you, Miss Browne?" He smiled. "As a favour to me? Of course, if it will cause you any trouble with Sir Reginald . . ."

His intimate smile had stirred her to the very depths. "Of course not," she said. "I can manage Uncle Reginald. Only get Sir Francis there, and I will arrange for his room. He can stay as long as he needs to. Perhaps," she said, looking at Francis thoughtfully, "it will be a good opportunity for you to get to know Uncle Reginald better and to get him accustomed to the idea of your marrying Eleanor."

Francis looked with terrified eyes from his cousin to Miss Browne. "I swear I do not know what will be worse—facing Sir Reginald or Aunt Margaret! Oh, Jack, perhaps I shall just take a horse and ride away somewhere—anywhere."

Nancy took his arm. "You have nothing to fear from Lady Selbridge—"

"My mother is a tartar, Miss Browne, and Francis has never come up to her expectations of him."

"Well, never mind," she said comfortingly to Francis. "Pack a few items of clothing, leave by the servant's stairs, take one of Lord Selbridge's horses and go to Ellwood. Wait in the wood along the drive, and no later than five minutes after you see our carriage pass, I will send Bowen out to you." She smiled. "He owes me a favour, for I persuaded Uncle Reginald to put him in charge of the male servants, and he revels in it. You will not have to wait long, and early next morning I shall explain it all to the family."

"Bless you!" cried Francis, before he flew up the stairs to his room.

Selbridge turned to Nancy and took her hands in his. "I cannot thank you enough, my dear. You are so capable that sometimes you quite take my breath away."

Nancy was pleased and startled. "Oh, I . . . it is nothing, Lord Selbridge. You have been very kind to me and to my family, and I am happy to do anything . . ."

He was drawing her closer, but she persisted in looking at his chin and not at his eyes. "I want to be more than kind," she thought she heard him say . . . but suddenly one of the drawing-room doors was flung open, almost knocking Nancy into the earl's arms. It was Eleanor.

"I could not bear it any longer," she said, completely oblivious of the mood she had just destroyed. "What has happened to Francis?"

Lord Selbridge quickly explained, and by the time he had gotten Miss Chetwynd calm enough to go inside again, he looked about for Miss Browne, but she was gone, having apparently slipped back into the drawing-room, safe in the large crowd.

CHAPTER TEN

NANCY EXPLAINED Sir Francis Garrard's presence at Ellwood the next morning by informing the family that Gervaise had invited him. Since Gervaise, with his new-found dedication, was already at Marbelmeade again by the time everyone descended to a late breakfast, no one could contradict her. Strangely, they were all preoccupied.

Lady Verena was wondering why Lord Selbridge, having told her son he was in love with Eleanor, had paid the girl so very little attention the night before.

Sir Reginald had greeted Francis almost politely and, to Nancy's delight, had not seemed to mind the extra guest. "All of that freckle-cream foolishness is your own business, sir, but mind you don't talk my grandson into joining you in such an enterprise," he had said when told that Francis was Gervaise's guest. "The youngster is just now settling down to some honest work, and I don't want his head turned."

Osbert was, as usual, thinking only of his own affairs and scarcely regarded Francis's presence. While Eleanor spirited her beloved away for a walk, Osbert rose from the table and asked Nancy to come to his study.

Sir Reginald looked up at once. "Go along, children," he said in kindly tones that they hardly recognized. He winked at his son, nodded encouragingly at Nancy, and his grim mouth even sketched a smile.

Nancy smiled back uncertainly and followed her red-faced cousin from the room, eager to rid herself of this burden of misunderstanding. As for herself, Nancy knew she could not realize her dream. Since the day he had presented her with Mischief, the puppy who even now followed obediently at her heels into the study, his lordship had treated her with flattering and distinguishing attention. He had listened to her support of Francis with gravity and respect, and she had an inkling that he had been so generous to his cousin because he desired her good opinion. Last night he had turned to her at once in his need, trusting her to help him. But none of these things, she told herself, meant that she was justified in encouraging her feelings.

Seeing the earl surrounded by his elegant friends amidst the splendour of his ancestral home had made Nancy feel the gulf between them even more. Selbridge had only turned to plain Nancy Browne for friendship and consolation.

If her heart were not so deeply involved, his friendship would have been enough. But she had taken the first opportunity last night to run away, afraid that if he continued to speak in those soft tones, with that look of tenderness in his eyes, she would reveal her feelings and cause herself even more anguish.

"Please, Nancy, I did not ask you here to daydream," Osbert was saying reproachfully. "Even now father probably thinks we are planning our wedding."

"Have you finally decided to speak to your father about Caroline?" she asked. "Every time Sir Reginald sees us together, I am more eager than ever to have him know the truth." She picked up Mischief and placed him in her lap, where he promptly went to sleep.

"Not yet," Osbert admitted. "I have another problem, Nancy, and I require your advice. Selbridge has invited me to shoot tomorrow morning with him and some of the gentlemen, and Papa knows about the invitation. If I refuse, he will see that I do not get a moment's peace. But I really do not wish to go.''

''I think you ought to go, Osbert,'' Nancy said at once. ''It will make Uncle Reginald happy, and you cannot afford to antagonize him before you break the news to him about Caroline.''

''B-but, Nancy,'' Osbert protested. ''I have not even asked her yet, let alone told father about her. As for shooting, I could not hit a tree trunk were I aiming from three feet away. I would make an utter fool of myself shooting at Selbridge's game!''

''That need not stop you,'' Nancy told him briskly. ''Simply pretend you are having a bad day. That is what gentlemen do,'' she assured the agitated Osbert. ''No one will care. You can simply fade into the background.''

''Why, so I could,'' said Osbert thoughtfully. ''I doubt anyone will even notice I am there. And if it will prevent Papa from being annoyed with me...''

''That it will. Now you had better tell him. I must go and speak with Mrs. Walker. As you know, Uncle Reginald is taking the unprecedented step of having a dinner party tomorrow night after Selbridge's shoot, and we must confer about the menu.''

''Nancy, do you think Papa is entertaining because he thinks that you and I will soon...?''

Nancy laughed. ''You needn't sound so horrified, Osbert. You are fortunate I have managed to learn so little from Eleanor and Lady Verena, else I would be swooning from such an insult by now! Don't worry,'' she said as he hastened to apologize, ''I have taken no offence, but I think you are right about Uncle Reginald's sudden hospitable mood. He undoubtedly sees me as Ellwood's future mistress. Never mind, he will soon come about when you tell him about Caroline.''

Osbert still looked unconvinced.

That afternoon Francis was with Nancy and Eleanor in the sitting-room, when a note arrived from Selbridge. It was addressed to Francis, and it tersely said that the countess was too fatigued from her journey to see him. She had been informed that he was visiting at Ellwood, and she would see him the next day at the shoot.

Francis read it aloud in a trembling voice. ''Whatever will I do, Miss Browne? You do not know Aunt Margaret. Felicity can always turn her up sweet, but my aunt regards me as a spineless wastrel. She must be furious at having discovered how I have disgraced the family name. Aunt Margaret is very proud of the Selbridges' heritage, you know.''

Nancy pondered this, while Eleanor comforted her beloved. ''If it would do any good, Francis, *I* would face the countess for you,'' Miss Chetwynd said bravely.

''My dearest, I would not ask it of you.''

Nancy smiled at the solemnity of the pair, wondering at the change in her self-absorbed and sometimes very affected cousin since falling in love with the intrepid young inventor. She must help them, as they were obviously meant for one another. A pang of wistfulness attacked her. Would Nancy Browne spend her life assisting the love affairs of others and never meet the man for her? Her heart told her she had met him already, but would never have him.

She determinedly put her mind back on the problem at hand and finally arrived at a solution. ''You will be sick, Sir Francis,'' she declared.

''Sick?'' Eleanor and Francis asked in unison.

''Yes, Sir Francis. Nothing serious, just a slight indisposition. A cold will do. Anything to keep her ladyship away from you until I have time to speak to her. I shall find out exactly what she has heard about you—it may not be so very bad after all—and then endeavour to bring her around to seeing what an accomplishment your invention is.''

"Would you, Miss Browne?" Francis's eyes were alight with gratitude.

"Oh, thank you so much, dear, dear Nancy!" cried Eleanor.

Nancy smiled. "I can hardly believe that two confident people like yourselves are so terrified of such an elderly pair as Sir Reginald and the countess! Though I have not met her ladyship, I feel certain that she will see reason, if only I stand up to her.''

Francis shook his head doubtfully.

Early the next morning Nancy went outside to see off a pale but determined Osbert. He was fully equipped and accoutered for the shooting party, and Sir Reginald watched with pride and happiness as his heir went off to take his place among the gentlemen, where, he said stoutly to Nancy, Osbert belonged. As the carriage pulled away with a wretched-looking Osbert imprisoned within, he said, "You've made a man of him."

"With respect, sir, that is all a humbug. Osbert has always been a man, but simply a different kind of man, with talents and interests that are not your own." Nancy took the old man's arm as they strolled back into the house. To her relief he appeared to be listening without anger. "Osbert simply needed a little encouragement to try unfamiliar things." With her great-uncle in this balmy mood, Nancy thought she might as well get in a good word for Caroline Phillips, but Sir Reginald cut her short.

"And I want to thank you, my dear, for arranging this party tonight. You know I'd just as soon never see most of those neighbours of mine, except Selbridge, and as for those fine folk from London, I wouldn't invite them except out of respect for the earl, but I thought we should celebrate your coming to us, Nancy. Tonight the party is in your honour my dear, for you have made this house come alive again.''

Nancy was surprised and touched to see the old man's eyes gleam with tears. ''It has been a damned uncomfortable and lonely place since my wife left us, but you made it well again.''

Nancy impulsively hugged him. ''It is I who must thank you, Uncle Reginald. I have found my first real home at Ellwood, and I have been very happy here.''

Nancy had sent off a note from Francis excusing himself from the shooting party and from visiting his aunt at Marbelmeade, and was wondering if the poor young man would have to miss the dinner party that night as well. She wished she could confer with Lord Selbridge about the problem, but it was impossible.

She was ill-prepared, then, and dressed in one of her oldest gowns, only suitable for the stables, when the countess herself arrived at Ellwood. Nancy had, in fact, been in the stables, and had just returned to the house when she was faced with the untimely visitor, who was at that moment being shown in.

Nancy saw Bowen greeting a tall, thin woman with a stern face and iron-grey hair, severely dressed and carrying an ebony walking stick tipped with silver. She knew at once who it must be. The strongest hint of her identity was her eyes, which were very like her son's except for the fact that they did not look as ready to smile. Bowen was about to bring her to the drawing-room, then caught sight of Nancy.

''Lady Selbridge, miss,'' he announced. ''Lady Chetwynd and Miss Eleanor are in the garden. Shall I inform them her ladyship is here?''

Nancy, in spite of her dismay at being caught so untidy by her august caller, was hard put not to laugh at Bowen's recently acquired solemnity.

She straightened, and trying to forget she looked a complete fright, hurried over to the countess. "I am so sorry, my Lady, that you find us scattered. Please, come into the drawing-room, and my cousins will be with us in a moment." She nodded at Bowen, who left in search of the ladies, while Nancy herself ushered the countess inside.

So far Lady Selbridge had merely accorded this poorly dressed young person a very slight inclination of the head, but she graciously allowed herself to be seated on a settee. "I take it that you are the Miss Browne I have been hearing so much about," she said.

"Yes, I am Nancy Browne, my Lady. I am a great-niece of Sir—"

"I know who you are, girl." Lady Selbridge's interruption was sharp. "What I do not know, however, is why you are receiving a guest dressed in that dirty rag. It is most unsuitable for a young lady, and most unbecoming."

She examined Nancy critically from head to toe. Nancy was for once left speechless and blushing.

"Well, no doubt you will look better when you are properly dressed." Lady Selbridge appeared to have dismissed the matter and was now looking at the drawing-room with interest, noting, perhaps, the new curtains, the clean rug and the high polish on the furniture.

Nancy could not bear to be so lightly dismissed. She lifted her chin. "I have been in the stables, my Lady. Pray forgive me. I am only waiting for my cousins' arrival before excusing myself to repair my appearance. I do not customarily receive visitors in this attire."

Unexpectedly Lady Selbridge smiled. " Yes, you do have backbone, and I can see how it is that you may have that

dreadful old Reginald Drakes twisted about your finger. He
hates a coward, you know, and obviously you, Miss
Browne, are no coward. Unlike my foolish nephew Francis
Garrard. Hmph!''

Nancy was startled by the sudden introduction of Francis's name, but before she could leap to his defence, Lady
Verena and Eleanor entered. Eleanor glanced pleadingly at
her cousin before assuming her usual demeanour, and Lady
Verena greeted the countess fawningly only to be told, ''So,
Verena, still trying to dress like your daughter, eh? A woman
your age should know better.''

Nancy escaped with relief to change her gown. When she
returned, the ladies were sipping tea and the countess was
holding forth with great energy on the improvements at
Ellwood. ''And you admit that before Miss Browne came
you had no idea how to manage the servants? For shame,
madam!'' Lady Chetwynd smiled nervously and gave Nancy
a pleading look.

The countess also turned to Nancy, who was now attired
in her new morning dress, a gown of cream-coloured muslin trimmed with green ribbons. ''I must tell you, Miss
Browne, that I am most favourably impressed. My son had
told me about the young lady who swept down upon Ellwood.''

''I felt it only my duty, ma'am, to do something for my
cousins, who took me in so kindly.'' Nancy did not tell her
the other reason, which was that she could not bear to live
in such uncomfortable circumstances nor see anyone else
living that way.

''Duty...'' mused the countess. ''Yes, that is a word one
does not often hear from young people these days. I find
you quite refreshing, Miss Browne, and now that you are
properly gowned, almost as pretty as my son said you were.''

Lady Verena exchanged a startled glance with her daughter at this. Eleanor, however, had no jealousy left, her only thought being for Francis.

Nancy was equally startled, and she was warmed at the thought that Lord Selbridge not only thought her pretty, but had told his mother so. Danger, danger, whispered her heart, but she paid it no heed. Even if she could never admit her love, she told herself, there was no reason she might not at least enjoy knowing that the man she loved admired her looks.

"Now, I came here to see that silly nephew of mine. Down with a cold, indeed! I know for a fact that neither he nor his sister have ever suffered a day's indisposition except when it was convenient for them to do so."

Nancy's face reddened, as the feeble deception had been hers, and immediately the countess ignored Eleanor's attempts to explain Francis's illness and fastened her gaze on Nancy again.

"I apprehend that you know something about Francis's avoidance of his dear aunt, Miss Browne. Come." She rose majestically and leaned upon her ebony stick. "Give me your arm and let us take a turn in the garden."

Nancy could not but obey, and once outside, she began to defend Eleanor's beloved.

"Of course, you are right, my Lady, about Sir Francis's illness. It is not of the body, but you might say rather of the spirit. He is anxious for your good opinion, and he fears that you have heard some news of him that might cause him to forfeit that."

The old lady glanced up at her. "Very shrewd, Miss Browne, and diplomatic. They ought to have sent you to Vienna with Castelreagh."

Nancy could not help but let out a chuckle, and to her relief, the countess smiled approvingly. "A sense of humour, too. Well, you are of barely respectable birth, no fortune, and are certainly no paragon, but you are a good girl, Miss Browne. Now please have the kindness to tell me why my nephew is hiding from me.''

Nancy tried to evade Lady Selbridge's glance, but it was impossible. "It . . . it is the Whisper Balm, my Lady.''

Lady Selbridge looked astounded. "Why, how did he know I had even heard of it!''

"I believe it was something you told Lord Selbridge upon your arrival, ma'am.'' Nancy was already more hopeful, for the countess did not yet look angry.

"Francis has ever been a widgeon, and I imagine he always will be,'' her ladyship said with a deep sigh. "I suppose the foolish boy thinks I have descended upon the neighbourhood in order to rake him over the coals.''

"Precisely, my Lady. And . . . you have not?'' Nancy asked.

"Of course not, you silly girl! Why, when a lady who has always been accounted handsome, with a good complexion, reaches a certain age, she is grateful for every invention that will delay the ravages of age, or at least diminish them.''

She stopped walking, let go of Nancy's arm and removed one of her gloves. Her hand, though heavily veined, was white and smooth, showing none of the brown discoloration that Nancy had seen on so many elderly ladies. Nancy's mouth began to turn up at the corners. How ridiculous she and Sir Francis had been!

"Do you see, Miss Browne, not a single brown spot! And on my face as well, in only a fortnight. Why, I have been searching for this very thing, and as soon as I heard about it, I had some sent to me from London. Then to discover that it was my own dear clever nephew who created Whisper Balm! My dear, I was ecstatic. It is the first useful thing Francis has ever done.''

By now Nancy's chest ached with laughter, and she could no longer hold it back. ''But to think of the terror your sudden visit has caused, and all because you approved of Whisper Balm! Why, we have all been beside ourselves since we learned that its inventor's identity has become known and that the lotion is now publicly linked with Lord Selbridge.''

''Indeed,'' declared the countess, ''I cannot believe you were such a parcel of ninnies. Why, I admit it is not the thing for a gentleman to have his name connected with trade, but my nephew has done nothing disgraceful, and as for Selbridge's name being bandied about...'' She frowned. ''Well, I cannot like it, but I suppose it was inevitable, and it will not do this family any harm. Selbridges,'' she told Nancy proudly, ''have been earls since the fourteenth century, and a hint of scandal will do no harm to such an old, respected name. We are above such trifles.'' She drew on her glove again, and they turned back to the house.

''Pray send for Francis and let me speak with him. You may assure him that I have come only to congratulate him and to ask him to get me a large supply of Whisper Balm.''

Nancy sent word up to Sir Francis that all was well, and she left him and his aunt alone together, while she explained their mistake to Eleanor.

''Oh, this is above everything wonderful, Nancy!'' cried Eleanor, more animated than her cousin had ever seen her. She was fairly dancing about the room, more like the seventeen-year-old girl she was than the mature, fashionable beauty she had pretended to be. ''If Lady Selbridge approves of Francis's making his living this way, then Grandpapa can hardly put a rub in our way. And Mama will finally be convinced that Lord Selbridge is not on the point of offering for me. She is forever scolding me about not having kept his interest." She hugged Nancy. "Come, let us go up and decide what we will wear tonight. Perhaps Francis will go to grandfather now and ask for my hand. This could be the very night my engagement is announced!"

So excited was Eleanor that Nancy found it difficult to get an explanation of her remark about Selbridge, but finally Eleanor became calm enough to discuss it sensibly.

"Why, I was sure you knew! Gervaise came back with some foolish tale about Selbridge's being in love with me and only waiting for encouragement to make an offer, but, of course, he was wrong. That is just like my ridiculous brother!"

Nancy, however, put some credence in Gervaise's report, for she knew him to have steadied a good deal in the past few weeks. After all, he was at Marbelmeade nearly every day, and was in a position to hear such gossip. She tried hard not to show her hurt. This was just another reason, she told herself sternly, to guard her tongue and her heart. It would not be at all surprising if Lord Selbridge loved Eleanor. By now, however, he must know of her secret betrothal to Francis. Poor man, to have a heart broken twice so soon! She determined that nothing in her demeanour toward him would change and that she would be kind and allow him to seek her friendship, no matter how much it might hurt to know that she could be nothing more.

That evening Nancy appeared in the second of her two new evening gowns, and Sir Reginald, Francis and even Gervaise and Osbert took in the sight appreciatively. It was gold tissue over yellow satin, with lace panels in the skirt and at the bodice and gold trimming at the neck, hem and sleeves. Lady Verena's maid had done her hair a little more elaborately than usual, and Nancy felt completely unlike herself.

She stood in the drawing-room to greet the guests with the rest of the family, trying to hide her eagerness to see Lord Selbridge again. She feared, now that she had met his formidable mother, that she would not be able to hide her feelings from that sharp-eyed lady.

Her ladyship declared herself delighted to see Miss Browne again, then progressed along the room in a stately fashion, and Nancy was free of the woman's observation when she finally spoke to Selbridge.

They had only a moment. "Miss Browne, you are looking exceptionally lovely tonight." His voice was completely sincere, and Nancy timidly returned the pressure of his hand. "Thank you, Lord Selbridge." She lowered her voice. "All is well, between Sir Francis and the countess."

He smiled, still holding her hand. Nancy's heart was beating rapidly, and she willed herself to be calm, but she knew that her breath was coming quickly from between her lips.

"I cannot thank you enough for all you have done, my dear," said Selbridge softly. "Will you give me the pleasure of a moment's private conversation later?"

But the next guest was arriving, and she had time only to nod before the earl moved on. For the next hour she was preoccupied with his strange request, but told herself that it could mean nothing. She was afraid to be alone with Selbridge, not because of what he might do or say, but of how she might reveal herself. She could not bear to see him pitying her.

The dinner was not as elaborate as the earl's had been, but it was, Gervaise told Nancy, of a much higher standard than any they might have had at Ellwood before she had arrived. She was sorry to be seated next to Osbert, who seemed terrified of the London lady at his other side and scarcely let Nancy talk to Gervaise on her left, but finally she managed to leave him to his own devices while she conversed with the younger man.

"I . . . I do not know if Francis has told you, but it is almost settled between Miss Garrard and me," said Gervaise shyly. "Although Sir Francis knows, we have not told Selbridge nor the countess yet. Soon everyone will know." How changed he was from the drunk, ill-mannered youngster who had spent his time chasing housemaids!

Nancy had long suspected an attachment between her cousin and the pretty Miss Felicity Garrard, as Miss Garrard's public attentions to her noble cousin had diminished quite noticeably since Gervaise had begun working at Marbelmeade. Francis had told her that Gervaise had been accompanying Felicity every morning to pick herbs for the formula of Whisper Balm.

"I proposed in the meadow," Gervaise said after Nancy wished him joy. "Miss Garrard is the dearest creature, and I can only be grateful that Selbridge is being so generous with her dowry." He smiled secretively. "But then, at one time he appeared to have ambitions to strengthen the ties between Marbelmeade and Ellwood. Poor Eleanor and Mama! I'm afraid I should not have told them. His lordship must have been frightened away by their renewed attacks. But I'm glad. Selbridge deserves better than my sister."

It meant very little to Nancy that the threat of Selbridge's being in love with Eleanor was apparently over. It brought him no closer to falling in love with Nancy Browne. She twitched impatiently in her chair, unable to stop thinking about the promised private talk with Selbridge.

Finally Lady Chetwynd began to rise, and the rest of the female guests were about to follow suit, when Sir Reginald stood, wineglass in hand, and thundered, "Ladies and

gentlemen, my dear friends and neighbours..." There was
immediate and startled silence as the ladies sat down again.

Nancy looked up at her great-uncle in dismay, wondering what rudeness he was about to commit, and was even
more worried when she saw how unfocused his eyes were
and how red his face. It was plain he had overimbibed,
which was not his usual practice, and it was this, and perhaps happiness, that had inspired him to rise to his feet and
address the table. If only she had been seated near him, she
might have been able to forestall it. But it was too late. There
was no way to stop him.

"I am pleased and honoured to have you all at my table
tonight. This is the first time this house has been filled with
guests and laughter for a very long time. We owe our present happiness to a young lady who came to Ellwood a
stranger and is now very much part of the family. To our
good fortune, she will become more than that in the future.
My great-niece, Miss Nancy Browne."

There was a rumbling accented with the ladies high-
pitched squeals of surprise. Several guests stared at Nancy,
some smiling, some in amusement. Nancy stared meaningfully at Lady Verena, hoping to induce her to lead the ladies away to the drawing-room, but her cousin only
shrugged helplessly. If only, Nancy prayed, Sir Reginald did
not go any further.

She turned to Osbert for help, but he only looked back at
her in fright. Obviously, she could depend on no one but
herself.

"You do me great honour, Uncle Reginald," she began,
blushing furiously, for all eyes were now on her. "I am most
grateful to you and my family here at Ellwood."

She began to rise to her feet, after a frantic glance at
Eleanor, who rose with her, but Sir Reginald raised a hand.
"A very pretty speech, my dear, and modest, as becomes

you. But since my son is apparently too shy to speak, I wish to announce that, very shortly, our dear Nancy will be making Ellwood her permanent home and as Mrs. Osbert Drakes, will one day be its mistress.''

Nancy was too mortified to look at Osbert, but she heard a stifled groan from him, hidden from the others in the sudden babble of conversation. The guests, after a second of shock, were talking to cover the embarrassment of having an announcement of that sort made in such a fashion. Heedless of etiquette, people offered Nancy and Osbert their best wishes, and it was several minutes before she could escape with the ladies to the drawing-room, leaving the miserable and stammering Osbert with the men.

Nancy's second thought, after her own shock, was for poor Caroline Phillips. She sought her out immediately, but the girl, barely holding back tears, would not hear her, and Mrs. Phillips, with a sympathetic glance at Nancy, bore her away.

At least, Nancy thought, her friend Mrs. Phillips did not believe Sir Reginald's nonsense and could not think her guilty of such great cruelty to a sweet child like Caroline. But then she realized that it must be because Mrs. Phillips suspected her feelings for Selbridge, and that thought did not comfort her at all.

As for the other ladies, the Londoners scarcely cared, and Lady Chetwynd was startled but on the whole pleased. She would have chattered to Nancy about it all evening if she had not been shouldered out of the way by Lady Selbridge.

Nancy could barely face the countess, but managed to look the old lady in the eye for at least a few seconds. "Hmph! I shall tell you at once I do not care for the hole-in-the-corner way in which this affair was managed. I have been here two days and if anything of the sort was going on between you and Mr. Drakes I ought to have heard about it.

What's more, the Drakes men have always brought home brides of rank and fortune, and you've neither.''

At Nancy's stricken look, the countess patted her cheek. ''There, my child, you and Drakes seem an unlikely couple to me, but I do wish you happy, and I have the consolation that at least the second house in the neighbourhood will have a proper mistress.''

Felicity and Eleanor seemed to be the least startled by the betrothal, but they sensed her displeasure and believed it to be about the manner of the announcement and not the announcement itself.

''I hope, my dear Miss Browne,'' said Felicity, fluffing up her hair before one of the drawing-room mirrors, ''that you will ask Mr. Drakes to treat his nephew with more respect. Why, he seems to think that Gervaise is only a boy and not a man with a brilliant career ahead of him.''

Nancy numbly agreed to do what she could. Eleanor was watching her closely. ''I know that you do not approve of what Grandpapa did, but really, Nancy, you really ought to try to look happier about it for Osbert's sake. If you are to marry him, you must not go about with that Friday face.''

Impossible, Nancy thought, to explain that she had not the slightest intention of marrying Osbert and that her expression was caused primarily by her worry over poor Miss Phillips's broken heart.

She was terribly angry with Osbert for having put her in this situation, and for twopence she would have announced to all the world that it was untrue, but she could not. She must discuss it with Osbert first, and was certain that if they simply announced that the engagement was dissolved, it would all blow over. But to cause a scene tonight would create a scandal, and she could not do that to the family.

Nancy got through the ensuing hours, she knew not how, and endured the congratulations, speculation and talk of weddings with a weary smile. As for Osbert, she had hardly a chance to talk to him, for he was being put through his own sort of purgatory on the other side of the drawing-room. She vowed she would not seek her bed that night till she had given him an ultimatum. Either he proposed to Caroline Phillips the next morning or she would inform Sir Reginald herself about his son's real love.

On impulse, Nancy looked across the room and caught Lord Selbridge staring at her. It appeared that he had forgotten his request to speak privately to her. Indeed he had not yet offered congratulations, but then she had been so distracted by other well-wishers that she had not noticed. Now she met his glance and forced herself to smile. He gave a short nod, but did not return the smile. She had no idea what he was thinking, but obviously he had changed his mind about speaking to her. She felt tears spring to her eyes, but made herself play the part of the acquiescent, if not eager, bride to be. It was with great relief that she bid the guests good-night. Selbridge offered only quiet good wishes as Nancy stood with Osbert at her side, and left without having that private conversation he had requested.

Sir Reginald was obviously too flushed with wine and pride to listen to reason that night, so Nancy let him go to bed without suspecting that she was unhappy about his abrupt announcement. But she cornered Osbert in the corridor as he was creeping to bed with his candle.

"Osbert, you must propose to Caroline tomorrow, as early as possible, before she has too much time to brood."

"I...I cannot, Nancy! You see how Papa has trapped us. Everyone in the neighbourhood believes we are betrothed."

"That makes no difference. Betrothals can be broken. You must do as I say, or I will go to Sir Reginald with the truth."

"You would...you would do that?" Osbert's hand holding the candle trembled.

Nancy sighed. "I am out of patience with you, Osbert. You know I have tried my best to help you, and I will try only once more, until I take matters into my own hands. You will propose to Caroline, and then I will tell Sir Reginald of the change in plans. If you do not agree, your father will hear the story anyway, and you will not even have the advantage of having secured the hand of the woman you love."

Osbert stood silent for a long time. Finally he raised his head. "All right, Nancy," he said softly, "I have been a coward for far too long. I do want to marry Caroline, and I see that if I do not speak now it may be too late."

In spite of her relief that she had convinced him, Nancy had little confidence in Osbert and worried about her interview with Sir Reginald on the morrow. It would be unpleasant to have to disappoint the old man, but at least if she could offer him a fine girl like Caroline Phillips for a daughter-in-law, that might take some of the sting out of it.

That night she tossed in her bed, until Mischief, curled at her feet, awoke from his canine dreams and whined. She sat up and took the pup in her arms, burying her head against his silky hair. He was all she had left to remind her of the fleeting moments of happiness spent in Selbridge's company.

CHAPTER ELEVEN

OSBERT DRAKES STARED miserably at his breakfast. Although he had always regarded food as an annoying necessity, he had never before suffered from an actual lack of appetite. Across from him, his father was eating a chop with gusto and was positively beaming at him between bites.

This completely unfamiliar sense of being approved of ought to have given Osbert joy. Instead, knowing that the approval would soon be withdrawn, Osbert felt his stomach twist itself into knots.

"Has love killed your appetite, my boy?" enquired Sir Reginald, his jovial air a trifle rusty from disuse.

Osbert hastily shoveled a large forkful of egg into his mouth. Sir Reginald chuckled. "Never mind. Our Nancy will see to it that you don't fade away. By God, son, do you realize what a lucky man you are?"

His heir gulped some cold coffee. His food felt stuck in his throat. "Y-yes, indeed, sir."

Osbert knew he had to make his exit and get to Caroline before Nancy lost patience and told the full and awful truth to his father. "If you will excuse me, sir, I must call at the rectory..."

Sir Reginald nodded. "Of course. Set it all up with Phillips. Fine man, the rector. Tell him to spare nothing about the ceremony. Flowers, music. The best is not too good for Miss Nancy." He smiled, and there was a mist in his eyes. "What a bride she'll be, eh, son? Now I should recommend you set the day no more than two months ahead. Just enough time to order the bridal clothes and get your lazy sister, Verena, to bestir herself about the guests and food.''

Osbert nodded, rose and made his escape. He shivered as he wondered what Reginald would say if he knew that it was Caroline Phillips and not Nancy he would bring to Ellwood as his bride. At the thought he straightened his shoulders and his cravat. Why, he was actually going to do it!

Although he had been ignoring his father's expectations and keeping to himself for many years, Osbert had never before directly disobeyed Sir Reginald. At five and thirty, he was initiating his first truly independent action. This novel thought spurred him on, and he drove the gig at a smart pace to the rectory, eager to convince his Caroline that he loved her and that the betrothal to Miss Browne was a mistake.

Nancy did not awaken till after ten. The dreadful events of the night before burst upon her as soon as she opened her lids, and she shut them again quickly, pretending that it was a morning like any other, and that her publicly announced betrothal to the wrong man had never occurred. But it was useless to pretend, and she made herself get up and dress.

She was relieved, when she came down to the breakfast parlour, to discover only Eleanor there. Her cousin greeted her with unusual affection.

''Good morning, dearest Nan! Grandpapa was positively angelic to me this morning, even teased me about getting a husband of my own, and he said Osbert has already gone to the rectory to arrange the wedding. Mama is still upstairs.''

Nancy was delighted to hear that Osbert had already gone to the rectory, although everyone attributed his visit to the wrong reason. She ate and tried to answer Eleanor's ex-

cited queries about Osbert's courtship without generating
any suspicion. She certainly had no wish for anyone to know
the truth until it was all arranged between Caroline and Osbert—and, of course, with Sir Reginald.

"I daresay Grandpapa is in a good-enough mood even to
accept my betrothal to Francis. What do you think,
Nancy?" asked Eleanor.

"Very likely," said Nancy cautiously, "but I advise you
to wait at least till tomorrow." By then the old man would
either have accepted the news that she would not marry his
son or have thrown her out of the house.

Nancy blinked back a tear. She dearly loved Ellwood, and
the thought of leaving and very likely never seeing Selbridge again made her heart ache. Though it might be
painful to watch him some day marry, and to be treated by
him only as another neighbour, she knew she could not bear
to have him out of her life completely.

At that moment the door of the breakfast parlour was
pushed open. Sir Reginald leaned his regal silver head into
the doorway and smiled at Nancy.

"How are you this morning, my child?"

Nancy stood up, forcing herself to smile. "I am well, sir.
If you can, I beg you will give me a few moments of your
time. There is much we have to discuss."

"Of course." Sir Reginald offered Nancy his arm. She
gave Eleanor a quick smile and went with her great-uncle to
the morning-room, which had become her favourite place.

She sat in the small, satin-upholstered armchair that was
set in front of a little gilded secretary and turned toward Sir
Reginald, who stood before the marble mantel, regarding
her fondly.

"It was just so that my Eleanor used to sit when she
would call me in here to take me to task about what she
called my 'cheese-paring ways.'" He sighed. "How I wish

she could have met you, my dear. Now do not worry about my tendency toward economy. You shall have a free hand as mistress here.''

Nancy dreaded what she must say, but she steeled herself, even forcing a playful smile. "I...I wish you would sit down, Uncle Reginald. There is something I must say, and I cannot be comfortable with you towering over me."

Sir Reginald looked surprised, but took a seat opposite her on a sofa. "What is it, my child?" His brow furrowed. "That fool of an Osbert has not offended you, has he? If he has, I'll—"

"Certainly not, Uncle Reginald!" He must not become angry with Osbert. That would do their cause no good. "Osbert has been very kind and a good friend to me," she said gently, holding Sir Reginald's gaze with her own, "but I am afraid that...your announcement last night was rather premature."

Sir Reginald simply stared at her for a moment and then gave a hearty guffaw. "So Osbert is vexed because I beat him to the finish, eh? Well, well, it makes little difference. It was perfectly obvious to me and to everyone that he was on the verge of offering for you."

Nancy sighed and looked down at the floor. "I am very sorry, Uncle Reginald, but you have been mistaken. Osbert and I had no intention of marrying. We are not in love."

The door to the morning-room flew open, and Osbert, a bright-eyed, flushed Osbert, with hair rumpled and neckcloth askew, stepped confidently into the room.

"Excuse me, Father, but I could not wait. I have something of the utmost importance to tell you."

Sir Reginald leaped to his feet. "What is the meaning of this interruption?" He glared at his son, and then at Nancy. "And what do you mean you have no intention of marrying my son, miss? A fine fool I shall look after announcing it to the whole neighbourhood last night.''

Osbert paled but clenched his jaw with determination. "I am afraid, Father, that you should have been more certain of your information before you made such an announcement.''

"Why, you impertinent—"

"Oh, please, sir, allow him to speak,'' cried Nancy, frightened.

"Indeed, sir,'' said Osbert. "I must ask that you hear me out. I daresay Nancy has told you that we are not betrothed. But I have the pleasure and honour of informing you that Miss Caroline Phillips has consented to be my wife, and beg that you will receive her with the kindness and respect she deserves.''

For a long moment Sir Reginald simply stared at his son. Then his mouth opened, closed again, and he slowly sat down, holding out a shaking hand to make certain that the sofa was still there behind him.

Nancy was at his side, worried, for his face was ashen. Osbert seemed oblivious. "I had the devil's own time convincing her, sir, after that announcement of yours last night, but finally I told her that she must be mad if she thought that I had spent all summer dancing attendance on her only to marry my cousin!''

Nancy saw the colour flow back into Sir Reginald's cheeks, saw a gleam come to his eyes, and relaxed. She turned to her cousin. "You didn't, Osbert! What a thing to say!''

Osbert grinned. "Was it not? She still wouldn't believe me, so I finally had to kiss her. Then she was convinced.''

"Ha!'' erupted Sir Reginald, and Nancy felt relief sweep over her at this favourite but long-unheard monosyllable of the baronet's. "You are my son, at that, sir! I can hardly believe you had it in you, but blood will tell, by God."

He stood up, apparently recovered from the severe shock, delight on his face. He slapped his son heartily on the shoulder. Osbert smiled at Nancy and bore it bravely.

"The infernal impudence of you, to fool your old papa into thinking it was Nancy you wished to marry, when all the time it was that pretty little Phillips girl." He frowned, and turned to Nancy. "My dear, if this youngster has toyed with your affections—"

"Not at all, Uncle Reginald," Nancy hastened to inform him. "In fact, it was I who introduced him to Caroline and encouraged him to come with me to the rectory to see her." She smiled up at Osbert. "I hope you will forgive me, but I knew all along that you two should make a match of it."

Sir Reginald's shoulders were shaking with laughter. He rang, and when Bowen appeared, too swiftly to have been doing anything but listening at the door, he ordered wine. "At this time of the day, sir?" asked the scandalized servant.

"Yes, idiot, we have something to celebrate! Ellwood is to have a new mistress."

Bowen looked at Nancy and smiled uneasily, as if suspecting that his employer had lost his wits. "Yes, Sir Reginald, we had heard...the staff hopes that you and Mr. Osbert will be very happy, ma'am."

"Not Miss Browne, dunderhead, Miss Phillips!" roared Sir Reginald.

Bowen glanced at Nancy and Osbert in fright and confusion. Their smiling faces seemed to reassure him. "Wine, sir, instantly," he muttered, bowing his way out of the room, hastening to the lower regions to inform his fellow servants of the incredible news.

"I fear you will have a great deal of explaining to do, Uncle," Nancy said to Sir Reginald, taking his arm affectionately.

"Minx!" he said, patting her hand. "You have made us all dance to your tune, Miss Nan, ever since you stepped off that ridiculous cabbage-wagon—oh, yes, I heard about your mode of arrival here. But as long as you are telling the truth about not wanting to marry Osbert, and my son has shown the sense to get himself engaged to a pretty and well-born girl..."

Osbert cleared his throat. "I fear, sir, that you are out there."

Sir Reginald scowled. "What do you mean? She is a pretty thing, though she hasn't much to say for herself..."

"I mean, Father, that Miss Phillips is not precisely well-born. Her father was a noted scholar, of course, and on her mother's side she is distantly connected to an earl, a marquess and a duke, but her paternal grandfather—"

"Pray do not bore me with this genealogy, Osbert. I know who the man was. A low-born, but gentlemanly and intelligent fellow. Just the sort of blood this family needs."

Osbert's relief was palpable, and Nancy was enjoying the heady sensations of freedom and success, when Bowen, slightly breathless, reappeared with the wine.

"Lord Selbridge is here, and requests an interview with Miss Browne, sir," he said, putting down his tray and glancing eagerly at the three occupants of the room in turn to see how they received this news.

Nancy's face burned, and she turned away with the glass Sir Reginald had just handed her, for she could not bear for him to see her trembling reaction. Osbert looked at Bowen curiously, and Sir Reginald smiled.

"Show his lordship in, and bring another glass. I know he will be happy to hear this news. He has agreed with me for years that Ellwood should have a proper mistress," he said, conveniently forgetting that last night he had already informed Selbridge and everyone else that the house was about to acquire a chatelaine.

"But, Uncle Reginald..." Nancy began in despair, hoping to avoid a confrontation with the earl, which would undoubtedly involve an explanation of her recently broken engagement.

"What is it, my dear?"

"Nothing sir." What difference would it make? Selbridge might be surprised at the news, but it would not change a thing.

He was in the room in a moment, sweeping off his hat, then offering his neat, square hand to Osbert and Sir Reginald, while his eyes searched the room—for her, Nancy realized.

His eyes held no humour now. They were somber, searching. He held her glance for a moment, and Nancy's chest became tight. His expression was inscrutable. She looked away.

Sir Reginald's booming voice had been filling the room all the while. "You are always welcome, Selbridge. Have some wine. We are celebrating, you know."

"I know, and I have come to offer my good wishes to the betrothed couple, as I could not...I did not have the opportunity last night to properly express my...happiness."

"Well, you are a trifle late for all that, sir," said Sir Reginald with a laugh. "My son is not betrothed to our Nancy after all. You and everyone else will think I'm a doddering old fool, but it seems that engagement was all my idea and not what the young people had in mind at all."

Selbridge looked from one to the other, his eyes wide with astonishment. "They are not betrothed? But last night..."

"Perhaps I should explain, my Lord," said Nancy in a small voice. "It was a rather embarrassing mistake. Sir Reginald was under the impression that..." Under Selbridge's stare she faltered. "That Osbert and I were something more than friends. He was not aware—not many were—that my cousin had been addressing his attentions to Miss Phillips. I only hope she was not too distressed last night."

"When I first arrived she wouldn't see me," Osbert replied cheerfully. He too, had finished his wine, and the unaccustomed drinking at such an early hour had affected him so that he swayed gently as he talked. "I begged Mrs. Phillips to put in a word for me, told her it was all a mistake about you and me. Finally, Caro was brought to believe in my sincerity." He smiled a little fatuously.

"How fortunate, Mr. Drakes. May I offer my congratulations?" said Selbridge stiffly. Nancy had not heard him sound so little like his usual friendly self since Gervaise's escapade with the bull.

"Thank you, my Lord, thank you very much," said the dazed Osbert, unaware of the edge of steel in the earl's voice.

"If you would be so good, Miss Browne," said the earl. "I would be pleased if you would honour me with your company for a few moments. There is a matter I would particularly like to discuss with you."

Before Nancy could reply, Sir Reginald put down his glass and said, "Of course! Probably needs our Nan's advice on some problem. You cannot do better than to ask Miss Browne's opinion on any estate matter, my lord. She's as knowledgeable as my old bailiff, and certainly much prettier." With that, he shepherded his son out of the room.

Nancy's heart was thumping, and to cover the noise she was sure it must be making she said, "Please, sit down,

Lord Selbridge," seating herself on the sofa and gesturing to a chair nearby. Her legs were beginning to tremble. To her dismay, Selbridge ignored her gesture and promptly sat beside her, which made her feel not a whit more serene.

"I must confess, Miss Browne," said the earl, "I am quite startled at this news, much more startled than I was at last night's announcement. Sir Reginald had confided in me that he thought you and Mr. Drakes would soon be engaged. But last night . . ."

She darted a glance at him and to her relief saw that he did not look so solemn. The corners of his mouth were turned up ever so little, as though he might smile if he found reason to do so.

"I am afraid that it was all a mistake, Lord Selbridge. It was always Caroline Phillips for Osbert, you see," she began, but he stopped her with an upraised hand.

"Please, do not explain. I had originally come here because I felt it my duty as a neighbour and . . . friend, to offer my good wishes and ask if there was anything I could contribute to the celebration of your nuptials. But now that I know the truth . . ." His voice became softer, and he leaned closer and took both of her hands.

Nancy was too surprised to do anything but stare at him, wide-eyed, as he continued. "Now I must say how very sorry I am, my dear Miss Browne, that you were so taken in. I hope that, as I have been a sufferer from unrequited love myself, you will accept my most heartfelt sympathies."

"Y-your sympathies?" Nancy was trembling from his nearness and the warmth of his hands enveloping hers, and she wondered if she had heard him correctly.

Selbridge gave her a gentle smile of pity. "Of course. I saw how matters stood between you and Osbert, and I was ready to be happy for you last night, but now . . ." His face darkened. "Surely Sir Reginald and Mr. Drakes have trodden most cavalierly over your tender feelings."

"But, Lord Selbridge, you do not understand, Osbert never offered for me to begin with," Nancy cried. She knew she should have taken her hands back and moved away, but it was heavenly being so near him, even if he completely misunderstood her feelings.

"The more pity that Sir Reginald exposed you to the gaze of the world in this fashion, only to reveal your disappointment now that Miss Phillips is to be Mrs. Drakes," he said vehemently.

It was incredible, Nancy thought, but he felt sorry for her, thought she had been ill-used.

"As a friend, Miss Browne, I merely wish to offer my support in your hour of distress."

Nancy slowly pulled her hands from his grasp and looked down. It was only as a friend that he was angry about her apparently beind the victim of a jilt. It was only as her friend that he offered her sympathy. The last of her foolish hopes died.

She rose, the tightness in her throat choking her. His startled face was a blur through the tears welling in her eyes. "Thank you," she managed to say before a sob broke through. "You are very kind." And then she turned and fled upstairs to her room. It would have been even kinder if he had not come at all, she thought, flinging herself on her bed.

Nancy stayed in her room until she was calm and had erased all traces of her tears. Then she went about her usual business, having only to endure the surprise and questions of the family now that the news of Osbert's real betrothal had spread.

Lady Verena seemed undisturbed by the change, except when she heard that Selbridge had been to call while she was still in her bedchamber. "I hope you saw him, Eleanor," she said to her daughter, who sat near a window sewing, gazing out at the towers of Marbelmeade in the distance, thinking of Francis hard at work in one of them.''

''No, Mama, I did not.''

Lady Verena frowned. ''Well, my child, I see it has been of no use encouraging you to do the best for yourself. You saw how he has lost interest, all but ignoring you, and it is your own fault for not taking the trouble to attract him. Mind you, I shall take you to London, but you will hardly be thrown among very many wealthy earls there, with the pittance we shall be obliged to live upon.''

Nancy shot her cousin a warning glance, but Eleanor, her nerves taut from keeping her secret for so long, stood and tossed her sewing aside, and her mother looked up in surprise.

''I have no interest in becoming countess of Selbridge, Mama,'' she announced, tossing her head back. ''In fact, I—''

''Eleanor, perhaps this is not the time to discuss it. I see Gervaise and the Garrards coming up the walk,'' Nancy intervened.

Nancy was grateful for this fortuitous circumstance, as it was just the distraction Eleanor needed to prevent her from making an unfortunate and premature announcement of her betrothal to Sir Francis.

Lady Verena, too, was distracted and surprised to see her son home early from his labours at Marbelmeade. ''Why, Gervaise, why has Lord Selbridge sent you home?''

Gervaise smiled. Felicity was on his arm, and Nancy knew in an instant what had happened.

''It is nothing of the kind, Mama. In fact, I was sent home with his lordship's blessing, to tell you—'' he smiled again at Felicity, who was blushing and staring down at the floor ''—that Miss Garrard had honoured me by consent-

ing to be my wife, and that Lord Selbridge and the countess have given us their blessings.''

A commotion broke loose in the drawing-room, as Lady
Verena first dropped to the sofa in an histrionic attitude and
called for sal volatile, and then sat straight up again when
Gervaise went on to inform her that Lord Selbridge was
prepared to dower the bride.

Eleanor recovered her composure quickly, and with
Nancy's encouragement, welcomed her brother's betrothed into the family. To Nancy's relief, the timely announcement released her from the pressure of being the
centre of attention.

Mrs. Phillips and a shy but glowing Caroline arrived next,
and when Osbert came in to stand by his beloved, Nancy
took one look at their faces and knew that all the trouble
had been worth it.

The room was soon noisy with the clatter of teacups and
a great deal of excited chatter. Mrs. Phillips left her sister-in-
law to the attentions of her future family and took Nancy
aside. ''Well, my dear, we have accomplished it, although
you have been put to a great deal more trouble than any one
ought to be. I thought I would give it away when I saw your
face last night as Sir Reginald betrothed you to Osbert!''

Nancy laughed. ''I am quite recovered from the shock,
my dear Mrs. Phillips. I am only happy that Osbert finally
discovered the courage to fight for the woman he loved.
Caroline, I trust, has forgiven me?''

''Oh, yes. In fact, Osbert and I have both told her that
you intended them to marry from the very start, and she is
sorry that she ever thought ill of you even for a moment.
Now, what about you, my dear?''

The question took Nancy by surprise. ''I do not precisely
take your meaning,'' she said, looking away.

''Nonsense, my child, you know perfectly well what I mean. Suppose,'' she said with a glance at Eleanor, ''your cousin does not take her daughter to London next season. What will you do in that case?''

Nancy shrugged. ''Why, I suppose I shall go back to Yorkshire, where there are friends of my father, and find a companion and a cottage somewhere—I could not live in a town on my small income, you know.''

''Why not stay here? Sir Reginald would hate to part with you, and we would all miss you terribly. Perhaps Lady Verena will take you to London anyway, or Eleanor, once she is married.''

At Nancy's startled glance, Mrs. Phillips smiled and whispered, ''I assure you that I am not at all fooled when I see Miss Chetwynd and Sir Francis Garrard together.''

''Fortunately, my dear Mrs. Phillips, you are much cleverer than most people when it comes to discovering attractions between ladies and gentlemen.''

''Yes, I am, am I not?'' replied Mrs. Phillips instantly. ''And as I once told you, I had an idea very soon that you and Lord—''

''I fear that you are too ambitious, ma'am,'' Nancy interrupted. ''As to my future, I believe I have outlasted my welcome here. Caroline will be mistress at Ellwood, and if I were here, she would not dare to put herself forward. Without me, she would soon learn to take the reins of the household and would grow out of her shyness. As you suspect, Eleanor may be marrying, though I pray you will not speak of it until we convince Sir Reginald to give his consent, and Gervaise has both a career and a bride now. No, I am no longer needed at Ellwood and shall have to make my own way.''

Mrs. Phillips fixed her with a look of kindness and concern. ''I do not believe that you are no longer needed,

Nancy. I do hope you will reconsider. It is kind of you to think of Caroline's comfort, but I assure you she will be much happier here with you to guide her. She is positively frightened of Miss Chetwynd and Lady Verena!''

But Nancy gave her friend no hope that she would remain at Ellwood. Both for the reasons she had given and because of the discomfort of remaining where she would constantly be seeing or hearing of Lord Selbridge, it was impossible.

The guests left, and Sir Reginald, who was doubly pleased now that his ne'er-do-well grandson would be linking himself to the Selbridges by marriage, asked Nancy to take a stroll in the garden with him before dressing for dinner.

Nancy agreed, realizing how soon these tranquil days would be gone and knowing that she would miss the difficult old man.

''It seems to me, Miss Nan,'' said Sir Reginald, ''that you have lost some of your sparkle since last night. Now, I may be nothing but a selfish old man, but I've grown fond of you, and I can pretty well guess what is troubling you.''

Nancy stiffened. She had been too sanguine in believing that she could fool sharp-eyed Uncle Reginald. He must have realized how much she had seen of Lord Selbridge, and have noticed her anxiety in his presence earlier that day. ''Can you, sir?'' she said in a shaky voice.

''Certainly, though it took a long time for my eyes to be opened to it,'' he replied. ''I watched your face when we had those happy lovers in the room, and though I know you are glad for them, you seemed more than a bit wistful. You have not found the happiness that you have given to others, my child.''

''No, Uncle Reginald, I suppose I have not,'' Nancy whispered.

''But there is someone you love,'' he prodded.

Nancy stopped walking, withdrew her arm from her uncle's and turned to bury her face in a fragrant rose. "Yes," she said in a voice barely audible.

Sir Reginald's impatient step crunched on the gravel as he paced near her. "I supposed as much, ever since you began telling me that Osbert loved another. Who is the fellow? Does he not love you in return?" he demanded.

Nancy gathered her pride. "I am afraid he does not, Uncle Reginald, but it is of little consequence."

"Let us have none of that foolishness, Miss Nan. Of course, it is of consequence. I shall flay the fellow alive if he is making you unhappy!"

Nancy could not resist the temptation to laugh in spite of her misery. "Oh, Uncle Reginald, pray do not be so Gothic! He has not offended me, and he cannot help it if he does not return my regard. You would be unjust in making him suffer, for I do not believe he has the slightest notion of what I feel."

Sir Reginald turned on his heel. "Ha! Fellow must be blinder than I am." He squinted at Nancy. "It is someone hereabouts, is it not? Unless you've taken to meeting strange men secretly in the village."

Nancy laughed again, more easily this time. "Of course not, sir. I swear to you the man is no stranger. In fact," she said with a sigh she could not repress, "I have spent much time with him since I came here, and he considers me a friend."

"Well, then, that is all right," said Sir Reginald with less than his usual certainty. "I suppose he is not . . . that is, he is eligible . . ."

"Quite eligible, though many might think a match between us unsuitable," said Nancy.

Sir Reginald ceased his pacing and turned to Nancy, his long nose almost quivering, much, Nancy could not help thinking, like a dog on the trail of a good scent.

"Considers you a friend...match unsuitable...ha! And he happens to reside at Marbelmeade, does he not?"

Nancy gasped, knowing that colour was flooding her face.

"Do not worry, I have your secret safe, my dear," Sir Reginald said with a paternal smile. "Though, again, you are too modest. A match there would be unexpected but not at all unsuitable. I shall speak to the young man and discover what his feelings may be. Perhaps he is only unsure of your regard."

"Oh, no, please, sir, I beg you will do nothing of the kind!"

"Pray compose yourself, girl." Sir Reginald cleared his throat. "I can be just as tactful as even your dainty Cousin Eleanor when it comes to affairs of the heart. I was a youngster in love myself once."

Nancy was contrite but firm. "I am sorry, Uncle Reginald, I know you mean to be kind, but really, I cannot allow you to do such a thing for me. I would be...I would be mortified, and *he* would be made to feel uncomfortable. It really would not do, sir, but I thank you with all my heart."

Sir Reginald looked down at her for a moment, then sighed. "I suppose you know what you are about, miss, but it seems ridiculous to allow you to suffer when a few words with the gentleman will settle it."

"I am grateful, Uncle, but I fear it will take more than a few words to make him fall in love with me," said Nancy.

"Hmph!" Sir Reginald resumed his customary gruffness as they returned to the house, and allowed the subject to drop.

Nancy was sure he had forgotten their conversation. It was fortunate for her that she could not read his expression well enough to suspect what was going on behind the bluster. If she had even suspected what he was planning, her rest that night would have been seriously disturbed.

As it was, she slept better than she had in many nights. The relief of revealing her troubles to someone else more than made up for the momentary discomfort. How kind it had been of the old man to try to solve her problem for her! But his proposed solution was, of course, impossible. She tried to imagine poor Lord Selbridge being confronted with an irate Sir Reginald accusing him of coldness to Miss Nancy Browne, who was suffering severely from unrequited love.

Selbridge would be astounded to hear it. Fortunately for her pride, she had been careful. Uncle Reginald would, she thought with a smile, be hard put to convince his lordship that Miss Nancy Browne had conceived a tendre for him. Luckily, she thought just before dropping off to sleep, it would never be put to the test.

The next morning Sir Reginald went out for an early ride, which was not unusual on a day when he was feeling well. What was unusual was his destination. Instead of surveying the farthest acres of his estate, he rode straight to Marbelmeade.

What was more surprising was that, when informed that his lordship was not at home, he asked at once to see Sir Francis Garrard. The well-trained footman conducted Sir Reginald into the morning-room and informed Sir Francis of his visitor's arrival.

Francis took off his apron, hurried down from his tower and greeted his guest with surprise and anxiety. "Good day, Sir Reginald. I am honoured—"

"No need to waste your sweet words on me, young man," said the baronet. "I've very little time, so I shall come directly to the point. There is a young lady at Ellwood who is pining, and I do not want to wait a moment longer than I have to until I can make her smile again."

"Young lady, sir?" Francis was a little frightened, wondering if he would spoil this moment by saying the wrong thing. But Sir Reginald must have finally noticed his discreet courtship of Eleanor and come to confront him with it. He must make the right impression.

"I am at your service, sir."

"Good. Now the poor girl doesn't know I am here, and I should like you not to tell her I came to see you. She's sensitive about these things, you know."

"Indeed she is. Her nature is so refined—"

"Enough, sir. I do not need an impertinent young scamp like you to sing her praises to me."

Francis subsided.

"But I suppose that means that you return her regard?" Sir Reginald looked at him keenly.

"I do, indeed, sir. I can hardly believe my good fortune that you came all the way here to assure yourself of it. If I'd had the least encouragement that you might approve of the match, I would have waited upon you at Ellwood and stated my case before you. But I had always thought—"

"Yes, you must have realized that I have no great opinion of gentlemen who don't live up to the name, but in your case I can see it has proved successful, and success is something I cannot help but admire. I will not disapprove of your suit. In fact, I shall see that the girl has a suitable dowry."

"Sir!" Francis was nearly speechless with gratitude.

"But for all that I cannot understand what she sees in you," his visitor went on. "She ordinarily has much more discrimination, though she is generous to a fault. I suppose she found something about you to her liking.''

He scrutinized Sir Francis, as if hoping to discover some virtue that had hitherto remained hidden from him. ''I do not pretend to understand women, sir, but I suppose if she loves you, then I must accept whatever will make her happy. Now, enough time wasted. You have my permission, nay my encouragement, to speak to her.''

Francis had a strong desire to kneel at the old man's feet, but he restrained himself to profuse verbal thanks.

''Never mind. See that you make her happy. I advise you to wait until this evening at the ball. Take her out in the moonlight, but mind you don't disgrace yourself, young man.''

''Certainly not, Sir Reginald. I would not dream of—''

''Good.'' With that the baronet left, grateful that the interview was over, but more puzzled than ever over Nancy's choice.

Francis dreamed over his new invention, savouring his unlooked-for triumph and imagining Eleanor's face that evening when he told her that they could now make public their intentions to marry. And a dowry as well! He had hardly expected the old man's approval of the match, let alone any fortune. It was most odd.

Then Francis grinned. It was all his Eleanor's doing, he was sure. She had been growing impatient of the secrecy. No doubt she had gone to her grandfather and shed a few maidenly tears and put the thought in his head to demand Sir Francis's intentions. Francis could not decide what he admired more about his betrothed, her beauty or her cleverness.

At Ellwood Nancy was going about her accustomed duties and amusements with a lighter heart. She had only one more ordeal to endure, and that was the ball at Marbelmeade that night. After that some of the earl's guests would be leaving, there would be far fewer entertainments and she would more easily be able to avoid meeting him. She had already ceased to take her morning ride and found that though she missed Selbridge's easy companionship, the peace of mind it gave her was worth the loss.

She distracted herself that afternoon by comforting Eleanor, who was losing patience with her secret engagement and was almost determined to confront her grandfather about it.

"Oh, do wait until after the ball," Nancy said. "Your grandfather has had enough surprises, after Osbert and Gervaise suddenly presenting him with future brides. Just try to have a little more patience. You and Francis have made a great effort, and I am sure it will be worthwhile. Now, what will you wear tonight?"

Eleanor was willingly distracted, for despite her impatience she feared her grandfather's wrath, and ran to her wardrobe to pull out several ball gowns. Unfortunately Sir Reginald's generosity had not extended to a ballgown for Nancy, and the latter looked at the lovely creations with envy. She had not mentioned this lack to her preoccupied cousins, resigned to wearing one of her new evening dresses instead. Although she knew that neither of them would do justice to this grand occasion, at least her dress would be fashionable and flattering.

"I shall wear the ice-blue satin. It is very demure, but Mama is sure to think it suitable, and it sets off my hair beautifully," decided Eleanor, holding the gown up to her. "But, Nancy, what will we do about you?"

Eleanor delved into her wardrobe and emerged with a gossamer creation that made Nancy gasp with delight.

It was a gown of green crêpe with an overskirt of gauze shot with gold threads. The low-cut bodice was caught up with a rouleau of pumpkin-coloured satin, and there was a billowing demi-train of the same satin embroidered with pearls, as were the tiny sleeves.

"You will wear this," Eleanor said, flinging it upon the bed for her cousin to examine. "It will suit you perfectly, and Mama's maid can thread some pearls in your hair. Come, try it on. We must make certain it fits you."

"But, Eleanor, it is so beautiful, and it is yours. I cannot—"

"Nonsense, put it on at once, we haven't much time," Eleanor replied. "I ordered it on a whim, when I was at school in Town, and Mama disapproved. She would never have let me wear it before my come-out. Besides, the colours are just right for you."

Nancy could not resist the temptation and found that her cousin was right. The colours set off her skin and hair, and with only a few minor alterations the gown would be a perfect fit.

Lady Chetwynd was called in to approve, and was persuaded that it was suitable, though she hesitated, saying, "It is not quite the sort of gown a young lady who is not out should wear. But then, I daresay we must consider you out already, Nancy, as you are almost one and twenty."

Nancy's delight was dimmed by this bald statement of her decrepitude. But perhaps her idea of a London Season had been unrealistic. How could she, even properly dressed and prepared for Society, ever compete with wealthy and beautiful girls of seventeen who would be filling the London ballrooms in the spring? She had been a fool to think it possible, and now it was almost certain Lady Verena would not need to take Eleanor to London at all, and therefore would not take Nancy, either.

Even if success in London were possible, Nancy thought, as she subdued her sudden restlessness while Lady Chetwynd's maid pinned the folds of the gown around her, it would be nothing but ashes in her mouth now. How could she in good conscience accept the offer of any gentleman, knowing that her heart was elsewhere?

That evening the family at Ellwood were among the select company invited to dine with Lord Selbridge before the ball. When Nancy came down from her room she was immediately accosted by Bowen, who said, "Sir Reginald requests that you join him in the library, miss."

Nancy found her great-uncle sitting at his desk, looking elegant and almost young again in his evening clothes. When he saw her he stood up and went to her with a huge smile on his face.

"You look charming, my child. But I shall curtail my compliments, as I have some very important news for you."

Nancy's throat was suddenly very dry.

"Now, I know you will think I am an interfering old man, but you will not be angry with me when I tell you what the results of my interference were."

Nancy felt as though her legs were about to give way beneath her. Fortunately her great-uncle's hand was at her elbow, and when he saw how pale she had become, he led her immediately to a chair.

"You did not . . . you haven't . . ." She choked and stared at him in utter dismay.

"I did and I have," Sir Reginald told her. "Do not be so distressed, child. Why, if I had not gone to him, the two of you would have remained ignorant of one another's feelings for perhaps months!"

"Oh, no," Nancy moaned, and buried her face in her hands. She could not bear knowing that Sir Reginald had actually spoken to Selbridge of her feelings. How shocked he must have been, and how much more he must pity her now—pity her and despise her, for what else would he think but that she was so unmaidenly as to ask Sir Reginald to plead a case of love for her?

"You do not understand, my dear. Come, look at me, and for heaven's sake do not cry. You will spoil your beauty, and you must be in your best looks tonight, because your young man will speak to you."

"He will...speak to me?" Nancy stared up at him in amazement.

"Am I growing unintelligible in my old age, girl? I said he will speak to you—make an offer. Why, I had hardly to mention you when he began singing your praises. I don't know where you got the ridiculous idea that he did not care for you. You should have seen his face when I told him that you returned his regard."

Suddenly the blood pumping through Nancy's veins turned to champagne. He loved her! But her natural caution forbade her to accept only one assurance of this, and she questioned Sir Reginald until he began to lose patience.

"I tell you, the fellow is heels-over-head for you, my dear, and I shan't say it again. I told him that I approved, and I advised him to make it all right with you tonight at the ball. Come, I hear the others in the drawing-room. We certainly don't want to be late."

Before Nancy could question him further, he hurried her out to join the rest of the family. The short journey to Marbelmeade might as well have not happened, so caught up was Nancy in a wondrous dream. Her wish had been granted, and it was gruff, self-centred old Uncle Reginald who had done it. And to think she had told him not to say anything!

She was still a bit fearful, but Sir Reginald's assurances rang in her ears. Emerging from the carriage, she straightened her gown, put a hand to her elaborately dressed hair and tried to make herself ready.

CHAPTER TWELVE

JACK WAS HAPPY FOR his Cousin Francis, but he had tired of the young man's ebullience long before the day drew to a close. Certainly, it was welcome news that Sir Reginald Drakes had approved Francis's courtship of Miss Chetwynd, and Jack was just as relieved as his cousin to know that the discovery of the true identity of the inventor of Whisper Balm had not rocked Society to its foundations after all. But must the fellow go about whistling with such infernal happiness?

"I must beg you to cease that cacophony, Francis," he said when he arrived in the drawing-room before dinner. "Our guests will be coming soon."

Francis apologized and replaced the whistling with humming, which was no less annoying to Lord Selbridge. He turned away, suppressing a sigh of irritation, to find that his mother had entered the room and was looking at him with disapproval.

"Let the boy make noise if he wishes. I want this to be a lively house. I am not like a certain young man who sent his mother into exile because he wanted solitude and then invited one hundred of his most intimate friends to a ball." Lady Selbridge eyed her son with disdain.

Despite his amusement at her keen aim, Jack was compelled to defend himself. "Mama! How can you be so cruel? I was truly grieving when I sent you away to Brighton, and it was not as though you were at the far end of the earth with nothing to amuse you. I assure you, I am delighted for my cousin, but his noise is driving me to distraction.''

''Pay him no mind, Francis,'' Lady Selbridge said to her nephew. ''Jack has a sour temper because he has not been lucky in love. Though what you see in that little Chetwynd girl I shall never understand.''

Francis only smiled at his aunt. ''I am sure you will soon come to love her, Aunt Margaret.''

''Hmph!'' was her reply.

Meanwhile, Lord Selbridge had been bridling at his mother's last comment. ''I beg leave to inform you that I am not in a sour temper, my lady, and I have long since forgotten the misfortune in love that sent me here to lick my wounds.''

He did not say more, as her comment had touched him on the raw. His reception by Miss Browne the day before had crushed him. Offering sympathy, he had been made to feel as though he had committed some act of cruelty.

It was simply not fair. Miss Browne had once offered him sympathy, without knowing that he no longer required it. It had been obvious to him that she was devastated by her Cousin Osbert's desertion of her. Why could she not, at least as a friend, accept his compassion? How much more than that would he offer if only she would give him the slightest encouragement!

Unfortunately it seemed Nancy had grown shy of him. He must make his own opportunity, and it must be tonight. Her appearance, a few minutes later, with the Ellwood party, only confirmed him in this decision. He had always thought her looks delightful, but why had he not realized until this moment what a beauty she really was?

Her hair sparkled with red highlights, her gown was breathtaking in its loveliness, curving gently round her graceful figure, and her skin was like rich cream. Jack noted

to his delight that a very light spattering of freckles still
dusted her nose, and when she turned her sherry-coloured
eyes up to his and said, "Good evening," he thought that
he had never heard anything so lovely as the breathy catch
in her voice or seen anything that so pierced his heart as the
sweet eagerness on her face. She seemed to have drunk a
draught of moonlight.

Dinner was a dream. Jack had dismissed formality this
evening and made certain that Miss Browne was at his side.
Other than making sure he had secured two dances, if
pressed he would not have been able to recall what he and
Nancy talked about between courses, only that her smile was
more delightful than he had ever known and that she appeared to have forgotten his clumsy pity and had made up
her mind that he and she were to be friends again.

If Nancy had harboured any doubts about Sir Reginald's
report of Selbridge and his feelings, one look at his face as
he greeted her at Marbelmeade that evening would have
chased them away instantly. She had never before seen any
man's eyes light up with such wonder and admiration at the
sight of her. He had taken her hand and held it for so long
that she'd had to look away, shy under the gaze of the
others. It had seemed for a moment that Selbridge might
even bring her hand to his lips, but when she glanced up
again, he was smiling a smile just for her and slowly released her hand.

His assiduous attentions during dinner reassured her. It
was as though Selbridge were savouring her with his eyes as
his tongue savoured the wine. Her embarrassment at what
Sir Reginald had done and her fear of revealing her love
were gone, and with every glance she knew she was showing Lord Selbridge just how much she yearned for him.

"You will save at least two dances for me, will you not,
Miss Browne? We have not danced together before, but my

instinct tells me that our steps will suit admirably.'' He was leaning close, and his hand brushed hers accidentally as he reached for his glass.

Nancy felt the heat rising in her face and was dizzy for a moment. Such a flame had rushed along her fingertips from that little bit of contact.

She poured all the happiness she could into her reply. ''I shall look forward to it most impatiently, sir.'' She hoped her eyes would tell the tale her tongue was too shy to utter—that she loved him and could not wait to be in his arms.

The short time before the ball began seemed to stretch out endlessly, but with her new confidence, Nancy was totally at ease among all the gorgeously dressed ladies. Lady Selbridge's keen glances did cause her a few moments' panic, but she forced herself to ignore them. Even if the proud dowager did not approve of her as a bride for her son, she could do nothing about it. Nancy's spirits were soaring by the time the ball began.

Her entire being was so concentrated on what was to come that she hardly noticed the other happy couples, or her suddenly full complement of partners, young men attracted by her radiance. She knew Selbridge was watching her from across the room, and when their eyes met, she had to look away or be devoured by his glance. She swung gaily into dance after dance, smiling and completely unaware of her partners, of Sir Reginald's puzzled frown as he watched from the side of the room, of Francis and Eleanor dancing together too frequently or of Lady Selbridge's smile of satisfaction. Then Lord Selbridge came to claim her for his partner.

Their dance was a revelation to Nancy. It seemed that Selbridge could not take his eyes from her face, and every time their hands met in the figures of the dance she felt their secret pass between them.

"Miss Browne, I hope I did not offend you yesterday. I...I only meant to offer you some comfort," he whispered as they proceeded down the set.

As they momentarily separated, Nancy could only wonder at his bringing up the subject now. When they drew together again, she said, "I am sorry I gave that impression. But, of course," she said, smiling shyly, "you understand now why your pity affected me that way. I could not bear it."

He stared at her in puzzlement, but before he could speak, the dance ended and he slipped his arm beneath her elbow. "Why could you not bear it, my dear?" he asked as he began to escort her off the dance floor.

The colour flew to her face, but Nancy was full of confidence and assured of his regard. The words so long repressed burst from her. "I could not bear your thinking I loved anyone but you," she said. She saw a fire kindle in his eyes, heard him draw breath and was delighted at the effect of her boldness.

"Could you not, my sweet?" said Selbridge with a teasing smile. He abruptly turned toward the doors opening onto the terrace. "Come," he whispered, "take a breath of air in the garden with me."

Nancy merely nodded and allowed herself to be borne away, hardly feeling the floor beneath her slippers. How foolish she had been to fear showing her real feelings for Selbridge! Why, had she not been so timid, he might have taken encouragement from her behaviour much sooner, and they might have already been betrothed, without the embarrassing intervention of Sir Reginald. But she pushed these thoughts to the back of her mind. The moment had come. Selbridge took her hand and placed it on his arm, holding it there tightly.

The moon and stars lit the way for them as they strolled, the warm air caressing Nancy's bare arms and carrying the scent of roses to her nostrils. Selbridge, still silent, at last released her hand, and they sat on a tiny stone bench.

His closeness, the rough feel of his evening clothes brushing against the soft crêpe of her gown, the warmth that came from him, roused Nancy from her reverie, and she realized that Selbridge had slowly drawn one arm about her shoulders while he reached for her hand with the other.

"My dear Miss Browne, I hope I do not frighten you, but I have been encouraged to hope..." There was an endearing break in his voice, and Nancy felt tenderness welling up in her as she saw the very real look of uncertainty on his face. It pleased her that despite all the assurances he had received, he did not take her love for granted.

Still, she wished to make everything as easy for him as possible. She returned the pressure of his hand and immediately felt him draw her closer to him. Catching her breath, she said, "I know. And please don't think you frighten me. I...I only wish I had not been such a fool. I should have been less reserved."

"You are not a fool, my darling Nancy. It would be too much to expect that you could read my mind, when I made such a muddle of things. How could you know I loved you, when I persisted in believing that you did not wish to hear those words? But I do love you, Nancy Browne."

Nancy gazed up at him, but before she could say a word, he had pulled her still closer and was kissing her. She delighted in the lingering touch of his lips, and the ease with which she fitted against him. It was so perfectly right that she wondered now how she could ever have mistaken his love for mere friendship. She rested her head against his shoulder, and he gently stroked her hair, careful not to disarrange it.

"I hope no one thinks that I am going about this with unseemly haste, my love, but I want to marry you as soon as possible," he whispered in her ear.

Nancy murmured her acquiescence against his shoulder, then said, "I...I think, my dear, that we ought to go in now and thank Sir Reginald," she said when she could speak again.

"Well, certainly, my love, if you wish it, but is it really necessary?" asked a puzzled Lord Selbridge.

Nancy sat up and straightened her gown. "But we owe so much to him. I should not like him to think me ungrateful. Besides, he must be awfully curious by now. I am sure he saw us leave the ball."

Jack, a bit confused, was nevertheless willing to follow his newfound love in whatever odd impulse took hold of her, and he admitted to himself that it would not be unpleasant to enter the ballroom with Nancy on his arm and have everyone suspect just by looking at them that they were betrothed. The official announcement, of course, would have to wait, but there was a certain delight in setting tongues to wagging, and in knowing that only he and Nancy could tell what had really happened in the garden.

Sir Reginald was, as Nancy had suspected, extremely curious about the outcome of her stroll in the garden with Selbridge, but for reasons of his own. He had thought it odd that his neighbour and host had paid so much attention to Nancy, while Francis Garrard, her declared lover, had all but ignored her, latching on to Eleanor in a most annoying way. Why, even now, he saw as he stood watching the dancers, the chit was simpering at him as they danced. The dance over, he saw that Francis was drawing Eleanor away to an alcove, and... By God, the fellow would not be permitted such despicable behaviour, the old man fumed to himself, and in a few moments he was beside them, tearing aside the drapery that had not entirely hidden them.

"What is the meaning of this, sir? You vile betrayer, how dare you disappoint my niece, after all those vows of undying love. And by what right do you trifle this way with my granddaughter? You, miss—" he turned to the frightened Eleanor "—are no better than a trollop, allowing yourself to be pawed by this creature."

"Grandfather!" cried Eleanor. "How can you be so cruel?"

"I would never expect a gentleman to go back on his word, Sir Reginald!" Francis said at the same time. They both stared at him accusingly as they clung to one another.

Sir Reginald's anger was dashed away in an icy shower of amazement. "What the devil? What do you mean, sir?" he demanded of Francis, more bewildered than enraged.

"Why, nothing but what you yourself encouraged me to do, Sir Reginald. You told me that Miss Chetwynd loved me and urged me to offer for her, which I have done," he said, glibly ignoring the fact that the offer had been made a long while ago. Francis gathered his dignity together. "If you have changed your mind, sir, I wish that you had found some less public way to inform me."

Indeed, the scene was attracting the attention of all the guests who were not dancing at the moment. Sir Reginald muttered a curse and steered the young people out of the ballroom.

"I have not changed my mind, you young fool. It was not Eleanor, but Miss Browne I gave you permission to court."

"Nancy!" Eleanor and Francis said the name in unison and looked at one another in surprise.

"But, sir, you never mentioned Miss Browne—" Francis began.

"I did not mention my granddaughter, either, and neither did you, you insolent puppy! But it appears that you heard only what you wanted to hear. And I—" Suddenly his face paled.

"Damme, I'm nothing but an old fool after all. The poor girl! My poor Nan!" To the amazement of Francis and Eleanor, he hurried away into the ballroom.

As he entered it, Selbridge and Nancy were walking in from the garden, and he made his way with assumed casualness to the couple. To his amazement, Nancy was glowing, and Selbridge looked proud and happy. Relief flooded him.

"There you are, dear Uncle Reginald! I wanted to thank you…" Nancy's voice was low but vibrant. She glanced up at Selbridge, who smiled at her gently and then pumped Sir Reginald's hand.

"Indeed, sir. I do not precisely know why Nancy insists on it, but I shall certainly thank you if she wishes it." He grinned at his elderly neighbour, as Nancy was temporarily distracted by the complaints of a young man with whom she had missed a dance. "And here I was priding myself on overcoming my doubts of her feelings, and being brave enough to win the woman I love."

Sir Reginald was immediately enlightened. Great luck had befallen him. By some miracle, his dear Nancy had not made a fool of herself, confessing her love to the wrong man. How could he not have known that it was Selbridge she had meant and that the young earl had been harbouring a secret love for the girl? Now it was apparent that all was well. But Francis and Eleanor…

Nancy dealt kindly but firmly with her importunate partner, promising a dance after supper, and she turned back to Selbridge and Sir Reginald. To her surprise her great-uncle made a strangled sound, turned on his heel and headed for the door, mingling with the guests who were leaving the ballroom for the cold supper, which was being served in the next room.

He caught up with Francis and Eleanor, who, with Lady Verena, Osbert and his Caroline and the Phillipses, were proceeding decorously to the supper room.

"Garrard, I want a word with you," said the old baronet, his hand coming down heavily on the young man's shoulder.

"Father, really," said Lady Verena, "cannot it wait until after the ball? I am sure you can discuss the marriage settlements with Sir Francis some other time." Lady Verena beamed at Eleanor and her accepted suitor, now fully reconciled to the fact that her daughter would never be Selbridge's countess, but only the wife of a wealthy baronet.

"Marriage settlements! Verena, have you gone mad?" Sir Reginald demanded. "I had no idea this fellow was buzzing around Eleanor. Was I to remain ignorant forever of the doings of my own household? I have yet to give my consent."

The little family group stopped, now alone in the hall. Osbert glanced warily back at them and hurried Caroline and the fascinated Mr. and Mrs. Phillips away to supper.

"Why, Papa!" cried Lady Verena. "You gave your consent to Sir Francis only yesterday, have you forgotten?"

"Of course, I haven't forgotten. I gave him permission to court Nancy, not Eleanor. And I told Nancy that Francis loved her. But now Nancy is going to marry Selbridge, another love affair going on underneath my nose, not to mention Osbert and the Phillips girl, and Gervaise and Miss Garrard and—"

Sir Reginald was reddening with impotent anger and confusion as his family gaped at him. "Oh, was there ever such a pack of infuriating relations! Why have you allowed me to make such an utter fool of myself?"

Eleanor and Francis were suppressing smiles, and Lady Verena fluttered anxiously over her father, encouraging him to sit down and sending a footman for a glass of wine. "Papa, do calm yourself. You will make yourself ill!"

"And so I should. No one has any consideration for all I have done. You young people make your own plans without even consulting me." But his voice had died to a bewildered grumble, and he consented to sit down and sip some wine. As he did so, he saw Nancy and Selbridge, who had emerged from the ballroom unnoticed, standing and staring at him in amazement.

At her great-uncle's words, the roses of happiness had faded from Nancy's cheeks. She realized with a sickening lurch just how close she had come to humiliating herself.

"I . . . I'm sorry, my child," said Sir Reginald, seeing her face. "It never occurred to me . . . Come now, do not look so miserable! It has all ended happily."

"Indeed it has, sir," said Selbridge in most decided tones, having realized from Sir Reginald's frantic discourse what had led Nancy to suddenly declare her love. "I am proud to announce that Miss Browne has consented to become my wife."

Lady Verena looked startled and put out, Francis and Eleanor were equally surprised, but on the whole pleased.

"Come here, my girl," ordered Sir Reginald.

She obeyed. "I will not say I'm sorry," her great-uncle continued, "for it was my foolish meddling that brought about this engagement, and I couldn't be happier. Now you may thank me, as you planned to."

"Yes, Uncle Reginald. Thank you." She smiled at him with affection, but her voice was subdued.

The others added their good wishes. Lady Chetwynd sniffed and said, "Well at least I shall not be put to the expense of taking you to London next Season."

"No, indeed, Cousin Verena," Nancy replied, exchanging a shy smile with her betrothed, who was barely restraining his amusement. "But perhaps you will visit us in London instead."

Mollified, Lady Verena smiled. Then a pleasing thought occurred to her. "Good heavens, just think what Lady Selbridge will say! I daresay she will disapprove of you dreadfully. But you will win her over, my dear." She sighed, and looked at her father. "You have managed to win Papa over, so her ladyship should be no challenge to you at all."

"We shall go in to supper," Sir Reginald announced, rising from his chair and looking only a few years older than he had at the beginning of the evening. He looked at his daughter accusingly. "Or do you intend to starve an old man simply for making a foolish mistake that has ended by benefitting everyone?"

The family withdrew, Eleanor and Francis still arguing with Sir Reginald over their marriage but certain, Nancy thought, to win. Uncle Reginald had been more proud than disappointed at his bungled management of the various matches, she thought. But, oh, how her cheeks flamed when she thought of how bold and forward she had been!

"Nancy, please, look at me." Selbridge's voice was tender, and she ached to see him smile at her again, but she was as yet too unsettled at her own close brush with humiliation to meet his gaze.

Jack was still floating in a sea of happiness at having discovered Nancy's love for him, but he could understand her shyness at this moment. He went to her and gently pulled her close.

She finally looked up at him, encouraged.

"You know, my darling, you took no great chance to-night after all. I was determined to take you away and demand to know whether you returned my feelings. I'd had enough of being your friend and being careful not to alarm you. I had to know. You gave me a great deal of joy to-night, my love."

"I can scarcely believe it is all true," murmured Nancy. "For so long I thought that you would never consider me fashionable enough, or accomplished enough, or well-born enough. I will never be so hesitant to believe in my own attractions again."

Selbridge kissed her forehead, cheeks and lips, just in time for a scandalized but delighted footman to witness these caresses. "There will be no need for you to be hesitant, my love," his lordship said, "for I shall tell you every day how beautiful and perfect you are. Besides, Ellwood will not need you much longer, and Marbelmeade certainly does. Did you forget that we will soon have a nursery wing to fill?"

"No, indeed, I had not forgotten. And I think that Mischief will be happier back at your kennels, too, for Lady Verena hates having him in the house.. Oh, and may I bring Trouble?"

"Trouble? I had hoped, Nancy, that you would bring me nothing but peace," said Jack with a grin.

"Come now, do not pretend that you have forgotten the kitten. Why, he was present at our first meeting, has since outgrown his basket and is becoming an excellent mouser," Nancy informed him with a laugh.

Jack pressed her close to him out of sheer joy. "We shall welcome the kitten as well, but pray let us change his name. And as for you, my dear, let me never hear you deprecate your unique talents. I do not care if you are unskilled in the harp or cannot embroider creditably or know nothing of poetry."

And when he added, "I am not nearly as clever as you are, and you are more than worthy to be my countess, Miss Nancy Browne," he bent to kiss her again.

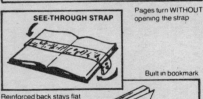
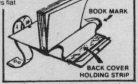